D1563921

WAIT WITH ME

AMY DAWS

This book is inspired by real-life events.

Except for all the hot and romantic parts.

My life is not nearly that exciting.

Author forward:

This book is inspired by real life events involving my own case of writer's block and a magical place called Tires Tires Tires. Unfortunately, none of the hot and romantic parts happened to me. Fiction is often better than reality.

But one awesome reality is that *Wait With Me* was optioned for film by Passionflix, and you can find more information about the film here at:

amydawsauthor.com/waitwithmemovie

WAIT WITH ME

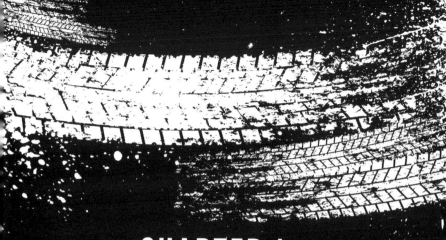

CHAPTER 1

Kate

Kate Smith. My name is literally Kate Smith. My parents couldn't even fancy it up and call me Katherine or Katelyn. Or God, if only they'd have named me something exotic like Katarina, my life could have turned out so differently.

Hell, I would have even settled for Katie. She sounds a tiny bit fun. Maybe.

But no…I'm just Kate.

I'm the eldest child in a bustling family of five from Longmont, Colorado. My parents have been married for over forty years and still magically like each other. My two younger brothers went off and married two sisters. The two perfect couples and their precious offspring live within a two-block radius of our childhood home. My parents babysit every Friday night so my brothers can wine and dine their hot wives like the good Christian husbands they are.

And what does boring ole, practically pushing thirty years old Kate do?

She writes porn.

In a tire shop.

In Boulder, Colorado.

"Excuse me, but you look familiar," a woman in her mid-sixties says to me with a starry-eyed look on her face. She's got that pleasantly plump look about her that reminds me of a vintage fairy godmother. The one that looks like a grandmother, not the one that looks like a character from Harry Potter.

I lift my hands from my laptop keyboard where they have been furiously typing away and pop out my earbuds. "I'm sorry…what?"

The woman's eyes blink rapidly. "Do you work at a hospital?"

I offer her a kind smile. "No, I'm afraid not."

"Do you work at a dental clinic?"

"Nope."

"A veterinary office? That's got to be it. You look so familiar. I'm Betty, and my poodle's name is Misty, the teacup black one?"

I smile again and take pity on the woman. "No. I'm sorry, Betty. I don't work at a vet clinic. I'm a writer. Maybe you've read my books?"

Her eyes light up. "Oh, what's your name?"

"I write under the pen name, Mercedes Lee Loveletter,"

I reply confidently. *Don't judge! I was making up for a lifetime's worth of hating my boring-ass name.*

"Is it Christian romance?" Betty asks, hand to heart with hopeful excitement.

"No," I reply, chagrin all over my face.

"Oh…is it Amish? How I love those Amish novels."

I inhale deeply. "Definitely not Amish." Betty is so not my people. I should have guessed, but you'd be surprised at the number of grannies who like dirty smut.

She frowns and glances down at my computer. "Are you writing now?"

"Yes." I hug my laptop to my body as she moves to look over my shoulder.

"May I see?" she asks, brushing up against my shoulder, the scent of vanilla all over her.

I close it. "I'm afraid I don't let anyone see my work in progress…they need an editor's touch." *And you'd probably have a stroke.*

"You were in here yesterday too, right?" she asks curiously.

My spine straightens. "Yes, why do you ask?"

"And the day before?"

I look around nervously. "Okay, what's the problem? Did management send you in here?"

Her eyes go wide. "Oh no, no. I'm just the baker!"

Realization dawns on me. I totally saw her bring in some pans yesterday. "Betty the Baker!" I cry out like she's the long-lost grandmother I've always wanted. "You do the cookies!"

She smiles proudly, and I sorta want to hug her, but damn, that's probably too much too soon. "Yes, I make the cookies. Normally, I only come in once a week, but I've been popping in a lot lately to see how the new product is being received."

"The scones!" I exclaim and shake my head, trying to calm down. "Holy cow, those scones are delish."

"You really think so?" She's practically glowing with pride. Jesus Christ, she looks like she's going to burst.

"Oh, yeah," I reply. "I dip them in my morning espresso, and the combination is life-changing. Almost as good as the white chocolate chip cookies dipped in the caramel almond latte I have in the afternoons."

She giggles happily. "Have you tried the danishes?"

"I haven't seen danishes!" I nearly screech with excitement and then try to reel it in. *Damnit, there are danishes? Who the hell is eating all those?* "I usually get here around ten. They must be gone by then."

"Well, that's a good sign!" the woman chortles, and then her brow furrows. "How many days have you been coming here? Is something terribly wrong with your car? I bet they could get you a rental."

I bristle instantly. *This is why you don't talk with the patrons, Kate! You're supposed to keep a low profile, not chat up the magical baking grandmother!* I take a deep breath and lie through my teeth. "Actually, I'm not really a writer, Betty. Can you keep a secret?" Her eyes go wide at my serious expression, and she looks around to make sure no one hears us before nodding eagerly.

This is the moment you've been preparing weeks for, Kate. Don't hold back now. "I'm with corporate. We've been worried about the service in this branch, so they sent me here to scope things out for a few weeks."

"Oh, but I've never heard any complaints before! And I so love the gentlemen at the front desk. They are always so friendly, and they love my chocolate chip cookies."

"I think everyone loves your chocolate chip cookies," I reply with a knowing wink. "But I need to ask you to keep my presence here quiet. We want to really see this branch's day-to-day customer service so we can make any necessary improvements."

She nods slowly, clearly excited she's in on my secret mission. "I understand." *Possible snitch, secured.*

"Thank you for your discretion." I reach out to shake her hand in a very corporate manner, and it feels like a sticky, limp noodle. "It was nice to meet you, Betty. Keep up the good work. We're not worried about you at all."

My wink has her shuffling away with a stark look on her face, and I turn to exhale heavily. That was close. Too close. I need to finish this book before anyone else notices that I'm here a lot.

I reopen my laptop and pick up where I left off in book five of my erotic *Bed 'n Breakfast* series. This book is the conclusion to an overnight international bestselling sensation that was recently optioned for film by Passionflix. My fans are dying for this book, and my mind can't help but drift off to recall the great lengths I went to deliver.

Sure, some might say it's unusual to write smutty

romance in the waiting room of a tire shop. But when you're a New York Times Bestselling author and suddenly all the words and characters in your mind disappear—you take extreme measures.

That's why the day I walked into the Tire Depot waiting room prepared to stare at my computer blankly while I got a new set of tires, I was stunned when the words started flowing again. Like seriously flowing. This wasn't a trickle but a flash flood of epic proportions.

After such a dry spell, I didn't dare tempt fate by walking away from that shit! I was like a prized athlete on a winning streak heading into the championship game. I wasn't going to wash my socks or shave my legs. I was going to eat the same shit, walk the same steps, and repeat every day like fucking *Groundhog Day* until I finished this book!

That is why I'm on my third week of work at the good old Tire Depot. And I've learned a lot in my time here. Like the fact that Tire Depot is so much more than a tire shop. For starters, they don't just sell tires. They perform oil changes and do maintenance and mechanical repairs. The other day, I overheard the manager say they did everything except paint and glass. *How neat is that?*

But if I'm being honest, I have to admit that I come here for one thing and one thing only:

The Customer Comfort Center.

The CCC at the Tire Depot, also known as my new mothership.

When I first brought my vehicle in three weeks ago and the counter guy gestured to a waiting room around the corner, I thought I'd find a crummy twelve-cup Mr. Coffee with generic stale coffee. If I was lucky, they'd have powdered creamer from this year.

When I turned the corner and walked into the thousand-square-foot Customer Comfort Center complete with a brick fireplace, leather lounge chairs, and a coffee machine that dispensed an incredible variety of gourmet coffee, I nearly fell to my knees and wept.

Within minutes, I had an almond caramel latte, a warm oatmeal raisin cookie, and a sweet spot at one of their high top tables right next to a convenient outlet. It was kismet.

Feeling more positive than I had in months, I cracked open my laptop, and after a couple of sips of coffee, the words I'd been struggling to find in my latest smutty story suddenly flowed from my fingertips. I had found my way out of the dreaded writer's block! It was a Christmas frickin' miracle!

I blinked, and three hours had passed. The customer service agent said my car was ready, but when they said they didn't mind if I stuck around for a while, all I heard was *jackpot!* Before I knew it, I had crushed five thousand words in five hours.

I had never written that fast in my career as an author! And they were good words too! That was the real clincher.

So, like a dog who'd found the best dumpster of leftovers, I decided to come back for seconds. At first, I brought in a few vehicles for oil changes … my neighbor's, my friend's. My two brothers even let me take their vehicles in, but they side-eyed me the whole time because I had to drive thirty minutes just to get their cars—judgmental pricks.

But then I got the feeling a guy at the counter was starting to recognize me. They get a lot of traffic at Tire Depot, and sadly, I don't exactly blend in. I'm a curvy redhead with skin that doesn't suffer the sun like so many of my fellow gingers. But I think what tipped the guy off was when I brought in my seventh car for service. At that point, I was bringing in a friend's co-worker's vehicle, so I was clearly fucking desperate and maybe a bit manic. But I knew I had to do whatever it took to get in my words!

Then I realized the comfort center had its own entrance. An entrance that bypassed the counter guys. They were the gatekeepers, after all. The only ones I ever spoke to. So why couldn't I just slip in the side door every day, quietly do my work, drink my weight in complimentary coffee, and sneak out with no one the wiser?

I mean…sure, my guilty conscience poked at me a few times, but the more I went, the easier it got. America's greatest serial killers probably lived by this same mantra. But so be it.

Give me complimentary coffee or give me death.

The CCC had become my Luke's Diner. I was Lorelai Gilmore waltzing in every day, and that little, nonverbal, automated coffee machine was the grumpy diner owner that I was slowly falling in love with. And now I've met Betty, the baker of the goods and direct cause of my poor diet these past few weeks.

But love is a wild creature. You can't contain it or control it. You can't break it and tell it no. It's a charging animal that you must accept as your destiny.

That is how I feel about the Tire Depot CCC: true, un-adulterated love.

So for now, I'm blending in with the crowd. Tire Depot is a busy place, and with four areas for seating, this makes concealing my identity quite easy. Gone are the days where I beg my brothers to ask their friends if their cars need oil changes. Finished are the moments I try to plan a road trip just to get my car closer to needing service.

For now, I'm incognito, and Mercedes Lee Loveletter is writing a book that's going to blow her horny readers away. *Wait…I punned. Oh man, that's good. I'm writing that down.*

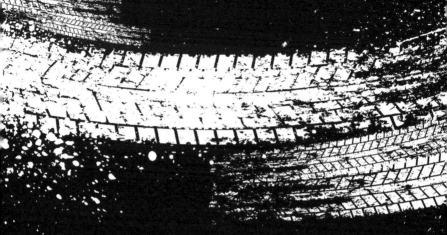

CHAPTER 2

Miles

Leaning against the outside of the building in the alley behind the garage, I lift the red rope of licorice to my lips and suck air in through the opening I just bit off. I take an actual bite and blow out, imagining the intoxicating rush I'd be getting if this were an actual cigarette.

If only I still smoked.

My head snaps to the left when the back door of the comfort center opens, and a blaze of curly red hair comes out. The same redhead is back. The one I've seen passing through this alley for several days now. I always get a glimpse of her red mane through the foggy shop window where my station sits. I keep wondering where she comes from and where exactly she's going.

Today, I have a much better vantage point. She's

dressed in plain black leggings and a loose, flowing T-shirt that has PIZZA scrawled across the front. From the drape of that top, it's clear she's well-endowed, and even in flip-flops, I can see the definition of those legs clear as day. Curvy and small in all the right places. She's low-maintenance hot, not the type to primp before going to the grocery store.

The redhead is moving straight toward me but looking backward like someone's going to come chasing out after her. I try to get the licorice out of my mouth fast enough to tell her to stop, but it's too late. She barrels into me like a bunny against a brick wall. In the scuffle, her flip-flop gets lodged under my work boot, and with an awkward twist of her ankle, she goes crashing to the ground, her gray satchel flying five feet into the alley.

"Shit, are you okay?" I ask, reaching down to offer her my hand.

Her blue eyes fly wide. "Oh my God. My computer!"

She doesn't even look at me as she scrambles across the hot asphalt for her laptop bag that landed a few feet from her. Crouched on her knees, she pulls the MacBook out of her bag and opens it quickly. With a sharp intake of air, the redhead finally says, "Not cracked but will it boot?"

After tapping the space bar, the screen alights with a login window. She falls off to the side on her hip and exhales with relief. "That could have been so bad," she mumbles to herself. "Ugh, this is why I email the file to myself after every session. Rookie mistake!"

"Everything okay?" I ask, approaching her cautiously as

she slides the laptop back into her bag. I feel really fucking weird about interrupting the conversation she's having with herself, but staying silent seems even weirder.

Her gaze turns to me, and her eyes widen as she takes in the full sight of me. As if she's only now noticed another human standing right next to her this entire time.

Her eyes slide up my body, taking in my rough, steel-toed work boots and oil-splattered, charcoal coveralls currently protecting my denim-clad legs. I've slipped my arms out of the top of the coveralls, revealing the black athletic tank I always wear underneath. My arms have a decent sheen of sweat, considering it's summer and the shop is not air-conditioned. And let's face it, some of that perspiration is from nicotine withdrawal.

Her eyes finally reach my face, so I decide to repeat my earlier question. "Everything okay?"

Her brows draw together, and she nods, her nude lips still parted with a dazed expression on her face.

"Are you hurt?" I ask, trying to make sure she didn't sustain a head injury in our collision because she's acting super fucking weird.

She shakes her head, so I offer her my hand to help her up. My hot, rough hand grips her cold, soft fingers as I pull her to a standing position. She's a good eight inches shorter than I am, but at six-foot-four, all girls are small beside me.

She clears her throat. "You…you…work here?" She closes her eyes like she's mentally chastising herself.

I cross my arms and can't help but notice her eyes watching my biceps flatten on top of my hands with interest. "I do. I'm a mechanic. Were you getting a service?"

She giggles. She giggles so hard that it turns into a laugh, and then she's slapping her hand over her mouth to muffle it. Mumbling against her palm, she replies, "Yes."

I frown and ask, "Then what brings you back here to the alley? Completed cars are parked out front. These back doors are employee entrances."

Her eyes flash back to the door, and she begins gnawing on her lip. "Right. I, erm…was just…" She eyes the spare strand of licorice I have tucked behind my ear. "Coming out for a smoke!"

My brows lift. Smokers come in all shapes and sizes, but something tells me this luminous, ginger bombshell does not smoke.

"Great, can I bum one?" I ask, calling her bluff.

"Weren't you just fake smoking with licorice?" she asks, pointing to the half-eaten piece that fell to the ground during the course of our collision.

My face heats. "You saw that?"

She laughs softly. "Before my triumphant fall, yes, I saw something that looked like a puff of make-believe cherry smoke floating all around you."

I roll my eyes and jam a hand through my short, black hair. "It's a thing I started doing when I quit smoking three months ago."

"Does it help?"

I shrug. "Doesn't hurt."

"Maybe hurts the ego." A dimple flashes in her right cheek as she fails to conceal a smirk. "How macho is it to fake smoke candy?"

Is she flirting with me? Or teasing me? I can't tell, but I can definitely retaliate, and I must admit that her dimple is adorable. I lift my hand to grab the licorice behind my ear and flex and relax so my bicep tightens impressively. "My ego is never in danger, babe." I pull down the candy and bite a piece off while shooting her a wink.

This makes her genuinely laugh. It's a rich, full-bodied sound that projects all the way from her toes. "With book boyfriend arms like that, it's no wonder."

"Book boyfriend?" I ask curiously.

"Book boyfriend," she repeats. "The leading male in a romance novel that readers claim ownership of because he doesn't likely exist in the real world. Basically, the ideal man."

"I've never heard this term before," I admit, leaning back against the wall and eyeing her curiously. "I take it you're into books or something?"

"Or something." She smiles and runs her hand through her wild red waves. They have to be natural because no girl would touch hair that beautiful if it had been styled. "And it doesn't surprise me you've never heard of it." She leans in and whispers loudly, "You're not my demo."

I frown curiously, and with a parting wiggle of her eyebrows, she turns and resumes her walk down the alley toward wherever she was going. After staring at the globes of her ass for far longer than is appropriate, it dawns on me that I didn't even get her name.

Cupping my hand to my mouth, I yell after her, "What

if you're my demo?"

She twirls on her heel to gaze at me, looking a hell of a lot more graceful than she did earlier. "We won't know that until *The End!*"

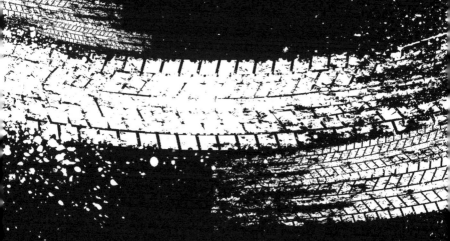

CHAPTER 3

Kate

"Fess up. Where have you been?" My neighbor and best friend since college, Lynsey's voice snaps, nearly making me fall into my front door and drop my keys in surprise.

"Jesus!" I exclaim, turning toward my tiny brunette compadre who's the scariest short person I know. "You're like one of those annoying bouncing min pins that leap up into the air just to be eye level with humans."

"Ha-ha, short joke, what a shocker coming from you. I'm serious, tell me where you've been."

"The library! I told you in my text," I reply, turning my back on her to resume my goal. Pushing the door of my townhouse open, I drop my mail, laptop bag, and keys on the entry table by the stairs right inside the door.

"Bullshit," Lynsey barks, following me in like a little puppy. She reaches out to fist the hem of my shirt. She pulls it to her face and inhales deeply. "You smell like coffee and rubber."

"Also known as freedom." I sigh wistfully and yearn to be back there. I would have stayed longer if I could survive on coffee and cookies all day. But curses, I need some protein or I might die.

"You actually went back to Tire Depot?" Lynsey seethes. "Kate! They are going to call the cops on you."

"For what?" I protest over my shoulder as I make my way through my living room and into the kitchen to grab a water bottle out of the fridge. "Stealing complimentary coffee and cookies? Come on. That's not a thing."

"But loitering is."

My face freezes around the mouth of my water bottle. "You think they'd really do that?"

Lynsey looks slightly unsure. "I don't know, but do you want the awkwardness of finding out?"

"I don't care, Lynsey!" I exclaim with a huff. "I've found my words at the TD, and I'm not letting go until I'm done."

"TD?" she repeats dubiously.

"Tire Depot is such a mouthful."

"You know what's a mouthful? Prison." I roll my eyes, but she continues with her lecture. "This is a crutch, Kate. You have to see that."

"It's not a crutch."

"You think you need it, but you don't."

"I do need it!" I snap, making my way back to the entry

table and grabbing my mail. "I couldn't write a thing before I went there. And writing is what keeps me in this posh townhouse on the outskirts of beautiful Boulder. If I want to continue being this stunning creature, living the high life in the foothills, I have to follow the vibe. And the vibe is strong at Tire Depot."

I move into my sitting area and drop into an overstuffed leather armchair to begin sifting through the envelopes in my hand.

Lynsey perches on the edge of my coffee table in front of me. "Can we stop dancing around what's really going on here?"

"Watch your hiney, Lyns, that's luxury reclaimed barn-wood that Mercedes Lee Loveletter afforded me."

"Stop changing the subject. This is about your ex who happens to still live with you." She points up the stairs to the master suite I shared with Dryston Roberts for the better part of the past two years before everything went to shit.

I scoff at that notion. "We're playing a game of chicken right now, and there's no way I'm letting that small-minded fucker take this house."

"Even though you can't even write in it? You want to fight for the house with no 'vibe'?" she quips.

"That's irrelevant," I exclaim and ball my hands up into tight fists. Every time I talk about Dryston, my hands end up like this.

We met two years ago at a pool party, and I fell for his suave moves. It took me way too long to see that he had Peter Pan Syndrome written all over him.

Unfortunately, leasing this townhouse for three years was the one grown-up thing we did together, and now, it's a disaster. Living for three months in the same house as your ex-boyfriend, a perpetual frat boy who will never mature, is about as bad as you can imagine.

The only silver lining in this situation is that he's away for the summer. *Thank God.*

"There's no way in hell I'm moving out," I grind through clenched teeth and swing my eyes to Lynsey in accusation. "I live next door to my best friend! You don't want me to move, do you?"

She rolls her eyes. "No."

"Exactly. So that's that. He's a spoiled brat who has always gotten what he wants but not this time. He's summering in the Hamptons, for God's sake, so he can afford his own place. I'm staying put."

"It's like a Mexican standoff with you two…I can't even!" Lynsey growls and runs her hands through her hair. "You enjoy living with your ex for the next year. See how that works out."

"I'm perfectly happy living down here. This bedroom is actually bigger." Never mind the fact that the upstairs room has the best views of the mountains. That room is tainted anyway. It reeks of preppy boy cologne and idiocy.

My thoughts are distracted when my eyes land on a familiar logo that I know better than my own for the Mercedes Lee Loveletter brand.

I look up at Lynsey with grave eyes. "It's a letter from Tire Depot."

"They've figured it out." She gasps and covers her mouth like we just found out one of our friends is a murderer.

"Stop being so dramatic!" I screech defensively as my fingers squeeze tightly around the envelope. "You don't know that they figured it out. This could just be like…junk mail or something. Maybe they're offering a special on oil changes next week?"

"Have they ever mailed you anything like that before?"

"No!" I bellow as the realization sinks in and dread washes over me. I look at Lynsey with wide, fearful eyes. "What if this is it?"

"What do you mean?" she asks.

"What if this is the moment I've feared all along? They might be taking my mojo away!"

"You don't know that," Lynsey defends. Clearly, we both process feelings differently because now we've done a one-eighty, and she's coming up with excuses while I'm circling the drain of despair.

"They would have no other reason to send me a letter!" I shriek and inhale a shaky breath. "Damnit," I growl and tear into the envelope to make my death swift.

I unfold the letter that's printed on the Tire Depot letterhead and read aloud. "Dear Ms. Smith, We've taken notice of your enjoyment of our customer waiting area. We are very glad that you enjoy spending your days with us. You have, however, exceeded the limit for complimentary refreshments. Per company policy, enclosed you will find an invoice for the refreshments you've consumed in excess of the limit."

"What?" Lynsey screeches. Jesus Christ, we're both a fucking mess.

"It's gotta be a prank," I force out a fake laugh and look at the second page that lists the itemized products that I've consumed. Like a shot, I stand, the mail on my lap falling to the floor. "Holy shit! How did they know?"

"Know what?"

"I mean…this invoice has to be bullshit, but this itemized list is scarily accurate."

"What do you mean?"

I thrust the paper at her and point to each line item. "I probably have drunk fifteen long espressos and thirty caramel almond lattes. That's like…exactly my jam. I start my days off with a long espresso and then do two lattes in the afternoon."

"Oh, Kate!" Lynsey gasps. "That's a lot of caffeine!"

"But I don't eat lunch!" I argue.

She nods, seemingly appeased by that reply. "So this is legit?"

"It can't be," I argue, but the growing pit in my stomach indicates I'm not fully convinced.

Here's the thing. I'm not mad at the one hundred and eighty dollar invoice. Charging four dollars for a beverage is cheaper than Starbucks. But I'm livid over the nerve of Tire Depot! What kind of respectable business would charge a person excess consumption of complimentary coffee?

"This seriously can't be real."

"Oh, Kate! You missed a page." Lynsey says, scooping a sheet up off the floor. "It's for the cookies."

"Shut up!" I snatch the sheet out of her hands and am

mortified at the list. "Wait a damn minute…this says danishes on there. I've never had a danish there in my life! I'm being punked!"

I swerve accusing eyes to Lynsey, but she looks way too caught up in this scene to be the culprit. I rack my brain for who else would possibly send me a fake invoice. It could be any number of the people I begged to let me take their cars in…which was an embarrassing number. Or it could be my brothers, but honestly, the logo on the letterhead is way too perfect for it to be any ole friend or family.

My blue eyes meet Lynsey's brown, and in unison, we both say, "Dean."

Minutes later, Lynsey and I are in my car to head toward our friend Dean's house about a mile up the road. This little complex of townhouses is a bit of a hidden gem situated on the edge of Boulder. Full of twenty and thirty-somethings with disposable income but no longer riveted by the nightlife of Boulder and needing to be living amongst it. And since the property is expensive everywhere in this area, this spot seems a bit more worth the cost. Out here, you get more space, the wilderness, the views, and still a nice sense of community.

After college, I lived downtown, but as I grew older and began writing full time, living there felt too crowded. I hated how I was constantly swerving around hundreds of joggers when I went for a bike ride on the trails. Jesus, there are a shit-ton of runners in Boulder.

But the idea of moving back to Longmont in the same neighborhood as my parents, two brothers, and their growing families was such a depressing thought. I could see all too perfectly my parents inviting me over on Friday nights while they were babysitting and feeding me hot dogs with mac 'n' cheese alongside my nieces and nephews. Don't get me wrong, I love those little rugrats, but it's really annoying being the oldest sister yet seen as the baby of the family just because I have a job that lets me wear sweatpants every day.

Not to mention, no family wants a smut writer to become their neighbor. *What kind of kinky mail deliveries will be dropped at her doorstep?*

Lynsey had moved out here about three years ago, and I followed with Dryston a year later. When we settled in, the words flowed like manna from heaven. The quiet roads were blissful, and the views were feeding my soul as well as my little fingers. I had my best friend right next door, and the words were plentiful.

Then, the breakup happened, and my creativity dried up like the homemade granola our complex manager gives us every year for Christmas.

Since really only one other douchebag on the planet knows of my struggles with words and my recently found solution to that problem, that means he's getting junk punched this fine Friday evening.

"Okay," I whisper to Lynsey as we stand in front of Dean's front door. His windows are pouring light down on us as the sun sets behind the hills. "Here's the plan. I'm going to kneel here…you knock on the door, and when he opens it, his eyes will land on you, and I'll give him a right hook to the ball sack."

"Kate!" Lynsey chastises, her thick brows furrowing together. "That's so extreme. What if he didn't do it?"

"Surely, he has a junk punch coming for something. He's a mountain manwhore. They always have it coming."

I stare back at my friend, and she looks so young with those big, brown, innocent eyes. It's no wonder Dean was drawn to her when they first met.

Shortly after I had moved here, Lynsey and I came across Dean during his daily run while we were out for a walk. I could tell instantly that there was a spark between them. They went on a couple of dates but ultimately decided just to stay friends. However, I think Lynsey still has a soft spot for the little prick.

Rolling my eyes, I concede to her wishes and stand to knock on the door. "Why are you so mature?"

A minute later, Dean whips his door open and props his arm on the frame in that impressive, masculine way he has about him. Dean is the picture image of a Boulder businessman—tall, dark, handsome, and bearded. Plus, he wears these dark-rimmed glasses that make him look really fucking smart, which he is.

But as a whole, he's part nerd, part mountain man, and part hipster rich guy. He wears these plaid slacks and slim button-downs with peach colored jackets and manages to look masculine and stylish while doing it. He's the only guy I know that could pull off a look like that and not have other people convinced he bats for the other team. Sometimes he wears no socks with his loafers, and I don't know why it looks good, but it does. Dryston tried to mimic the style, but it was awful. Super trying too hard.

But Dean, he's just got that undeniable swagger.

He's also got the coolest backstory. Dean inherited a boatload of money from his grandparents when he was eighteen. Instead of going to college and getting a high-priced education like his parents begged him to do, he decided to educate himself on the stock market.

Apparently, he had the Midas touch. Lynsey told me he doubled his inheritance in the first year. Now he's some kind of stockbroker during the day. I don't know much about what he does, but he has an office downtown that he goes to every day in his fancy, hipster suits.

Without warning, I thrust my fist into his meaty stomach. Okay, hard, chiseled stomach, but whatever. I don't think of Dean that way. All the air expels from his mouth as he hunches over, clutching his stomach.

"You're a dick, and I know that fake invoice was from you."

He growls in pain, but I know he's just being dramatic so I won't wallop him again. "Nice to see you too, Kate," he croaks.

"Just be grateful she didn't junk punch you," Lynsey chirps from behind me. "I saved you from that."

"Thanks, Lyns," he groans and steps back, silently welcoming us inside.

Dean's townhouse is identical in design to mine and Lynsey's, but he's got the minimalist bachelor pad thing going for him. Which is weird because he's rich. Maybe he spends all his money on clothes because the only furniture here is bean bag chairs and uncomfortable barstools. There's no dining room table in sight even though there's a light fixture where one should be.

I stride past him, head straight to his fridge, and help myself to a beer. I grab one for each of them and say, "You're so obvious."

"How'd you know it was me?" Dean asks, rubbing his stomach and still wincing in pain as I hand him a beer that he passes to Lynsey.

I hand him another, and the idiot actually untucks his button-down to apply the cold glass to his chiseled abs. He looks up at me and waggles his brows suggestively.

I ignore his lame move and reply, "The letterhead was too perfect, and I know you know how to use Photoshop. You should try to suck more."

He half-smiles and adjusts his black-rimmed glasses. "That's the first time I've heard that."

I roll my eyes and hoist myself up on the counter. "You're such a pig."

"You're such a weirdo," he retorts and twists the cap off his bottle. "I saw your Instagram story today. How do you think you can keep going back to Tire Depot if you post daily about it on social media?"

"Because my social media posts are my saving grace. It helps me feel less guilty about going there without being an actual customer."

He leans against the nearby wall that leads into the spare bedroom and takes a sip of his beer before replying. "So you think if you get busted and they see all the Facebook posts, they'll roll out the red carpet?"

"God, I can only dream!" I bellow dramatically and take a swig.

Lynsey giggles from her place on the barstool next to me. "You should have seen her, Dean. I thought she was going to start crying when she saw that bill."

I nod seriously. "No shit! That thing almost sent me into a state of depression. I was considering moving to a different city that has a Tire Depot because I know it's a franchise."

"You are so basic." He shakes his head and takes another swig. "I tried to get you to come check out my co-working space. We have great coffee there too without fear of being caught red-handed with stolen lattes."

"That place is for wannabe business moguls. Those aren't my people."

He crosses his arms over his chest while still fisting his beer. "And the patrons in a tire shop waiting area are? How great can they really be?"

"You need to see it to believe it, man," I state and look over at Lynsey. "But it might not have the same effect on you guys as it does on me. It's all about the *vibe* and if it comforts your inner chi. Tell Dean about the hospital cafeteria the other day, Lynsey."

Her face heats, and she shakes her head at me, her brown hair covering her face as she does. "That was a one-time thing."

"A one-time thing you should be repeating if you want to get your damn thesis finished," I state with a serious lift of the brows. "I'm telling you guys. The three of us have the best life. We can work from anywhere we want. All we need is a laptop, Wi-Fi, and an outlet, and we're golden. But our productivity is closely linked to our state of mind. If you find the vibe somewhere, you gotta fight for it. A cool vibe is like a modern-day muse. Tire Depot is to me what Fanny Brawne was to John Keats! That's poetry in motion that you cannot walk away from! They'll probably write about this in history after I croak."

"You sound like a lunatic!" Dean bellows, shoving a hand through his dark hair that's always flopping into his eyes. "I bought this place out here to make the days I work from home peaceful and quiet. If you want to subject yourself to the noise of the general public, go ahead. Knock yourself out."

"It's not noise, it's a vibe," I argue and kick my flip-flop off at his chest. He bends over to pick it up, and instead of handing it back to me, he tosses it out the kitchen back door. *Dick.* "What if you could work even better elsewhere? What if you found a place where you finished your workload in half the time? You'd have more time to hike, screw chicks, prank your friends, buy more plaid trousers."

This forces a lazy grin to spread across his face. "Have you been noticing my slacks, Kate?"

"No," I scoff defensively. "And don't change the subject. There's something to be said for waiting areas. Places where people are waiting aimlessly are mental gold mines. I feel like a fucking champion when I'm blasting out words and sitting next to a gal wasting her life away on Facebook. It's a great morale boost for Mercedes Lee Loveletter!"

Lynsey giggles. "I still can't believe you hit a bestseller list with that pen name."

I chortle knowingly. "My readers get me."

"They'd have to," Dean mumbles but shoots me a proud smile.

"I just like to keep it real." I sit back casually, relaxing into my spot on the counter. "But I will say, if there's free coffee where you find your vibe, you do sort of feel like you've pulled one over on society. We live in a world that charges for damn near everything. Parking. Cups of ice. Office space. So when you get to enjoy the little things in life, like complimentary coffee, it restores your faith in humanity. And free frickin' tastes better, that's just a fact."

"So you're going back there tomorrow," Dean states, his demeanor clearly not as euphoric as mine.

"Hells yeah! This smut won't write itself." I raise my beer to them and decide to make an impromptu toast. "Wait with me, my friends. It's the revolution of the modern day millennials. You'll see."

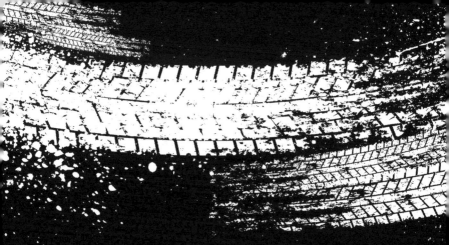

CHAPTER 4

Kate

Here's one thing I've learned after three weeks at Tire Depot: Confidence is everything. If you walk in like you own the place, no one will bat an eye. The Customer Comfort Center is mainly full of customers anyway, and those are new every day, hell, every hour. These guys are quick with a lube job.

However, there are employees who frequent the CCC. They usually come in to steal a cookie or refill their cups from the fountain pop machine. *Yeah, I know! A Coke Fountain Machine!* The only way the CCC could be more perfect is if they had *Gilmore Girls* playing on a loop on the television instead of cheesy soap operas. But honestly, I couldn't withstand that level of distraction, so shitty soaps are definitely for the best.

But since I catch sight of familiar employees on a regular basis, I carry a costume to protect my identity—my trusty baseball cap. I know I have noticeable red hair, but most people won't confront you on something so ridiculous as frequenting their waiting room without a car. At least, that's my hope.

Today, I'm deep in the word zone, baseball cap tucked down low, noise canceling earbuds in tight with some groovy synth beats that are great for anal scenes when the hairs on the back of my neck begin to stand.

My fingers pause on the keyboard, and I look up from my spot in the armchairs that surround the TV. Everybody is looking around curiously, accusingly even. Frowning, I glance around the room, and my blood runs cold when I see a pizza delivery guy standing in the enormous waiting room shouting something to the thirty-five-odd people here today.

With trembling hands, I pop out my earbuds and hear clear as day, "Mercedes Lee Loveletter, I have two large pizzas, parmesan breadsticks, and a pound of boneless chicken wings. With…" He pauses to look at the receipt. "Three dipping sauces."

Why is he bellowing the delivery receipt out loud? Is that a thing? I don't think that's a thing.

He adds, "Claim it now, or it's going in the trash."

My inner frugal girl roars to life, and my face turns red fucking hot as I croak, "I'm Mercedes."

The eighteen-year-old with greasy hair and acne scars looks at me with dead eyes. "I've been calling your name for like five minutes."

Is he seriously scolding me in front of all these people? And OMG...five minutes?

"Well, I didn't order the pizza," I defend, shifting uncomfortably and closing my laptop as everyone's eyes are pinned to mine like I'm about to start a fucking flash mob or something. "Do you know who it's from?"

"No," the boy states and moves toward me while pulling out enough food to feed ten people.

"This is a prank." I laugh nervously and slide my laptop alongside me. His dead eyes meet mine again. "I could never eat all this."

"I...don't...care," he confirms, plops the hot food on my lap, turns on his heel with his pizza bag in hand, and exits the room.

I'm literally sitting with a mountain of hot food on my lap, and everyone is fucking staring at me. No one is smiling. No one is looking like they get the joke. They're all gawking at me and thinking, what kind of nut job has pizza delivered to herself while waiting for an oil change?

Awkwardly, I get up with my boxes of food and move over to a high top table that's out of center stage, but I can feel everyone still watching me. My stomach is roiling with so much humiliation, I'm not even hungry anymore.

I see the receipt stuck to the top of the chicken wings and tear it off for a closer look. At the bottom of the credit card transaction, I find a name I know all too well:

Hannah Martin.

Hannah is the queen of romantic comedy and was the

very first author friend I made in the independent publishing community. We both had breakout books around the same time and were so new in the industry, we kind of clung to each other for survival. She lives in Florida with her husband and three kids, but I see her a few times a year at book signings. We talk almost every day about book crap and everything that amuses us. Hannah was the one to push me to keep going back to Tire Depot, so I never saw this coming.

I shakily grab my phone out of my back pocket and type out a text to her.

Me: You fucking whore.

Hannah: What?

Me: You know what. This pizza!

Hannah: I don't know what you're talking about.

Me: Your name is on the receipt.

Hannah: CRAP! I thought it'd take you at least ten minutes to figure out it was me.

Me: Yeah, crap! I am fucking mortified, you idiot. I'm trying to keep a low profile, but that delivery guy probably had to go talk to the guys at the counter to figure out where I was. I am humiliated, and you are the worst! Don't you have your own book to write? How do you have time for this?

Hannah: I'm shaking so hard with laughter, it's difficult to type.

Me: I had my earbuds in, so I didn't hear him calling my name. He listed off the food you bought for a football team and then handed it all to me—the chubby ginger creeping in the corner. Goddamn you!

Hannah: Is it good, though? I got you extra dipping sauces for those parm breadsticks. That cost extra, you know. I ain't cheap.

Me: I can't eat it because my mortification has killed my appetite! But…this does give me an excuse to try out the fountain pop machine, so…silver lining.

Hannah: My eyes are wet from laughing so hard.

Me: Yuck it up, yucky yuckerson. God, I was in the middle of writing an anal scene, so I was super in the zone too…it's no wonder I didn't hear him.

Hannah: STOP. MY STOMACH IS KILLING ME… ON ACCOUNT OF ALL THE LAUGHING.

Me: Well played, whore. Well played. And it's the burn that keeps on burning b/c my inner cheap girl will NOT let me throw these leftovers away. So I'm going to have to carry them out of here.

Hannah: Oh, I was counting on that. Want to hear something horrible?

Me: What?

Hannah: I was going to do a sub delivery, but then I decided the pizza boxes were more embarrassing.

Me: You're dead to me.

Fifteen minutes later.

Hannah: So I've been picturing you sulking and refusing to eat for the past fifteen minutes and then finally giving up and eating it anyway. Am I close?

Me: OMG, it's like you're here with me. That's exactly what I did. This food is delicious btw. But I'm still not thankful.

Hannah: But you're always welcome. ;) Best $53 I ever spent.

After finishing my lunch, I tuck the pizza under the chair in the corner where I like to sit in the afternoons because it's close to the outlets and attempt to go back to writing. Honestly, I've had a full lunch, so that should gain me an extra three hours here today.

My hero is just busting out the lube when I notice a large frame standing peculiarly close to me. I glance up and nearly squeal in shock as the same hunky mechanic stares down at me.

How did he see me back here? This spot is super secluded, and no one ever sits here.

"Can I help you?" I ask, pulling my earbuds out and taking in the broad width of his shoulders. Today, Mr. Book Boyfriend is wearing blue jeans and a black, fitted Tire Depot T-shirt. He's much cleaner than he was yesterday in his dirty coveralls that made me reconsider the profession of my current book hero.

"You're back," he states knowingly, his stunning blue

eyes drinking in my yoga pants, T-shirt, and a baseball cap.

"I, um…had an issue with one of my tires. The guys are fixing it."

"Which guys?" he asks, crossing his tan, sculpted arms over his chest. I have to crane my neck back completely to even reach his face he's so tall.

"I'm not really sure."

"Okay, well, which car?" he inquires, running a hand through his trim black hair. Damn, he's really got that tall, dark, and handsome thing down to a T. He looks almost Mediterranean. Le swoon!

I swallow slowly. "Um…I drive a Cadillac SRX."

"A Cadillac?" He barks out a small laugh. "Isn't that kind of an old lady car?"

My brows furrow. "It's not an old lady car. It's a luxury SUV. It's wonderful. I have heating and cooling seats."

"Well, if you have that kind of money to spend on a vehicle, you should look at a Lexus or a BMW. Much more sexy feel to the body. You'd look pretty damn hot driving a Lexus LX."

"Maybe I'm not trying to look hot. Maybe I like looking like an old lady." That was a really unhot thing to say, but Book Boyfriend booms with laughter and squats down next to me.

"What's your name?" he asks, and now that he's eye level with me, I get a full-on assault of just how truly handsome he is.

Yesterday, I was such a flustered mess that I didn't really have the time to take him in. Now, I can't help but ogle his entire face. His skin is tanned and damn near flawless. His jaw is square and defined, even beneath that sexy dark, five o'clock shadow. His blue eyes are like sapphires and framed by the thickest, blackest, most mesmerizing lashes I've ever seen. His lush, ruddy lips seem to rest naturally in a sort of puckered state.

Like his default face is a smolder.

I got stuck with resting bitch face.

"My name is Mercedes," I reply and then frown. Why did I give him my pen name instead of my real name? Well, I guess at least this way he won't be able to look up my file and see how many cars I've brought in over the past few weeks. Plus, sometimes it's more fun to be my alter ego rather than boring Kate Smith, who often forgets to put on deodorant.

"That's perfect. You'd look damn fine in a Mercedes," he murmurs, his deep tone sending shivers over my skin.

"And what do you drive?" I ask even though I already know the answer.

"An Indian motorcycle."

I shake my head. "Why am I not surprised?"

He smiles, his teeth a brilliant white, and I sort of like that one sticks out a tiny bit farther than the others. "Am I that predictable?"

"More predictable than my old lady car," I reply with a wink.

He smiles again, and I get those butterflies in my stomach that I painstakingly try to describe in different ways with every book I write. Stomach flips. Stomach somersaults. Fireworks in my belly. Wait, that last one is terrible, it sounds like diarrhea.

"Well, it's nice to officially meet you, Mercedes. I'm Miles Hudson," he says, taking my hand in his and shaking it gently. His palm is warm and dry and so frickin' huge, I have to squeeze my thighs together because I feel like I may start emitting a fertility musk like an animal. "Now tell me why you're really here."

My head drops back onto the chair. This can't be the end of the road. I'm not done with my book yet! I glance down at the lukewarm pizza under my chair. "Would leftover pizza keep you quiet?"

He purses those beautiful lips and looks down at my stash of barely touched food. "It might buy you some time."

I smile excitedly and nearly leap off my chair to grab the goods. "Great, time is all I need." I thrust the boxes into his chest, and he clutches them with a laugh.

"You're serious," he states with an incredulous look, his blue eyes flicking over every single feature of my overeager face as I plop back down on my chair.

"Super serious," I reply, my eyes pleading.

He takes me in for a second, and I halfway regret only putting on mascara this morning. "Very well, Mercedes. I'll leave you be, for now."

He stands up to his full height, and I can't help but notice the bulge in his jeans because it's literally eye level with me. Not like a boner bulge, the kind of bulge that a man who's well-endowed walks around with on an everyday basis. With those big hands and giant feet, it's no wonder.

"See you around the water cooler, Miles," I state brazen-ly as I tuck my earbuds back into my ears.

He looks at me with curiosity, but thankfully takes his pizza bribe and walks away. I use the opportunity to admire his backside and am not disappointed. The things I do for research purposes.

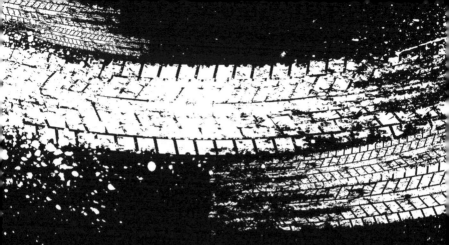

CHAPTER 5

Miles

"You haven't noticed a hot redhead in the comfort center, have you?" I ask my co-worker Sam, who's seated next to me at our favorite downtown spot, The Pearl Street Pub.

"Nope. Never seen her. She was there today?" he asks, stroking his ginger-tinged beard.

"Yes," I reply around a sip of my IPA. "And yesterday."

"What was she doing?"

I shrug. "She was just on a computer."

"What's the problem then?"

"I don't think she had a car getting work done at the shop."

"So she's syphoning free Wi-Fi? Call the cops, we've got a mooch on our hands," he says sarcastically and gestures to the bartender for another round.

I shake my head in defense. "I don't get a mooch vibe from her. It mostly feels like…desperation?"

Sam leans back and shakes his head. "Now it all makes sense. You have a fetish for desperate girls, bro."

"I do not."

"Yes, you do. You like to save them. Be the gallant protector, sweep in and guard them."

"This girl drives a big ole Caddy. She does not need saving."

"So she's nothing like Jocelyn?" he asks, his eyes narrowing seriously on me.

"Dude, I'm done with Joce. Can we please stop talking about her?"

"Miles, you got dumped by your longtime sweetheart for a rich, ugly prick. That shit sticks with you forever."

I growl and take a drink of my beer, trying hard not to squeeze the pilsner glass until it breaks in my grip. Jocelyn Vanbeek has wasted too much of my life already. Most twenty-something guys are sleeping with as many girls as they can while I spent the best years of my life obsessing over one girl. I was in a constant state of on-again, off-again hell with her for nearly a decade.

Now I'm thirty years old, and I've finally put that drama behind me. Never mind the fact that she's married and a mother now.

I take a moody sip of my beer and turn in my barstool to take in the handful of female prospects for this evening. "God, I hate that Boulder is such a sausage fest. Why do we live here again?"

"Uh, cuz my uncle is the manager, and no other boss would put up with our shit."

I smile and point out a hot brunette in the corner. "And maybe that?"

Sam shakes his head. "Making up for lost time—I get it. You do you, bro." He claps me on the back, and I proceed to make my move.

The next day, like some sort of stalker, I have my eyes glued to the window that overlooks the alley behind the garage. I'm on tire changes all day, which is nice in a way because it's mindless work. It's a little time consuming, though, because I have to clean out the wheel wells and readjust the alignment, but I'm not complaining. It makes it easy for me to keep an eye out for Mercedes sneaking around.

It's nearing the end of the day, and I'm beginning to annoy myself with how often I've looked out that damn window. Instead of cleaning up my station for tomorrow, I decide to clock out early, clean myself up, and brave the quiet Customer Comfort Center for a little coffee before I head out.

Coverall-free and dressed in jeans and a T-shirt, I walk into the empty waiting area and can't help but smile when the only soul in sight is a redhead standing in front of the coffee machine. The shop is due to close in fifteen minutes, but she's still hitting the caffeine like a boss.

Her back is turned to me as she waits for the machine to dispense her drink, so I take the opportunity to ogle the revealing cut of her denim shorts. They are frayed at the ends, true-blue Daisy Dukes that show off the muscular lines of her legs. A sliver of creamy skin peeks out beneath her gray tee when she reaches for a napkin, and I can't help but drool a little at the perfect curve of her waistline.

The brunette at the pub last night had a boyfriend, so I may be extra eager to figure out the redhead's story today. I raise my shoulders and stride over toward Mercedes with purpose. Our arms brush as I move to stand beside her and casually reach into the bakery case for a cookie.

Her head turns, and I look over to shoot her a smile. She stares down at my body first and then slowly moves her gaze up to my face.

I hit her with a wink and puzzle over the fact that she looks kind of pale. "Hey there, Red."

She looks like she's going to reply when suddenly, her face falls, and her eyes roll to the back of her head. She begins swaying, and with a cursed expletive, I fall to my knees and catch her right before her head hits the ground.

"Mercedes!" I exclaim, adjusting her head in my lap and pushing the strands of red hair away from her face. "Mercedes, are you okay?"

Her eyes blink rapidly, a little unfocused, then open. She looks first at the ceiling then over to me. "Miles, was it?"

I have to laugh a little at how normal she sounds. "Yeah, Miles."

"What's going on?" she asks, her vision becoming more

focused with every passing second.

"I think maybe you fainted. Have you ever fainted before?"

She groans and brings her hand to her face to pinch the bridge of her nose. "Only when I don't eat."

"You haven't eaten today?" I ask, shaking my head at her and glancing at the full rack of cookies next to the coffee machine. "How long have you been here?"

"Only since nine."

"Jesus Christ," I nearly growl. "Why didn't you eat a cookie at least?"

"I don't like to eat all the cookies," she nearly whines, still clearly a bit foggy from her spell. "Betty works so hard on them. It's bad enough I drink so much coffee." Her chin wobbles, and my jaw drops when I see tears filling her eyes.

"What's wrong?" I ask and try not to laugh as I brush away a wet tear path on her cheek. She looks so fucking cute, I think I might be in love.

"I just…I feel bad for Betty. No one ever tells her how good those cookies are. I got here early to try her danishes, and they were already gone. How crazy is that? Betty has to get up so early to make those fresh every day, and people gobble them up in seconds. I wonder if anyone appreciates her in her life? Do you know if she's married?"

My abs vibrate as I bite my lip and try to stifle back the laugh bubbling inside me. I don't know how much coffee she's had today, but I'm certain it was way too much. "Betty gets a hug from me every time I see her. She knows the guys in the shop love her baked goods."

"Really?" Mercedes croaks, her eyes filling with hope.

"Really."

"That's really sweet." Her chin does that trembling thing again. "I'm sorry, I get emotional when I'm hungry. You know how some people get hangry? Hungry and angry? I get emongry. Emotional and hungry. It's a thing. I got them to enter it in Urban Dictionary."

If she didn't look so pathetic, I'd be full-on belly laughing. "Well, let's go get you something to eat then. Real food, not cookies."

"I can take myself," she states, moving to sit up.

I haul her up to her feet, my hands snaking around her small waist to steady her when she sways slightly. "No way, Red. You're not driving like this. My bike is right out back."

"I just fainted, and you want me to get on the back of your motorcycle? How is that a better option?"

She makes a good point, so I pivot quickly. "Then give me your keys, and I'll drive your car. You're drunk on coffee and starvation right now, and I'm not letting you out of my sight until you eat some pizza."

"I love pizza," she replies tearfully.

"I know."

"How do you know?" She pins me with a serious look, her blue eyes bright and hopeful.

"Well, most people love pizza." I shrug. "And you had a pizza shirt on the other day and pizza delivered here yesterday."

"Oh, yeah." She tucks her hair behind her ears and makes her way over to her computer where it rests on an end table. She closes her laptop and slides it into her bag. "A quick bite and I'll quit bugging you."

"Nah, you're not bugging me," I reply, stuffing my hands into my pockets. *Maybe Sam's right—I do have a thing for damsels in distress.*

"Please," she retorts with an eye roll. "I practically fainted in your arms. We couldn't get more book-worthy if we tried."

She strides over and looks sheepishly up at me, the color already returning to her cheeks. I clasp her hand gently and pin her with a serious look. "Mercedes, there's no need to be embarrassed. This is not the first time I've had a girl faint at the sight of me."

She barks out a laugh and yanks her hand out of mine to smack me in the stomach. "Just feed me before you start reciting any more cheesy romance novel lines."

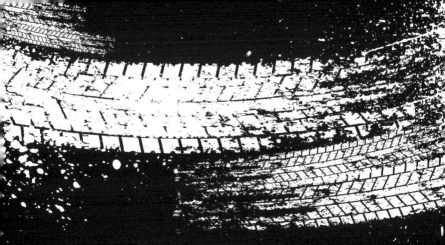

CHAPTER 6

Kate

I t's weird to hear Miles call me Mercedes, but not really if I think about it. I go to book signings all over the world where readers and author friends alike all call me Mercedes. A few people in the book world actually know my real name, but they never use it because they don't want to make the mistake of outing my real name to readers. So in the book world, I'm Mercedes, through and through.

But my Boulder friends know me as Kate.

And now Miles knows me as Mercedes.

This could get tricky.

But then again, we're just getting pizza. It's not like we're becoming Facebook friends or something. I'm making a big deal out of nothing.

Miles pulls my car up in front of Audrey Jane's Pizza

Garage. It's a hot spot in Boulder that serves tasty New York-style pizza. My mouth is already watering before we even get out of my vehicle.

I slide out of the passenger door, and Miles is right there, grabbing my hand like I'm some kind of surgical patient who just got a boob job. I pull my hand out of his. "I can walk, Miles. I feel better already. The fresh air is helping."

He nods and respectfully gives me my space while closing the door for me. "Why don't you grab one of the open patio tables, and I'll go order us a pie. Any topping objections?"

"No onions," I state seriously. "Those things are nasty and have no place on pizza."

"What about red onions?"

I narrow my eyes.

He holds his hands up and smiles. "Okay, okay, no onions."

He turns and takes the steps up to the restaurant entrance, two at a time, looking like some sort of mammoth gladiator in a world built for mere mortals. Jesus, he's so big, the steps are almost too tiny for him. And I swear he gets hotter every time I see him. Those jeans hug his ass perfectly, and I gotta say, I never thought combat boots were my thing, but on Miles, paired with those worn jeans, that tight black T-shirt, and his tanned skin? The whole mechanic-biker look is seriously working.

I find a table far away from the acoustic guitarist crooning in the corner. Boulder in the summers is like a haven for happy hours on restaurant patios with live music everywhere the eye can see. The city is bursting with aspiring musicians looking for a mic and an amp.

A few minutes later, Miles is back and has a couple of bottles of water, a bucket of beer, an order number on a stand, and a basket of steaming breadsticks.

He sets them down in front of me and says, "I had to kill a guy for these."

"I hope you didn't get blood on them," I nearly growl as I grab one of the long, swirled golden sticks and instantly pop it in my mouth like a savage. I'm too impatient to even dip in the marinara sauce at this point. "Mmmm," I groan, my eyes closing as I bite off another chunk and nearly orgasm over the taste. "You are my murderous hero."

I stuff another buttery bite in my mouth, continuing to moan my appreciation. Once I've finished an entire breadstick, I finally open my eyes to find Miles staring at me. His jaw is slack, and his hands are frozen in place on the armrests of the chair. He hasn't grabbed a beer out of the ice bucket, and he's not eating. He hasn't even opened a bottle of water. He's just…staring.

"Jesus, now what?" I ask, slicking my tongue across my lower lip to catch the dribble of garlic butter on the run.

"You are a walking, fucking tease, you know that?" he states with a shake of his head. He grabs a beer, twists the cap off, and drinks half the bottle in one go.

"How so?" I ask with a laugh, my mouth still full of doughy goodness. "I just stuffed my face with a breadstick like I haven't eaten carbs in years."

"Carbs look good on you," he replies and takes another swig.

I glance down at his hard body, scoffing because it doesn't look like he has a single soft spot anywhere. With a wistful sigh, I reach for a beer, and he quickly pulls the bucket out of my reach.

He eyes me firmly, those sapphire blues turning to slits. "Drink this whole bottle of water, then you can have a beer."

I tilt my head and hit him with my own withering stare. "I'm twenty-seven years old, Miles. I think I know when I can have a beer."

"Well, I'm thirty, and on a day you didn't faint in my arms, I would agree with you. But please, for my own sanity, will you drink some of this first?" He holds the sweating bottle of water out to me and softens his eyes in a way that makes me realize he's probably used to getting what he wants from the ladies. Maybe even a bigger manwhore than Dean.

Exhaling heavily, I take the bottle and chug down half of the contents in several obnoxious glugs. I lower the bottle, and he shoots me a satisfied smirk that actually makes him look even more handsome. He grabs a brown bottle out of the ice bucket, twists the cap off, and offers it to me.

"Thank you," I chirp and take a sip, enjoying the taste of alcohol after a long day of writing. Well, writing and fainting.

"Come on, let's hear it," he says, setting his beer down and propping his elbows on the table.

"Hear what?" I ask, batting my lashes innocently at him.

"What are you so busy doing every day at the Tire Depot Customer Comfort Center that you starve yourself into a fainting spell?"

I grab another breadstick and pop it into my mouth, chewing with a cocky smirk teasing my lips. "All I can say is that I was 'in the zone.'"

He smirks back. Damn, I wish my smirk looked half as sexy as his does right now.

"You gotta give me more than that." He gestures to the space between us. "Let's call this a safe space. You can share openly, and nothing will be held against you."

I exhale heavily because I knew there was no way I could break bread with this guy and not fess up. So I proceed to tell him my entire saga, all the way down to my favorite coffee, the pranks, and the side-eye looks.

He's not really laughing so much as biting his lower lip to stop himself from reacting at all. I continue to rave about the vibe and the people and the coffee. I even go on and on about Betty for a good five minutes. I vomit up everything I've been preaching to Lynsey and Dean, as well as my fans on social media. How the Tire Depot is like an unpretentious coffee shop that's inclusive of everyone. Well, everyone who owns a vehicle, I guess.

By the time I finish, I'm nearly out of breath.

Miles gives me a slow, disbelieving shake of the head. "And you've been doing this for over three weeks now?"

"Basically." I shrug.

"And you're writing a book? What's the book about?"

I grimace at that question. "It doesn't matter. I'm getting work done."

"Why won't you tell me what you're writing?" he asks, his head flinching back at my curt response.

"Because it weirds people out."

"How so?"

"If I tell you that, then I'll be answering your question, and I don't want to answer your question."

"I won't judge!" he argues, grabbing his beer and taking a drink.

I roll my eyes. "You'll judge."

This makes him chuckle with disbelief. "I mean, it's pretty much obvious now." I purse my lips, and he finally gives up. "Okay, fine, we don't have to talk about what you're writing." I sag with relief. "Although, I will tell you I'm a bit of a historical fan, so if you tell me you're writing the next *Game of Thrones*, we'll basically have to get married and live happily ever after."

This makes me giggle so hard, I nearly spew out the beer in my mouth. We're interrupted by the pizza's arrival, and since I still haven't had any protein for the day, we drop what we're talking about and focus on the food. The slices are bigger than my face, and we both carefully fold a piece in half and tuck into it like starved animals.

Even after three breadsticks, I'm still hungry enough to finish a whole huge slice, which is nothing compared to Miles's three slices. He just double-stacked the last two into a pizza sandwich. A pizza sandwich! I marvel at where the hell that all goes because his body looks shredded beneath that stretch cotton shirt.

Another beer later, I finally ask the question that's been in the back of my mind. "So are you going to tell anyone?"

His brows lift. "Tell them there's this hot redhead frequenting the waiting room and could we please get rid of her? Um, pass."

I giggle again. Goddamnit, this guy is turning me into a damn girlie girl. "Do you think anyone else knows about me?"

He shakes his head. "No, I asked my buddy Sam, who works at the front counter, and he didn't know what I was talking about."

"Will he say anything?"

"Nah, we're friends."

This relaxes me. "So you're a mechanic then?" I ask, realizing I've been doing nothing but talk about myself.

"Yep," he replies, wiping his mouth and sitting back in his seat, his long legs spread wide, his big feet taking up all the space between our chairs. "I started in bodywork, paint and some design stuff, but I got tired of wearing the gear, so I went back to school for mechanics. It's a good gig. Decent pay. Easy hours. No weekends."

"I know," I groan obnoxiously. "I hate that you guys close on the weekends."

That makes him chuckle. "Don't you ever take a break?"

I shake my head. "I'm a workaholic. It's the book business. The faster you release, the more you stay in people's minds. I was lucky to have my first book break out, and I don't want to lose that momentum."

He nods thoughtfully. "That's why you work through lunch."

I shrug. "That and sometimes I forget to eat."

He huffs out a polite laugh and adds, "Well, I think it's incredible that you write. I can't even think of enough words for my weekly email to my parents."

"Where do your parents live?"

"Utah. I was born and raised there. I came to Boulder for college. Well, tech school, I should say."

"That's a long way to go for tech school. Surely, they had places like that in Utah?" I pry.

He gets an uncomfortable look in his eyes. "I was following a girl."

"Ooh, yikes. Did I just stumble into a sore subject? You'll have to tell me when I push too far. I'm a writer, so I'm curious about relationships by nature. My instinct right now is to shoot rapid-fire questions at you about this woman and what happened between you two, but say the word and I won't."

"Word," he says instantly, his face losing all humor.

I swallow slowly. "Got it. No ex girlfriend talk." This works well for me too because who wants to hear about the fact that I still technically live with my ex?

"I mean, I'm over her," he offers, "but I don't like to think about her."

I nod knowingly. "I know the feeling."

Our eyes lock for a tense moment, and it's as if our

bodies have some instinctual understanding that our minds haven't caught up to yet. You can almost hear the sexual tension crackling like dry kindling in a fire.

Miles clears his throat and states, "Well, Red, don't worry. Your secret is safe with me." He gives a silly 'Scout's honor' pose and adds, "If you're all done, we should head back to Tire Depot for my bike."

"That's right!" I exclaim and quickly stand from my chair. "Yes, I'll totally take you back." My eyes wander off for a moment before I add, "You don't happen to have a key to the Customer Comfort Center, do you?"

"Mercedes!" he chastises and stands up in front of me, grabbing my shoulders in his big, manly paws. "You need a damn break, girl. Working this hard can't be good for your 'vibe' or whatever you called it."

I stare down at his warm hands on me. They are rough and hard looking, but not greasy, as one might expect of a mechanic. And the way his mouth curved when he said vibe has managed to send an instant jolt of awareness through my entire body. I actually feel my pelvis tilting toward him like it's developed a mind of its own.

"What do you do when you're not working?" I husk, and my hand flies up to cover my mouth. *Did I seriously say that out loud? Jesus Christ, Kate. Get hold of yourself. This isn't one of your books!*

Miles seems amused by my mortification, but then a wall comes down over his features, something that I haven't seen before. "I like to…ride my motorcycle. Hike. Read. Occasionally, I go to the lake."

I purse my lips together and nod. "Cool, I'll go shopping for a Harley this weekend."

"You do that." He smiles and throws his arm around my shoulders in a friendly, bro sort of way. "Come on, let's get out of here before I start boring you with why you should get an Indian instead of a Harley."

I giggle at that. "Oh, mechanic talk, sounds kinky."

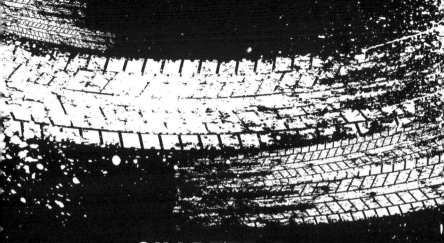

CHAPTER 7

Kate

Y ou know that moment in the movie *Sandlot* when Squints sees the lifeguard, Wendy Peffercorn, walking on the sidewalk? He quickly cleans his Coke-bottle glasses with his shirt, romantic music swells, and the video shifts to slow motion of the curvy blonde?

Well, for the next week at Tire Depot, I'm the creeper, Squints, and Miles is Wendy frickin' Peffercorn.

The first day I came back to write after Miles and I had pizza together, I ended up stopping at the open garage door in the back alley. I had a perfect view of Miles hard at work, and I just stood there, laptop bag on my shoulder, jaw dropped, heart racing.

He was stacking a bunch of tires. *So many tires.* They must have just gotten a shipment in or something because he was sweating profusely. At one point, he stopped what he was doing, unzipped his charcoal coveralls and pulled them off his shoulders to cool down. He was wearing another one of those hot, tight athletic tanks. Nike brand. Black. But I could tell it was soaked through with sweat. His arms were glistening in the light as he wiped his brow on his grease-covered forearm. He grabbed a bottle of water, took several long drinks, his thick neck contracting with each swallow, and proceeded to pour the remaining contents down his face.

You just can't make this shit up!

The next moment, he turns to look over his shoulder at a co-worker, and his blue eyes were glowing so brightly against his tan complexion that he didn't seem real. I seriously felt my knees wobble and it wasn't because I skipped lunch that day.

Suddenly, the billionaire I was writing about in my novel seemed all wrong. His six-pack too artificial. Sex appeal wasn't created in a gym with weights and treadmills. No, it was born in powerful, grungy garages where men, real fucking men worked with their hands. Where they got so dirty, they had to use a special manly soap to clean themselves up. You can't find that shit at Bath & Body. Pure fucking testosterone.

Feeling inspired like never before, I scurry off to the comfort center to take two pages' worth of notes for a new series. Jesus Christ, why had I never considered a mechanic before? My readers would salivate all over this! I can't help myself as I begin writing the first chapter, the voices of the characters so clear, I have to get them out. Right fucking now.

It's hours later when I'm ripped from my fictional world by a strong, overwhelming presence in the room. I look up from my laptop to find Miles watching me from the doorway, his mouth tipped into a lazy smile. His eyes are smoldering with something I've never seen before.

I pop out my earbuds when he walks over to me. "You look hyper-focused," he drawls as he drops down on the leather chair next to me.

My eyes fly wide as I quickly take my pen out of my hair and nervously mess with my top knot. "Yeah…I, erm…got a new book idea today."

"Oh, really?" he asks, running his hands down his denim-clad thighs. The smell of his manly soap invades my nostrils. He's showered. The sweat and dirt that were all over him hours ago are long gone, and he smells like a fucking mountain after a fresh rain.

"Do they have showers here?" I ask curiously, so I can make a mental note for my work in progress.

He laughs at that peculiar question. "Yes, why?"

My cheeks flame red. "You smell nice and fresh. Your hair is even still damp, right?" I reach out and comb my fingers through his short, black strands, moisture coating all five of my digits. My insides squeeze at the intimacy behind this embrace.

His eyes flutter closed like he's enjoying my caress as much as I am, so I take the opportunity to continue my path from the top of his head down to the base of his taut, strong neck. Jesus, this guy is all man.

I suddenly realize we're not alone and quickly force

myself to stop petting the hot mechanic.

Miles's blue eyes flutter open. "Does that mean you abandoned your other story idea?"

I laugh at that notion. "Lord, no. I just have to write stuff when it comes to me, or it's gone forever. These are only notes and the first chapter, so I can dive in easier when I come back to it. I'm still very much working on my original story."

"Well, I'm glad the comfort center is still giving you good vibes." He looks down at my computer. "Are you almost done for the day?"

I bite my lip. "Maybe?"

"Do you want to go grab something to eat?"

"Like a date?" I ask because Jesus, I have a big mouth and no filter, and I can't help myself.

His brow furrows. "Nah, just food." He shrugs.

"I like food," I reply, trying not to take his reply as a complete rejection as I begin closing my laptop.

Suddenly, reality crashes in on me. "Shoot, I'm sorry…I actually can't. I promised my girlfriend I'd go for a walk with her like…" I quickly look at my phone for the time. "Now. Shit, I need to go."

He nods and smiles, looking slightly disappointed. "I understand."

"Rain check?" I ask, and begin packing up my gear.

"Definitely." And with that, he gives me a friendly wave goodbye and exits the room like the stunning fucking stallion he is.

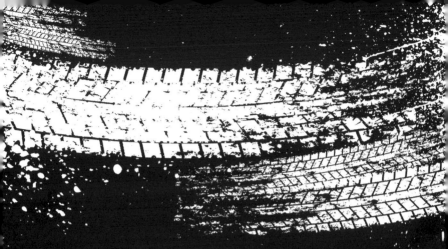

CHAPTER 8

Miles

I've never been more excited to come to work each day. I've certainly never entered the Customer Comfort Center this much in one week. I keep telling the guys at the front desk that I forgot my lunch and I'm stocking up on Betty's baked goods, but honestly, it's just to see Mercedes.

She's so fucking cute when she's writing. I find myself pretending to be on my phone in the doorway so I can watch her work for a while. Her eyes drift off into space a lot, and occasionally, she does some weird physical movements, like she's trying to figure out how to type an action in a book. One time, I had to bite my fist to stop myself from laughing out loud when she dreamily closed her eyes, licked her lips seductively, and air-kissed the room. She totally writes dirty books.

I love how she's in her own little world, completely herself, and completely unaware of the world around her. And she's doing it in a tire shop waiting room. I've never met a girl like her.

I find myself drawn to her every day. I like to stop in before I leave to see how her day was. Sometimes, she tells me how many words she wrote, which means nothing to me because I have no clue how many words it takes to write a book. But she seems excited by her progress, and I love the look on her face. Then she usually asks me how my day was, and I watch her eyes gloss over when I start talking cars and tools to her. It's a game we play, drenched with flirting, but nothing ever comes of it.

I haven't asked her to hang out after work again like I did earlier this week. I feel like the first time was a mistake, and the more I talk with her, the more I realize she's not just some chick I can hook up with. She's…cool. It's best to keep our relationship "Tire Depot exclusive." Lord knows I can't be trusted around someone who's beautiful, funny, and not crazy.

"Another week of work down," I state, dropping into the seat beside her and looking around the empty comfort center. It's the end of the day and Friday, so nobody is coming in for a late service.

"Big plans for the weekend?" Mercedes asks, closing the laptop on her legs and resting her hands on top of it. She's adorable today in a little red sundress, quite different from the typical activewear I usually see her in.

"My buddy and I might go down to Golden Gate Park

tomorrow. We try to hit this great hiking trail there every summer."

"That sounds fun and suuuper masculine," she states, turning to face me. Her blue eyes drop down to my lips, then she quickly looks away.

I frown and shift to face her more as well. "What about you?"

She exhales heavily. "Oh, I'll probably do some more writing. Maybe check out a real coffee shop."

I gasp dramatically. "But you'd have to actually pay for your coffee."

She deadpans, "I know, but Tire Depot doesn't have a suggestion box for me to ask if they'll start offering week-end hours."

"I'd rip that suggestion right up," I retort with a serious tone. "I like my weekends. Don't encourage them to mess with my weekends."

She smiles, and I get a flash of that dimple in her cheek. "Fine, go. Be a man. Catch some fish. Get some dirt all up in ya."

Her eyes drift down my body, and she pulls her lower lip into her mouth. Her brows pinch together in the most adorably intense way. Goddamn, she's cute. And if I could read her mind, I'd swear she's picturing me naked. I sure as hell have pictured her naked about eight times a day since the moment she collided with me in the alley. But I'm a dude, we do those things. Girls are usually a lot less obvious.

That's why I'm ninety percent sure she writes erotic books. I get the feeling that she has a dirty mind, and I really fucking dig that. I tried googling the author name Mercedes, and with only a first name, I didn't find anyone resembling her. And if I asked for her last name at this point, I'd be too obvious. So for now, I shall respect her wishes and not push for intel on the writing part of her life. Especially because she asked me not to.

"Well, you have a good weekend," I state. Leaning across the armrest, I kiss her on the cheek. I pull back and freeze, staring into her wide and clearly surprised eyes. She smells like fucking flowers, but that's besides the point. "I have no idea why I just kissed you on the cheek."

"Me neither!" She giggles, her cheeks and neck turning a rosy hue before my very eyes. "You know, since we're basically co-workers, this could be grounds for a sexual harassment claim."

I groan and stand, running my hand through my hair with embarrassment. "You should. I'm pathetic. And horribly inappropriate."

"You're not pathetic, and it's too soon for me to tell how inappropriate you *really* are." She smiles and waggles her eyebrows mischievously at me. "If you knew the dirty thoughts that run through my mind every day, you'd know I'm certainly no victim."

"I knew it!" I laugh and snap my fingers in triumph, reaching out and stretching my arms out wide. "There's something about you that screams...dirty mind. I think it's your red hair."

She bites her lip and eyes my torso, her gaze slowly falling to my groin area. My dick does a jump. More like a thump considering the fucker has its own pulse right now.

With a simple shrug, she replies, "I blame a lot of my problems on the color of my hair. Redheads have it rough as kids."

"Your hair is fucking gorgeous, and little kids are pricks." I close my eyes and pinch the bridge of my nose, grateful no one else is around to hear me make a damn fool of myself right now. "On that note, I'm going to go, and I swear to you that I usually have way more game than this. I hope this interaction doesn't negatively reflect on my book boyfriend status in your mind."

She laughs heartily. "Don't worry about it, Miles. Your book boyfriend status is still very much secure."

With a big smile, I turn and head out, calling over my shoulder, "See you Monday, Mercedes."

"See you around the coffee machine, Miles."

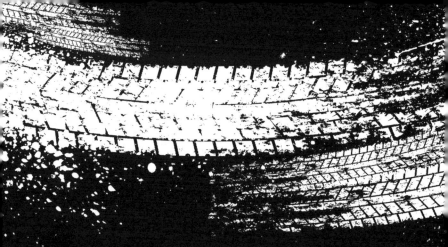

CHAPTER 9

Miles

"**W**hat are you fucking waiting for, bro? She tells you she has dirty thoughts and you don't think…'yep, I'm gonna tap that'?" Sam shouts, slamming his beer down on the bar and running a hand over his blond buzz cut.

"Nah." I shake my head adamantly and shoot a dirty look at the dude pressing up against me to order a drink. It's Friday night, so The Pearl Street Pub is packed, but that doesn't mean I need to be able to smell this guy's deodorant. The dude smartly takes a hint and gives me some space. I turn back to Sam. "I can't tap that, she's too cool. Then I'd have to see her every day in the comfort center. It'd be awkward as fuck."

"You wouldn't have to see her. Just don't go in there

anymore after you bang her. Problem solved."

"I like seeing her," I reply and frown over the fact that seeing her is one of the best parts of my days.

"You're so lame," Sam says, pulling his phone out of his pocket and checking the time. "Shit, we'd better get going. My buddy goes live at eleven, and I don't want to end up stuck in a line."

We pay our tabs and walk the two blocks down Pearl Street to The Walrus Saloon. It's a dive bar that's partially underground and usually swarming with college students, but since it's summertime, it shouldn't be too bad. Plus, I'm single. It's good for me to hit the meat market venues on occasion.

I don't necessarily dig younger chicks, but I'm guilty of taking home a college girl once last year. I could tell she was a lot younger than me, and I was so fucking paranoid that I asked to see her ID before we left the bar. I'm not proud, but I needed someone to help get over the final breakup of many with Jocelyn.

That girl fucked me up.

Ten years of 'will they or won't they?' We were worse than Ross and Rachel. And the mind games she played will stay with me permanently, I'm sure. Whenever we were broken up, which was a lot, she would find out what bar I was at that night and show up just to make out with a random dude right in front of me. She was fucking nuts. I'd probably still be living that sweet hell if she didn't get knocked up by some rich prick during our last "break."

After some dark days, I'm in what I like to call my 'bang

and bail' period. One night. No repeats. No strings. Time to add some long-neglected notches on my bedpost.

Tonight, I'm looking forward to finding a girl who will help take my mind off the redhead I know I shouldn't bang.

The music is loud as we make our way down the stairs to the Walrus Saloon. It's got a dark, grungy feel to it, but it's the only place in Boulder that offers any kind of real dance floor. My boots crack on the peanut shells scattered all over as Sam and I head to the two newly vacated stools at the end of the bar.

Sam works on flagging down a bartender while I stand behind my stool and do a sweep of the bar. It's mostly dudes except for a big group of girls hoarding most of the dance floor already. They are all surrounding a girl in a little white dress with a veil tucked into her hair. Bachelorette parties are usually a good time, and I tip my chin to a couple of girls who are eyeing me and whispering to each other. Being big and tall is always a draw for the ladies. And the fact that I'm not ugly makes it pretty easy to take my pick of a group like that.

I pass over another group of girls collectively sucking blue liquid out of a giant fishbowl-sized drink and think I see one that might interest me when a familiar shock of red catches my eye.

I swivel my gaze to see Mercedes walking down the entrance steps. She's laughing hard at something someone behind her said, but to be honest, I'm not looking at her face for very long.

She's dressed in a skimpy black and white striped skirt,

her sculpted legs on full display and looking even sexier than the time I saw them in those Daisy Dukes. She has a low-cut black tank top on with a long pendant necklace hanging right between her full breasts. I'd be concerned she wasn't wearing enough clothes if it weren't for the sexy, tight black leather jacket unzipped and layered over the top of the ensemble. At least that covers some of her body.

Her red hair is straight and shiny over her shoulders, like a curtain of color, and styled in a way I've never seen before. It's a lot less natural than usual but definitely still sexy. This is a far different look from what I see at Tire Depot.

She's a fucking knockout.

My dick roars to life between my legs, and I have to close my eyes and concentrate, so it doesn't get a mind of its own and say hello to the crowd. Dicks can be such…dicks.

She turns her head and smiles at the guy who follows her down the steps. Draping his arm around her shoulders, he's wearing glasses and dressed like he's headed to a fucking wedding, not a dive bar on Pearl Street. A small brunette flanks her other side and is digging in her purse to pay the cover charge to the bouncers.

Mercedes laughs again at something the glasses dude says. Her smiling eyes begin to peruse the bar and finally land on me. I tower over pretty much everyone here, so it's no surprise she spotted me. But the look on her face isn't the easy smile I've grown used to seeing this past week.

She pulls her lip into her mouth and snaps her head to the guy who's suddenly tightened his grip around her shoulders. He leans down so she can whisper in his ear and my eyes follow his other hand as it cups her hip. His thumb is dangerously close to the underside of her breast, and the familiarity of their embrace has my blood running hot.

What. The. Fuck?

"Jesus man, what's up? You look like you're ready to rip someone's head off!" Sam says from beside me as he shoves a beer into my chest.

"What?" I nearly growl, wrapping my fingers firmly around the cold bottle.

"What's going on? You look like…" His voice trails off as he sees where my steely gaze is focused. "Is that the same redhead?"

I nod, my jaw tight.

"I thought you were just friends with the girl."

"I am," I snap, sneering down at him.

"Well, then fucking cool it, bro, because you look like you're itching for a fight." He stands up off his stool and tips his chin up to rumble into my ear. "You look how you used to when Joce was fucking around."

His words are like a bucket of ice water tossed in my face. I instantly sag against his hand clasping my shoulder and turn away to take a big gulp of my beer. Exhaling heavily, I hunch over and prop my elbows on the bar, running a hand through my hair.

Fucking hell, what's wrong with me? I barely know Mercedes. I've only seen her outside the shop once. That doesn't mean I can go all beast mode on her when I see her with another guy.

A gentle tap on my shoulder has my head snapping to

the right.

It's Mercedes.

My adorable redhead.

Up close and personal like this, she's not adorable, though. She's super fucking sexy. Her eyes are lined with a thick black pencil. Brown eyeshadow on her lids makes her blue irises brighter than ever before. Her glossy, red lipstick emphasizes her lips. The plumpness of them reminds me of the time I watched her wrap her mouth around that bread-stick and—

"Hey, Miles," Mercedes says, tucking a strand of silky hair behind her ear.

"Hey, Mercedes," I husk, clearing my throat and standing to my full height.

In her heels, the top of her head reaches my chin, and I can smell the floral scent of her shampoo from this vantage point.

"Fancy seeing you here!" She laughs awkwardly and gives me a chummy punch to the shoulder. She glances behind her at where Sam has retreated to give us some privacy. "I thought you were going camping?"

"I thought you were writing," I retort and look over her head to see Sam sliding his pointer finger across his neck, silently telling me to cool it.

Her cheeks deepen in color, but she holds her chin up high and replies, "Well, as you said, I need to take a break on occasion."

I nod, clenching my jaw as my gaze finds the dude she came in with. He's staring us down like we're the live entertainment tonight instead of the DJ up in the booth.

"That your boyfriend?" I ask, nodding to Mr. Fancy Pants.

Mercedes looks over her shoulder and begins laughing. "God, no. That's Dean. He's my friend. And that's Lynsey standing next to him, my other friend. We're all neighbors, kind of?"

I nod, narrowing my eyes at the guy in annoyance. Whatever he's trying to communicate is a different language than the one Mercedes is speaking right now. He's certainly not watching her like he's just a friend.

Turning away, I point over at Sam, who's doing a poor job of pretending to look for something in the giant barrel of peanuts while eavesdropping on our conversation. "This is my buddy, Sam."

Sam's head pops up like he hasn't been listening to every word we've said so far. *Smooth move, Sam.* In one giant step, he's next to Mercedes and shaking her hand.

"Hi," she says with a genuine smile.

"Nice to meet you…"

"Mercedes," I finish when she doesn't look like she's going to. I look at Mercedes and add, "Sam works with me at the shop."

Mercedes nods slowly, clearly more cautious of him now that she knows where he works. "Nice to meet you."

"We're going camping tomorrow," Sam offers, clearly trying to make up for my current lack of social skills. "We head out in the morning."

She looks up at me through her thick mascaraed eyes

and smiles. "I'm heading to the coffee shop in the morning."

I offer a half-smile back to her, and our eyes hold each other for a long moment. It feels like we're both thinking the same thing at this moment. A thought resembling the question, *why have we not hung out again?*

But for some reason, I think we both know the answer to that.

Mercedes breaks the silence. "Well, I'll lea—"

"Can I buy you a drink?" I ask quickly before she makes her great escape. I know it's stupid, and I know it's probably not wise, but I'm not ready to see her go yet.

That dimple in her cheek catches my eye as she glances back at her friends for a split second. "A drink sounds good."

"Please, take my seat," Sam rushes out, turning his stool to her and all but shoving her down into it. "I'm going to go say hi to my friend. He's the DJ tonight."

"Thanks," Mercedes says, and he runs off like an overeager puppy dog retrieving his mommy's slippers.

I exhale heavily and take the seat adjacent to her that I've been propped on this entire time. "What's your poison? I can ask if they serve coffee in an IV drip if you'd like."

My familiar teasing has her laughing, and she swats my arm comfortably. "I'll take a beer. I've been drinking liquor already, and it's never good for me to stick with liquor all night."

Our knees brush together as I angle myself to her. "And why is that?"

"Well, I either get mean, or I get slutty."

"Slutty?" I cock a brow at her and slap my hand on the bar. "Bartender! Let's get this girl a shot!"

She laughs that deep, rich laugh, and I can already feel my growly demeanor disappearing. "Beer!" she corrects, pointing at what I have in my hand.

The bartender nods and pops the top off a beer and slides it down the bar to land perfectly in her hands. She takes a sip and smiles her thanks at me. "So what have you been up to since I saw you six hours ago?" she asks.

"Oh, I cured cancer and decided to go out and celebrate with my buddy, Sam. You?"

"Same." She shrugs with a serious look that she's having trouble maintaining. "Do you live downtown?"

I shake my head. "Nah, I live nearby, in Jamestown. I bought a fixer-upper there last year."

She splays her hands out on the bar and drops her head with a groan. "Oh man, you're one of those painfully handy guys, aren't you?"

I chuckle at her question. "I don't know about handy, but I can usually figure most stuff out. Or I google it after screwing it up and then figure it out."

She props her stunning face in a hand. "I bet you clean your own gutters too, don't you?" she says with a speculative look and takes another long pull of her beer.

"Yes, I do. But I usually end up cleaning them out in the rain because I only remember to do it when it's pouring outside, and the water is spilling over the top of them."

She nods and bites her lip like she's really deep in thought. "So you're all wet on a ladder and digging into your gutters to get the leaves out?" She uses her hands to gesticulate the action, then shakes her head.

"Yes." I chuckle. "What the fuck are you doing? Why does your face look like that?"

She takes a deep breath. "I'm painting a pretty picture in my head."

I roll my eyes. "Am I shirtless in this picture?"

She giggles knowingly. "Noo, you're wearing one of those tank tops you wear under your coveralls."

"You're very observant," I murmur around the mouth of my bottle. "Always plotting." I shoot her a wink as I take a sip.

She shoots one back.

By the time we're on our second round, neither of us is feeling any pain, both clearly having indulged prior to this moment.

Mercedes licks her lips and turns her body to face me straight on so her legs are pressed together between my sprawled out ones. "Miles," she states with a twinkle in her eye.

"Mercedes."

A peculiar look shoots over her face, but she brushes it away and sets her beer down. "Why have you never asked me to hang out again like you did that night we had pizza together?"

She must be tipsy to be coming in hot with questions like that. I eye her for a moment, noting that her eyes are a bit more hooded than before, but I'm not exactly sober either, so I'm not one to judge.

AMY DAWS

I shrug nonchalantly and hit her with honesty. "Tire Depot seems safer."

"Safer," she repeats, grabbing her bottle, but pausing before she takes another drink. "Meaning, I won't run into you again and catch my flip-flop under your boot?"

"Something like that." I chuckle, picking at the label on my beer with my thumbnail. "Which is probably for the best because, in those sexy shoes, I'm pretty sure you'd end up breaking an ankle or worse."

Her posture straightens, and the corners of her mouth turn down in a pleased smirk. "You think my shoes are sexy?"

She lifts the black strappy sandal up between us, causing her skirt to ride up dangerously high. I see a whole lot of tanned thigh and a flash of black panties, and instantly, my dick pushes up against my zipper.

Mercedes notices what she's just done and quickly drops her leg and turns toward the bar. Pursing her lips together, she demurely shimmies her skirt back down her thighs.

I lean in to whisper in her ear. "Really sexy."

She clears her throat and turns to look at me. "So what are your real plans for tonight? Were you really just here with your buddy to hang? Or were you on the hunt?"

"On the hunt?" I question her phrase because it sounds funny coming from her.

"For tail!" she chirps, twirling in her seat to look at the bar that's now filled to the brim. "For chicks. For a one-night stand that gets super awkward in the morning

76

because she wants to make you pancakes and you want to chew your arm off and sneak out before she wakes up."

I belly laugh at that very apt description. "Well, considering I was with my ex for the better part of my twenties, yeah, I guess I'm looking for casual."

She nods intently, eyeing me down her nose. "I could tell that about you."

"How?" I ask, disbelieving.

"You wear those T-shirts that show off your biceps." She reaches out and snaps the material around my arm. "This can't be comfortable. Why do you wear shirts like this?"

"This is how most shirts fit me." I look down at her creamy legs. "And that little skirt you're wearing is for comfort, I suppose?"

She shrugs innocently. "It's stretchy."

"Well, so are my shirts."

We both laugh and take another drink.

"So what's your type? What draws your eye? Gimme a hair color, something to work with." She's looking out at the people again like she's seriously going to help me find someone to bang.

My gaze lingers on her hair, sliding down the smooth strands that fall softly over her chest. I clear my throat and reply, "Brunettes. My ex was a blonde. I'm over blondes. They do not have more fun."

"Brunettes, it is. Let's see." She claps her hands and analyzes the crowd until her eyes land on someone. "Not my friend, Lynsey. She already dated our friend Dean, and it was so awkward for months after that."

I eye her friends who are at a table with a few other people, and they don't seem the least bit concerned that I've monopolized their friend for the evening. "Okay, friends are off-limits. That's fair."

"How about that one?" She points at a girl sipping on a cocktail in a corner booth. She's trapped in by a couple of other girls who look like they are having a major bitchfest about someone.

"She's swarmed by other chicks. I try to avoid the packs. They get awkward."

"How so?"

"Well, there's always one friend who tries to cock block. One friend who tries to steal the guy. And another who'll make her friend feel bad about herself for being a slut."

"Man, girls can be mean."

"You're telling me." I take a pull of my bottle. "What about you? Why aren't you on the hunt? You said you were over your ex, right?"

"Oh, I totally am. He's vile."

"And your friend Dean isn't a prospect?" I ask, feeling annoyed at the fact that I still seek that verification.

"No." She shakes her head. "He reminds me of my brothers."

I doubt your brothers touch you the way he did earlier.

She slaps her hand on her knee and bellows gallantly, "But you know what, Miles, you're right! I should totally find a random hookup tonight."

"Whoa, I never said anything about random."

"Well, you're doing it, so why can't I?"

I narrow my eyes. "You don't seem like the random type."

"Maybe I should be." Her eyes narrow when she leans in and whispers against my lips. "Can I tell you a secret, Miles?"

"You can tell me anything, Mercedes."

She giggles and crooks her finger for me to lean in even closer. I'm so close I can smell the faint scent of her cherry lip gloss, and it's not helping the half boner having a party in my pants.

Her lips graze my ear when she whispers, "My writing makes me horny."

I nearly choke on my beer. "I'm sorry, what?"

"My writing makes me horny." She pulls back and nods her confirmation. "I'm serious. I have a sex toy that works really well and really fast, but I miss the heat of a man, ya know?"

My eyes scrunch together, and I rub my fingers in the sockets to make sure I'm awake and hearing this all correctly. "I mean...I don't really ever miss the heat of man, so I don't think I know exactly what you're saying."

"Fine, the heat of a woman." She rolls her eyes dramatically "You know what I'm talking about. The heat."

I frown and shake my head. "You're going to have to elaborate because I think of a lot of things when I think of women, but their body temperature isn't one of them."

"You asked for it." She laughs and leans in so she's speaking low and soft and directly into my ear. "The heat of a woman is so much more than temperature. It's the soft, sensual curves of the female form. The way your fingers dig into the meat of her thighs when she's wrapped around you. Her smooth, sunken tummy when she's on her back, the delicate bumps of her ribcage when she's throwing her head back in pleasure. Tight little nipples in pillows of creamy softness. The fact that you could fold yourself around her and envelop her body almost entirely and still want more. You're saying you don't miss that kind of heat?"

I blink slowly, recovering from what just happened. Her voice was a sensual, verbal caress straight on my cock. Then there was the warm heat of her breath on my ear. The deep husk of her tone. The way her warm palm rests softly on my thigh.

Fucking hell.

My dick immediately went from a halfy to a fully, and I'm so turned on that I don't even give a fuck.

"You totally write erotica," I state, my voice deep and gravelly with arousal. I sit back and shake my head at her.

"Damnit!" She snaps her fingers in front of her, clearly annoyed that she let herself get carried away. "I didn't want you to know!"

"Why not?" I nearly growl. "What's the big secret?"

"Because it changes the way you look at me."

"How so?"

"Well, you'll either one, think I'm some kind of sex freak who's super frickin' experienced in the bedroom."

"That's completely accurate." I laugh.

"See!"

"I'm kidding, go on."

"Or two, you'll be embarrassed by what I do and not want to tell anyone."

"Are you joking?" I bark and lean forward to turn her face so she's looking at me. She actually looks kind of sad, and that blows my damn mind.

"Well, your buddy doesn't count. He's probably a horn ball," she corrects. "I mean, anyone that's super important to you."

"Fuck that," I argue and shake my head adamantly. "Then you don't know me at all, Mercedes."

"I know your kind," she retorts with a cocky edge to her voice like this doesn't really bother her. But I can clearly see that it does. "You dudes are all alike. You want a lady in the streets and a freak in the sheets."

"Bullshit."

She shrugs. "I don't believe you."

"Why not?"

"Because it was a huge reason my ex and I broke up. He asked me to lie to his family about what I did for a living."

My blood runs cold. "What?"

The shamed look on her face has my jaw clenching with rage. "Yeah, I thought it was weird that we'd been together for so long and he still hadn't introduced me to his family. Then his sister was getting married, and he sort of had to bring me to the wedding. That was when he asked me to tell everyone that I wrote cozy mysteries."

"What a fucker." I growl and take a huge gulp of my beer to try to tamp down my rage.

"Well, he is that, but I write some really kinky shit in my books, and that's not exactly easy to tell your grandma about."

"Fuck that." I growl and slam down my beer. "I'd tell my grandma about you."

"You would not!" she argues with an incredulous laugh. "Grandmas hate me! *My* grandma hates me."

"Your grandma can't possibly hate you. You're perfect!"

"She hates me. She's really religious, and every time I come home, she tries to arrange a meeting with me and her priest. She thinks I need an intervention or an exorcism or something."

I can't help but laugh. "I'm sorry, it's not funny." I reach out and touch her thigh in apology.

She shrugs and picks at the label on her beer. "It's a little funny."

I watch her for a moment and hate the way her posture has hunched. She went from a feisty, hilarious, sex-talking hottie to this slightly uncomfortable, semi-muted version of the Mercedes I've been getting to know the past couple of weeks. Her ex is a fucker, and if he was here, I'd make damn sure he knew it.

Jaw tight with determination, I hold out my hand to her. "Come with me."

She scowls at me. "Where are we going?"

"We have to go outside for a minute…just trust me."

I pull her out of her seat and exhale heavily through my nostrils at how high her skirt has ridden up. She smiles sheepishly and pulls her hand from mine to pull it down.

Damnit, she's way too sexy.

She gives her friends a one-minute sign by holding her finger up as I pull her through the crowd to the exit. The bouncer stamps both of our hands and takes her half-drunk beer as I haul her up the stairs and out the front door.

It's balmy out, the night air damp and hot against our skin. The blue neon lights of the Walrus Saloon sign glow against our skin as I look around for a private area away from the noisy drunks. Yanking her around the corner, I pull my phone out of my pocket and find a contact on my screen. I turn it to Mercedes.

"Press the call button," I state.

She squints at the screen, and her eyes fly wide. "Are you insane?" she exclaims and shoves the phone away. "It's after midnight, Miles. We are most definitely not calling your grandma!"

I roll my eyes and shrug. "She won't care. She fucking loves me. I'm her favorite grandchild. Press call. I want to tell her about your dirty books."

"I will not! I'd never call a sweet old grandmother in the middle of the night and tell her about my smut. Oh shit, I need to take a note. I just thought of a really funny line for one of my books."

She thrusts her hand through the low-cut neckline of her tank top and pulls her phone out of her bra. I frown down at that image. "How long has that thing been in there?"

"What do you mean?" she snaps. "The whole time. I didn't fucking *magic* it into my shirt, you idiot."

I chuckle at the ease of which she just insulted me. "Fine, we're calling my sister then. She'll tell you the truth." I press send.

"Your sister could be asleep too," she grumbles while typing a note in her phone, slightly swaying on her feet.

I shake my head at that comment. "She's taking summer classes at the University of Utah. She's probably out partying."

The phone rings a few times and then picks up with loud, riotous noise in the background. "Megan," I shout into the phone and press my other finger to my ear because I don't know how I'm going to hear her with all that noise.

Mercedes giggles and presses a finger to my lips to shush me. I bite playfully at her finger and mouth, "Sorry."

"Miles," Megan shouts back into the line.

"Megan," I repeat a bit softer this time. "Can you go somewhere quiet for a second? I want to ask you a question really quick."

It sounds like she's on the move because already I can hear her a little bit better. "Miles, how is it possible for you to cock block me from five hundred miles away?"

"Big brother intuition," I state and stand straight. "Who is the fucker anyway?"

"Miles," she chastises, and then the sound softens as she moves into what I believe to be a bathroom because I hear a toilet flush in the distance. "Shut up and ask your question."

I look at Mercedes and give her the quiet finger as I click the speaker button on my phone screen so she can hear what Megan's saying. "So Meg, I met this girl tonight.

She's super fucking hot, like suuuper hot."

"Gross, Miles!" Megan groans.

Mercedes rolls her eyes.

"Okay, so this chick writes sexy books. Like that's her job. Kinky, dirty shit, I think. And she was saying grandmothers hated her, and I told her our grandma would be totally into it…true or false?"

"Duh, Grams is a freak, so that's totally true."

I thrust my fist into the air and laugh heartily as Mercedes's mouth drops open in pleased surprise.

"Mom would be into those books too, don't you think?" I ask and smile even wider when Mercedes cups her hands over her cheeks, listening in rapture.

"Dude, Miles, of course, she would. You should get her name so Mom can look her up. Hell, Dad would probably read her stuff too. Don't you remember when I was ten and found those porno books in Mom and Dad's bathroom? I had to ask you what milk jugs were, and you flipped out and turned all red?"

I laugh so hard I have to brace myself on the brick wall. "Oh shit, I had forgotten all about that!"

"Yeah, our parents are hornballs, bro. You know this, why are you asking?"

"Because this chick wouldn't believe me."

"Well, give her the name of Mom's book blog website."

"Oh yeah, what's it called again? I forget."

"Dirty Birdy's Book Blog. She even passes out business cards at church. She's so embarrassing."

I can't wipe the satisfied smile off my face as I stare into the phone. "You read the books too, I thought, right?"

"Oh God, yes. Mom's the one who got me hooked. It's totally weird when she pushes her blog shit in everyone's faces. Like God, Mom, try not to be so desperate."

"Agreed," I reply and look up at Mercedes. My smile falls when her wide eyes are glossy in the dim lighting. *Is she upset?*

"So who is this girl? I want to read her," Meg asks.

A tear slips down Mercedes's face, so I know I need to get off the phone pronto. "I'll find out, but I gotta go, Meg. Don't fuck that dude tonight or I'll kill him."

"You don't even know who it is."

"It's probably one of my friends."

A sharp intake of air breaks through the phone line. "How could you possibly—"

I hang up, my mind completely wrapped up in the tears running down Mercedes's cheeks. "What happened? What did I say? Was it something my sister said? I wasn't trying to offend. I swear I'm not judging you. I was just—"

I can't talk anymore.

I can't defend myself.

I can't say another damn word.

Because her lips are on mine, and they taste like fucking cherries.

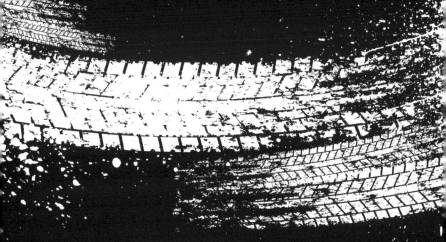

CHAPTER 10

Kate

You know that moment in a love story when two enemies are arguing and fighting and screaming and thrashing and so fucking mad at each other that they can't see straight?

Then suddenly, there's this bolt of lightning, and they crash together like two fucking cars colliding head-on at a hundred miles an hour?

That's me right now as I press my lips to Mile's perfect mouth.

I don't even know that much about him, but I have to kiss him. It's a knee-jerk, instinctual thing that tells me this guy is worth kissing. I have to shut him up and kiss the person that has been talking nonstop to his sister for the past five minutes.

With one simple phone call, this hot mechanic has squashed every thread of doubt I have been lying to myself about not having. I joke about writing at a tire shop. I call myself a porn writer and let's face it, I kind of am.

But deep down, I know I'm more. I'm a creator of stories. Stories that have a plot and an arc and a journey. Yes, they experiment in BDSM. Yes, they do anal. And yes, you will probably get horny when you read them, but they still mean something to me. I'm still proud of them when I type The End. And I love the fact that I have readers who get to escape their regular lives for a while and pretend that they're someone else.

I give them book boyfriends like Miles.

But he is not fictional. He is real, and he went to great lengths to prove how many fucks he doesn't care that I write smut for a living.

And fucking hell, this giant of a man feels so good under my hands. I had to yank him down by his neck to bring our lips together. God, he's tall and firm. So firm. Every muscle in his body is tight and hot beneath my touch. I can't help but run my hands appreciatively over his triceps as our lips dance together in the best kiss I've had in years.

Years!

Dryston was a terrible kisser. His name totally matched his romantic abilities. Let's just say it'd be a cold day in hell before I ever used the name Dryston in a book.

He never used tongue and never moved his head. He kept it at one angle and just opened and closed his mouth over and fucking over like a guppy fighting for his life on the shore.

Miles, on the other hand, kisses like a shark.

I may have started it, but damn, this guy has taken the lead. He moves his hands all over my body—squeezing, groping, and fondling as he wishes. He even turns his head from side to side, like a shark nipping at his dinner, savoring every scrumptious bite. It's pure frickin' magic. When his head tilts to the left, he gives me tongue. When he tilts right, he caresses my lips. And just when I think I've figured out his pattern, he changes it up. Biting my lower lip, he pulls it into his mouth. His big hands squeeze my ass and pull me flush against his hard groin, leaving me with no doubt about the effect this kiss is having on him.

Jesus Christ.

And the fact that I'm wearing this short, stretchy skirt makes the barrier between us basically nonexistent. If I was writing a book about this kiss, now would be the point where the bad boy steals his hands up the girl's skirt, rips off her panties, and marvels at how wet she is for him. He'd pick her up, press her against the wall, and slam his bare, hard cock into her tight, soaked cunt.

Or something like that.

I'm making out with a hot guy, I can't be a great writer right now!

"Mercedes," he husks, pulling away from my lips, panting. "What are we doing?"

I drag in huge gulps of air, not realizing how much I needed oxygen while swallowing down the stab of guilt that he still doesn't know my real name. But I don't want him to know me as Kate. I am Mercedes at this moment. I'm not the girl still living with her ex because she can't get him to move his shit out. I'm Mercedes, sex goddess in fiction and in life!

"I don't know," I reply, touching my fingers to his hot lips. *God, they are sexy.* "I just kissed you, I guess."

"Yes, you did," he replies, and a muscle in his jaw ticks like he's in pain. He presses his forehead to mine and pulls his groin away from me. "And as hot as that was, we have to stop."

I swallow and nod. "Totally. We're in public."

"And I don't think this is a good idea." He pins me with his steely blue eyes that sparkle even in the darkness. Piercing through his dark lashes like shining beams of sapphires.

"Wait, what?" I reply, pulling out of his arms and mourning the loss of his warmth immediately. "After all that shit you said inside and just now on the phone with your sister…you…don't want this?"

He grimaces as if I kneed him in the balls. And maybe I should have. "I like you, Mercedes. But I'm not in the position to like someone right now."

I have to laugh at that. What a line for a book! And what a twist—the sex writer who can't get laid. How perfectly ironic. "Got it. Well, sorry to put you in such a difficult situation."

I turn on my heel and move down the sidewalk to go back inside the pub. Fuck this guy. Fuck this bar. Fuck leaving the sanctuary of my fictional story and trying to live in the real world for one night.

A large hand snakes around my elbow and spins me back around. "Mercedes, wait. I don't…want things to be weird."

"Well, maybe you shouldn't have flirted with me so much then!" I snap and bite my lower lip, hating the fact I'm being so uncool about this.

It's not like he proposed to me. He flattered me and bought me pizza and beer. Miles didn't even make a move except for that one kiss on the cheek, and he was clearly uncomfortable about that.

Jesus. I write about this shit, but I don't see it for myself. Idiot, Kate. Idiot, Mercedes. Whichever personality you are, you're an idiot!

Miles runs a hand through his hair, causing his shock of black locks to stick out all over. "I'm sorry. I…don't know what to say."

I sigh and take mercy on him. "There really is nothing else to say. I'll just…I'll see you around, Miles."

I turn and stride away, humiliated by the fact I was just rejected by my real-life book boyfriend.

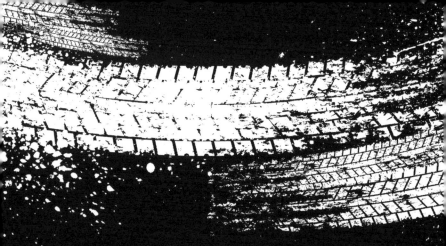

CHAPTER 11

Kate

Miraculously, my black moment with Miles matched up seamlessly with the black moment in the book I've nearly finished writing. Just a couple of more pages of depression, cue grand gesture, and *bam*...happily ever after. If only I could fucking write from home!

"Why are you here?" Lynsey asks, opening my front door without a knock to find me sitting cross-legged in my living room with my laptop open on my pretentious barn-wood coffee table. Her face falls. "Oh my God, what is that horrible smell?" She opens my front door wide and waves the stench outside as my face heats with humiliation.

"It's nothing!" I blow out the candle next to my computer and pop the lid on the tin to quickly stash the source of my embarrassment underneath the coffee table.

"It's not nothing. It smells like…burnt rubber." Her eyes go wide with realization. "Is that a fucking tire scented candle?"

She leaves the door open and dives on top of me, flattening me to the floor as we both grapple for the tin.

"Stop it! You're going to make me spill wax on the floor!"

"Then let go so I can see what you're hiding!" she squeals and claws her way up my arm, trying to reach my tightly gripped hand under the coffee table.

"No, you're just going to make fun of me!"

"You're damn right I am!" She redirects her hands to my sides where she starts tickling me mercilessly.

"Stop!" I howl and start laughing and screaming in unison as she assaults my tender sides and squirms on top of me. The ruthless bitch is going to leave bruises!

"What theeee fuuuuck?" a masculine voice stops us both midmotion. Lynsey's face is only inches from mine, her hair falling around both of us providing a curtain of privacy.

I cautiously push Lynsey's hair back to see Dean standing in my open doorway, gawking at us.

"Oh, thank God." I exhale. "It's just Dean."

"Yeah, it's just Dean," he repeats and gestures with his hands for us to continue. "Please…don't stop on my account."

Lynsey and I both roll our eyes as she hauls herself off my body but not before she makes one more attempt for the tin. "Ah-ha, I got it!" she exclaims, but her face crumples in disbelief as she takes in the label on the tin. "Burnt rubber scented soy candle. I cannot believe this is a thing."

She hands it over to Dean, and he winces as he takes a sniff.

"How much was that?" Lynsey asks, crossing her arms and tapping her foot like she's preparing to scold me.

"Only $8.50 on Etsy," I scoff and mumble, "I paid extra for expedited shipping."

Dean booms with laughter. "Jesus H, you've got it bad, Kate!"

"I know!" I cry and stand up, staring at my manuscript still lit up in front of me. "I can't write a damn word, and all I want to do is go back to Tire Depot."

"Then go back!" Lynsey exclaims. "So you kissed him, and he turned you down? Big fucking deal! Your ex still technically lives in this house, and you refuse to move out, knowing full well he can come back any day. But one little kiss with the sexy mechanic, and suddenly, you're a recluse again? I don't think so!"

"She has a point, Kate," Dean adds, completely unhelpful. "It'll be awkward for a day, three days tops. It's not like you have to gaze into his eyes from the waiting room. He'll probably stay in the garage and avoid you too."

I groan and drop down onto my couch, scrubbing my hands over my face. "You're right. My house smells like shit now too, doesn't it?"

They both nod down at me.

Lynsey adds, "You're going to have to get someone in here to clean it."

"Or throw a raging party when you finish this book, and we'll trash it so badly that the smell of booze and puke will overwhelm the burnt rubber."

Lynsey and I eye him with disgust.

He shrugs. "Just an idea."

"Fine, I'll go back," I decide at last. "But only because burnt rubber is not the same as new rubber, and I couldn't find a new rubber candle anywhere online. I wasted an embarrassing amount of time trying."

I walk into the back door of Tire Depot with my head held high. I have a book to finish, damn it. Lynsey and Dean are right. I sure as hell shouldn't stop sneaking in illegally and pilfering complimentary coffee in the CCC because of Miles and his hot and cold treatment.

It was one kiss. One kiss with some heavy petting. One kiss with some heavy petting and a boner the size of a fucking giant cucumber. This is nothing I can't get over!

Thankfully, as soon as I sit down and sip my free long espresso, I get that buzz in my fingers again. The buzz that means I won't need to stop for food because inspiration will be nourishing my soul!

And thankfully, I don't even see Miles for the first few days I'm back. It's nice—like the early days when I was literally invisible to everyone around me. Even Betty doesn't notice me typing in the corner when she comes with a fresh cookie stash. And that's good because I have work to do.

But on the third day I come in, I muster up the courage to wave at him through the window in the shop. It seems like a normal thing to do, considering I walk right past the garage every day and can clearly see him working through the window.

When Miles sees me waving like a moron, he blinks several times, like he thinks he's seeing a ghost. Eventually, his face relaxes, and he gives me that lopsided smile that's still sexy as ever.

It's nice. It's mature. We're adulting.

The next day, it's as if my wave to Miles in the garage was an olive branch he's accepted because he comes striding into the CCC just as he's done many times before "the black moment."

"How's the book coming?" he asks while grabbing a cookie out of the case and turning to look down at where I sit in one of the big, comfy armchairs.

Smiling shyly, I look over at the last couple of customers seated at one of the high top tables. One is on her phone, and the other is flipping through a magazine. Both clearly uninterested in our conversation.

Miles leans back against the countertop and bites into a cookie, his long legs crossed at the ankles, posture relaxed and friendly. I take a moment to drink in the enormous sight of him.

Freshly showered but not freshly shaved. Still hot as ever in simple jeans and a T-shirt.

"It's coming along," I reply, exhaling heavily. "This is the point in the story where I rip the couple apart and ruin everything they thought they knew about each other."

"Ouch," he states, pressing his fist to his heart in mock pain. "Can't they just be happy?"

"What's dramatic about happy?" I ask with a laugh. "My readers like the pain, the torture. They love when I rip stuff up and put it all back together." I lean forward in my chair and lower my voice. "It makes the makeup sex that much hotter."

He chuckles softly and shakes his head. "You know, my sister texted me and asked for your full author name so she could read some of your stuff."

I raise my eyebrows. "Is that right?"

He nods. "I warned you that we were a family of readers."

I eye him speculatively for a moment. There's really no reason to keep my pen name a secret from him anymore. It's not like we're romantically involved. I squashed any chance of that several days ago.

Clearing my throat, I reply, "You're going to laugh."

"Why do you say that?"

I prepare to reply, but pause as a voice cuts through the overhead music and announces, "Jeremiah Park, your Honda Civic is done." The couple sitting together both get up and make their way out of the CCC, leaving Miles and me alone once again.

Miles lifts his brows, clearly primed and ready for me to continue.

With a deep breath, I tell the unusual tale of how Kate Smith went from being a boring old copy editor to a bestselling erotic novelist, leaving out the whole real name part, of course.

"So my first book started off as a parody. I was actually working as a remote copy editor for a big publishing house and had no intentions of ever writing a book myself."

"Okay …" Miles replies, crossing his arms over his chest and listening intently.

I do my best to ignore the way his biceps stretch the sleeves of his shirt and continue. "So my ex and I had this horrible experience at a bed and breakfast."

"The ex who wanted you to lie to his family about what you did?" Miles asks, his jaw ticking angrily. I nod, and he clears his throat like he's holding back some words.

Fuck, it would be so book-hot if he was jealous right now.

"Anyway," I continue, "we show up at what we think is a normal bed and breakfast in the middle of nowhere Colorado only to discover that we've walked right into a secret BDSM club."

Miles's eyes are bright and blue when he exclaims, "You didn't?"

"We did! This is a true story!" I retort and keep going. "And somehow, they think we're their honored guests for the evening. We think the people they were expecting never showed up. I guess. I don't know, the details of that are still fuzzy."

"Jesus Christ."

"We kinda just rolled with it because we were tired and we thought, 'all we need is a bed to crash in, who cares what this woman is doing with a dude on a leash. That's her business.'"

"Your ex won't tell his family what you do, but he was open-minded to that kind of scene?"

I bark out a laugh. "He was as high as a fucking kite! He had consumed three edibles in retaliation to the fact that I forgot to book a hotel room. I don't know, he's an idiot."

"Agreed," Miles adds with a scowl.

I can't help but giggle at the serious tone in his voice. "I don't think he even realizes what he's seeing. Like I think he was actually seeing dogs on leashes, not human subs."

A full-on belly laugh erupts from Miles, and he eventually asks, "What happened?"

My brows lift. "You mean, did we participate?"

"Yeah," he admits with a shameless shrug.

"We did not," I reply with a sad smile. "Since we were the honored guests, we were only there to watch. The Head Mistress was very clear about that. She ushered us into this Western-looking parlor room and seated us in frickin' thrones, complete with sashes and crowns. Then, they basically put on a BDSM performance for us. It was frickin' insane!"

"Sounds like it."

"Naturally, I go to bed that night and think, I have to write down everything that just happened or no one will believe it. So I did. It wasn't super hard for me because I was already a copy editor and a huge reader. But I was pretty much writing it like a book, not a journal. It was complete with dialogue, descriptions, and the whole nine yards. I thought it would be really fun to take creative liberties with the story, so I kept going. Next thing I knew, I had a damn book!"

"I came up with this utterly ridiculous pen name when I was drunk one night. A crazy story deserved a crazy pen name, so I settled on…"

I pause for dramatic effect, and Miles rolls his hand out in front of him, encouraging me to continue.

"Mercedes Lee Loveletter."

I shrug and giggle, enjoying the stunned look in his eyes right before he asks, "What's your real last name then?"

I pause and bite my lip, quickly trying to decide how far I want to take this. It's a quick internal debate, though, because I know without a doubt that I love being Mercedes with Miles ten times more than I've ever loved being Kate, especially with men like Dryston. "It's Smith," I reply honestly because it's not like he'll find me on Facebook or something. I removed my personal account a long time ago because it was too much to monitor that profile as well as my pen name.

"Smith," he repeats with a nod, the corners of his mouth turning down with a concealed smile. "So why Loveletter then?"

"Well, because that was how the BDSM performance all started. This giant dominatrix removed a ball gag from her slave's mouth so he could read a love letter he'd written to his mistress. It was really sweet actually. He even cried."

Miles shakes his head. "That's how your journey began then?"

"Yep," I reply with an audible pop. "I self-published the story and didn't even know it hit the New York Times until an agent emailed me to ask if I had representation."

"Holy shit!" Miles exclaims, clearly impressed. "That's an incredible story."

"Book-worthy," I correct with a grin. This is fun. It's been forever since I've thought back through the whole saga, and Miles is lapping it up like a dog. "And it clearly gave me the itch to write because once I started, I couldn't stop."

"Until your slump with this book."

"Until Tire Depot saved me."

He shakes his head in disbelief. "And you said this book is the last in the series?"

I nod my head. "Yep."

"And then on to the next book."

"It's like an itch I can't stop scratching."

I exhale heavily and watch Miles's face morph into a warm, affectionate smile as he stares down at me. He's mesmerizing when he looks at me like that, all sweet and masculine. It's also totally frickin' obvious that he's thinking of a hell of a lot more than just the story I told him.

Damn it, men are confusing. How the hell can he look at me like that and not want to kiss me? The level of my urge to kiss him is at an all-time high.

I decide to smash the tender moment into pieces using the giant elephant in the room. "So does this mean we don't have to be awkward?"

He chuckles, those crinkles in his eyes framing the steely blue of his irises. "I thought you telling me the story of you and your ex waltzing into a BDSM bed and breakfast pretty much confirmed that fact."

"Fair enough." I nod in confirmation. "So we're friends, then?"

"Friends," he approves with a panty-melting smile.

I pack up my computer and toss my bag over my shoulder. "Good, because, as a friend, I was wondering if you might help me with some research for my next book."

His brows raise. "What did you have in mind?"

CHAPTER 12

Miles

Smiling broadly, Mercedes looks like she could burst with excitement when I hand her a black helmet. "Okay, you're going to throw your leg over but don't let your ankles touch this area here." I gesture down at the exhaust pipes on the side of my motorcycle. "These will burn you and hurt like hell."

She nods, looking very serious as she frees the top knot on her head and shakes her hair out, sending a riot of red waves cascading over her shoulders. She pushes the helmet onto her head and shoves the strands over her shoulder so they run down her back.

I swallow slowly as I glance down at her skimpy attire. She's wearing a pair of loose, colorful shorts with a white, flowing tank top. She looks girlie and super vulnerable, and it bothers me. I considered making her go home and put on some jeans but figured I was being overprotective as usual, and I'm really trying to work on that. Especially since we're just friends and nothing more.

After a second's hesitation, I do the only thing that doesn't make me look like a total control freak and shake off my leather jacket. "This won't save your legs from road rash if we crash, but I'll feel better if you wear it."

She nods and grasps the heavy coat out of my hand and slips into it. It covers her shorts and hangs so far down her arms that you can't even see the tips of her fingers. She pushes the sleeves up so she can buckle the chin strap of the helmet.

"Let's maybe not crash, though," she chirps, her voice muffled inside the helmet.

I chuckle and reach out to grab the front of my jacket, pulling her close so I can zip it all the way. Her blue eyes are staring at me intently when I look at her and reply, "I'm not planning on it."

She gives me a small smile, and I swear I see her nose tuck into the jacket and inhale deeply as the zipper reaches the top. She suddenly shakes her head and steps back for inspection.

"You're swimming in that, but it's better than nothing." I slide the eye shield down over her baby blues and tell her to climb aboard.

Mercedes widens her legs before even putting a foot on the peg next to my boot. I try not to laugh because I guess I'm just glad she's being careful. Resting her hands on my shoulders, she throws her leg over and sinks down on the seat behind me. Her warm center is snug against my backside, and I have to fight the urge to reach back and touch her bare legs.

I don't fight hard enough. My hand reaches back and strokes her bare thigh as I turn my head toward her and ask, "Do you have anywhere you need to be later?"

She shakes her head, and her voice is muffled when she says, "Nope, I'm totally free."

"Cool," I reply, pulling my aviators out of the storage pouch on the center console of my bike. "There's a really great mountain that I love to ride out to, and we should be able to get there just in time for sunset."

Mercedes gives me an enthusiastic thumbs up as I slide my glasses on and turn on the power switch. Standing up on one foot, I press my foot down on the kick start. My bike roars to life, and I rev the throttle a few times to warm it up.

Her hands move from my shoulders to snake around my waist, her fingers digging into my abs in a tight squeeze as she squeals her excitement.

"You ready?" I yell over the motor, the vibrations warming my thighs as we idle.

"Ready!" she shouts back and gives me an excited hoot. Then we're on our way out of the Tire Depot parking lot and off to chase the sunset.

We cruise southwest of Boulder for about thirty minutes out to Twin Sisters Peak, a place Sam and I frequently go hiking when we're in the mood for something quick and not too challenging. We call it our hangover hike because we can do it no matter how shitty we feel.

No roads allow access to cruise all the way up on a motorcycle, but at the top of a hill is one lookout point where hikers pull in to park, and it boasts stunning views of the Colorado sunset.

I love Colorado in general. After Jocelyn and I broke up, my mom urged me to consider moving back to Utah, but I just didn't feel it. Boulder had become my home. I had recently purchased a house, I liked my job and the new friends I'd made.

I had already lost the woman I thought was the love of my life, so I didn't want to stack another big change on top of that. Jocelyn slowly migrated her way out of my life for good, and I was okay with that. I just threw myself into fixing up my house and doing a good job for Sam's uncle at Tire Depot.

Mercedes's grip tightens around my waist as I pull off onto the small lookout point. Behind us you can see the Gross Reservoir, to the left are the Aspen Meadows, and to the right is the beginning of the Twin Sisters Peak. This entire area is chock full of enormous pine trees, animals, and unblemished nature.

As I cut the engine and drop the kickstand down, Mercedes presses down on the top of my shoulders and lifts her leg up over the seat. I instantly miss her warmth and realize that was not one of the many descriptions Mercedes gave me when she described the warmth of a woman at the Walrus Saloon.

"God, that was incredible!" Her voice is muffled as she

yanks her helmet off and shakes out her red hair. The sun slices through her strands as it sets behind the far-off hilltops. The few clouds lingering in the distance shift the sky to a stunning blend of pinks and purples. It's the perfect weather to watch the sun set.

"Good. Were you scared?" I ask, recalling the fact that Joce never let me take her out on my bike because she never wore anything but dresses and she said my driving made her nervous.

"No, was I supposed to be?" Mercedes asks, her eyes wide.

I laugh at that, pulling off my glasses and tucking them into my shirt. "No, not at all. My ex hated the bike, though. She never wanted to go out on it."

"Your ex is a fool. I mean, I get that motorcycles are dangerous, but it's the danger that makes it all the more satisfying. Do you know what I mean?"

I swallow slowly. "I think so."

"Ugh, why do we crave danger?" she asks, tucking the helmet under her arm and pacing back and forth in front of me. I have a feeling she's doing that writer thing I've seen her do when she's working through how to describe something. Only this time, she wants to articulate an emotion instead of describe a physical act. "I mean, what is it about the danger that draws in the human mind? Is it a sexual thing? A sexual attraction? I mean, what is it about the danger that keeps bringing us back over and over and over again?"

Mercedes pauses and looks at me, giving me the approval to have an opinion. I shrug. "Maybe it's the thrill of not knowing what's to come," I reply and throw my leg over and stand to stretch. "We get bored if things stay the same for too long."

I look down and see her eyes staring at the bit of skin peeking out on my abdomen. Good God, I really wish I could just fuck her. Just once. Just to know what she feels like. Her softness to my hard. I'm certain it would be incredible.

"Do you think men feel that way about women?" she asks, her lids fluttering with nervous blinks as she looks up at me. She's so small wearing my jacket as a dress with her flip-flops.

"I couldn't say for sure," I reply, awkwardly stuffing my hands in my pockets while moving over to a big log that lines the edge of the gravel pit. I sit down on it and look back at her. "But I do think women get blamed for loving drama when men are equally as guilty. We get away with calling it macho."

Her flip-flops slap noisily as Mercedes makes her way over and sits beside me so we're both facing the sunset now. I glance over at her. Her cheeks are flush, and some freckles have sprouted across her nose, probably from sun exposure.

She tucks her knees up inside my jacket and rests her chin on top of them. "Do you want to tell me what you mean by that, or do you want to say 'word' again?"

I half-smile, marveling a bit over how easily she can read between the lines. I suppose that's writer's intuition, to see the signs.

Exhaling heavily, I reply, "Eventually, I hope that every cryptic thing I say in my life won't all circle back to my ex."

Mercedes smiles, her dimple peeking out from the collar of my jacket. "Probably, but life lessons come from hardship, so spill it, Miles."

I growl and run my hands through my hair, feeling the strands sticking up every which way. "I think I stayed with my ex so long because I liked the drama on some sick level. It was stupid."

She nods thoughtfully, processing what I've said before asking, "What kind of drama did you guys have?"

I lift my eyebrows and shake my head up to the sky. "You name it, she probably did it. But the thing I hated the most was when she'd try to make me jealous."

I glance over just in time to see Mercedes wince in sympathy. "Yeah, jealousy is no fun. Although, I will tell you, from a purely romance writing profession point of view…my readers love a possessive man."

I chuckle at that. "Well, there's being possessive, and there's being made a fool of. Unfortunately, I think I was the latter more often."

She shakes her head from side to side and wrinkles her nose. "Your ex sounds horrible."

"So does yours."

"Why did we ever date them?"

"I ask myself that all the time."

She pulls her legs out of my jacket and stretches them out in front of her to cross them at the ankles. She gazes out into the sky for a moment before saying, "Well, a fun way to look at our exes is that if we hadn't dated them, then we wouldn't be right here, sitting on this tree, and enjoying this incredible sunset."

Mercedes waggles her brows at me and turns to watch the last few inches of sun dip down behind a faraway hill.

But I can't seem to take my eyes off her. Her hair is kind of like a sunset.

She feels me watching. "You're missing something really beautiful," she sings teasingly.

My voice is serious when I reply. "No, I'm not."

Her smile fades, and she looks over at me with wide, wondering eyes. The soft pink sky lights up her face, giving her this angelic glow. She's enchanting.

Her voice is a whisper when she croaks, "I can't figure you out, Miles."

I swallow slowly and reach out to cup her cheek, running my thumb from her cheekbone to her lip, lazily tracing the lines of her mouth. "I can't figure me out either."

She inhales deeply when I lean in to taste the lips that I've been reliving the taste of all week, but suddenly a motorcycle engine growls loudly up behind us. I freeze mere inches away from her mouth, my hand still on her face, my eyes still trained on her lips.

Swallowing hard, I turn around to see another couple dismounting from their bike, probably up here for the same reason we are.

Clearing my throat, I pull back and offer a sheepish smile to Mercedes. "Should we head back before we lose all the light?"

She looks forlorn and replies, "I'm at your mercy."

I help her up and get her kitted up and back on the bike behind me.

Away we go, back to Boulder and back to the life I'm currently living…with no drama.

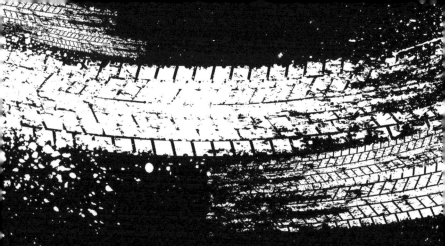

CHAPTER 13

Kate

When the day comes for me to write my epilogue, it's almost as if Miles knows because, in the middle of the day, he strides into the CCC dressed in his greasy coveralls that he has knotted down around his waist. The white T-shirt underneath is damp with sweat, and his hands look washed, but dirtier than I've ever seen them. Almost like he didn't bother to give himself a full scrub because he knew he was going back to work.

He grabs three cookies and strides over to me with a giant smile on his face. As if it's a normal day, and he takes breaks in the CCC all the time, he props himself on the stool across from the high top table I'm perched at and takes a big bite of his triple stack cookie sandwich.

I can't help but smile at the serendipity of this moment.

"Why are you smiling?" he asks, smiling back at me.

Seriously, so much smiling.

"Because life is funny sometimes." I tilt my head and narrow my eyes at him, drinking in all his manly glory.

"How so?" Miles leans across the table toward me, his black hair in need of a trim and his blue eyes bright amongst the dirt on his face.

Without a word, I turn my computer to face him and stand so I'm positioned beside him. When I lean down to press my fingers on the keyboard, our arms graze and a tingle of electricity sparks between us.

Steeling myself to be cool, I type out *The End.*

"No way," he exclaims loudly, clearly not giving a shit about the other customers in the waiting area. He turns wide, excited eyes to me. "You just finished?"

"I just finished." I smile and yelp when he drops his cookies, stands, and lifts me into the air, twirling me in a circle. He freezes when he remembers we're not alone and quickly sets me back down on my feet.

He leans in and whispers loudly, "Congratulations, Mercedes."

And I thank him, because right now, I *am* Mercedes Lee Loveletter, and I've completed my fifth and final book in the series. "I couldn't have done it without you, Miles," I reply with a humorous bounce to my voice.

His chest vibrates with laughter. "We should celebrate. Can I buy you a drink?" he asks, and his brow furrows when he sees the humor leave my face.

He said those same words to me the night I kissed him,

and the coincidence isn't lost on me. "Maybe another time."

He nods and stuffs his hands into his pockets, a bemused look on his face that's majorly killing my buzz.

"But hey, we're having a party Friday night at my house. My two friends at the pub from the other night and some people we still hang out with from college…you…want to come by? You can bring Sam!"

His lopsided smile is genuine, and we quickly exchange numbers so I can text him my address. It surprises me that for as many times as I've seen Miles now, we still haven't swapped numbers. I guess maybe that was his way of keeping me at a distance.

Miles stuffs his phone back into his pocket and asks, "So what are you going to do tonight then?"

My face heats with embarrassment, but I decide to own it anyway. "Well, I have this tradition that I used to do with my ex after every book I finished."

"Your ex?" he snaps, clearly confused at my mention of him.

"Yeah, we would…wear these onesie pajamas, order pizza, and read only the five-star reviews from my last book all while consuming an entire box of wine." I laugh awkwardly and marvel at the fact that it was the only truly original thing I ever did with Dryston. He probably only liked it because he had a dragon onesie, and the dude was kind of obsessed with dragons.

Miles nods, his brows still puzzling. "So you're hanging with your ex?"

"Oh, God no!" I exclaim and swat his hard chest

playfully. "No way, I'll probably just do it with Lynsey. Or Dean, most likely."

This doesn't seem to relax his stiff posture in the slightest. With a gruff voice, he replies, "You should find a new tradition."

My jaw drops. "Why do you say that?"

"Because it started with someone who didn't support what you do." Miles's jaw muscle ticks angrily, and I swear he grows even taller before me. "Why would you want to perpetuate his memory like that?"

"It's not *his* memory, it's just something I started when I was with him. I've done it for every one of my books, and it feels like bad luck not to continue it."

He shakes his head, disappointment all over his face.

"Miles!" I scold and look around the room to see a couple of people staring at us. "Chill out. What's your problem? This is supposed to be a happy day."

He takes a step back, and that mask I've seen on his face before returns with a vengeance. "Sorry, I don't mean to rain on your parade." Miles moves to leave but pauses to press a swift kiss to my temple. "I'm really proud of you, Mercedes."

I reach out and grab his hand, stopping his departure. "Are you okay?"

He nods. "Why wouldn't I be?"

"Because you're acting weird. As if I've…disappointed you or something."

His face softens at that. "You could never disappoint me, babe. I think you're incredible."

His use of the word 'babe' has my heart leaping up into

my throat. Being the idiot I am, I laugh awkwardly and reply, "Yeah, I'm so incredible that I had to sneak into a tire
shop day in and day out to finish a book I couldn't find the
courage to write because I was too wrapped up in my ex."

Miles dips his head, bringing us eye to eye, and pins me
with a serious look. "This isn't about your ex. This is about
you finding something that worked for you. You went after
it, balls to the wall, and did what you had to do to get the
job done. You don't care what anyone thinks, and that's really fucking cool, so don't go doubting yourself now."

His words stun me into a rare moment of silence. But
he's wrong about one thing.

I care what you think.

Instead of oversharing that fun little nugget, I decide to
shoot Miles a winning smile. "I had to stick with the vibe, so
thanks for waiting with me."

He offers me a soft smile. "Anytime."

I reach down to close my laptop and slip it into my bag.
"Will I see you Friday then?"

He nods. "You'll see me Friday." He looks like he wants
to say more but grips the back of his neck and steps back.
"Have a good night, Mercedes."

And without some gallant, final grand gesture, I let my
book boyfriend walk away, keeping him safe right where he
belongs, in fiction.

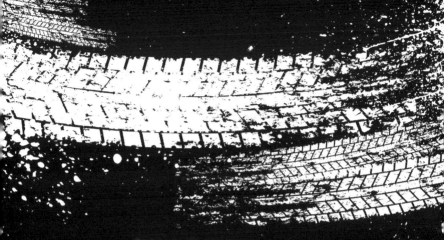

CHAPTER 14

Kate

"We're almost thirty years old. We're too old for kegs!" I groan as Dean rolls the huge silver monstrosity across my fancy plank wood flooring.

Dean sighs heavily and adjusts his glasses. "This isn't fucking domestic beer, Kate. This is IPA from my favorite local brewer. They don't sell this shit to just anyone."

"Yeah, cuz no one likes it," I mumble and kick the floor because damn it, what's wrong with Coors Light? It was good enough for us in college, and it should be good enough for us now.

But Dean didn't go to college with Lynsey and me. He self-educated himself on all things fancy. And ostentatious. Like IPA beer apparently.

He shakes his head and rubs the side of my arm. "You'll

like it, I promise. Just give it a chance."

Resuming his station, his polka-dot button-down stretches around his biceps when he lifts the keg and places it inside the garbage bag-lined wooden barrel he brought over earlier. He goes back to the front door and grabs the giant bags of ice he left on the front step and proceeds to pour them around the keg.

Lynsey comes striding through my back door. "The tiki bar is ready!" she exclaims with a swivel of her hips.

I have to stifle my laugh because she had to roll that thing all the way through her house and my house in order to get it to my back patio.

Even though we're neighbors, there's a giant privacy fence that separates our properties. When I first moved in, we got really drunk and tried to prop a ladder on either side of the fence so that we could flow freely between the two properties.

It did not end well.

Dryston ended up having to carry me up the stairs to bed because I hobbled into the house in pursuit of more vodka. But I lived to tell the tale so, silver lining.

"I also strung up my Edison bulbs back there," Lynsey adds with eager eyes. "It's great mood lighting. Perfect for meaningful conversation."

"Or random hookups," Dean adds, waggling his brows at me. "I invited some people from my co-working space, so there'll be some fresh faces for you to maul in an alley, Kate."

"Shut up, dick." I kick my flip-flop at him, and he tosses

it out the back door without even looking.

"Also"—I rub my hand over my forehead—"don't forget to call me Mercedes tonight, remember?"

Lynsey rolls her eyes.

"I mean it. It's the theme of the party since we're celebrating my typing '*The End*' as Mercedes. In my text, I told everyone coming that anyone who calls me Kate has to do a keg stand."

"What?" Dean gasps, horrified. "This isn't fucking cheap college beer, Kate!"

"Mercedes!" I correct. "And I'm banking on everyone hating that beer and no one wanting that horrific torture."

"You get used to the hops!" he cries like a huge fucking sissy.

"If by hops, you mean poison, then I'll pass," I reply and do a final check on the appetizers spread out on the counter.

Lynsey sidles up next to me as I stir the meatballs in the slow cooker. "Are you going to take my advice then?" she asks, her voice quiet, but Dean's comment of, "What advice?" means it definitely wasn't quiet enough.

"No," I groan and begin pointlessly readjusting the charcuterie platter.

Lynsey exhales heavily. "I told Ka—Mercedes that she should try to make Miles jealous tonight because it works. Tell her it works, Dean."

Dean stops monkeying with the ice and hits me with a look. "It works."

I frown, knowing that after what he shared with me out at Twin Peak the other day, there's no way in hell I'd do that to him. "I'm not going to manipulate Miles into liking me."

"He already likes you," Lynsey corrects. "He just needs to like you enough to sleep with you."

"He sounds like a tool, if you ask me," Dean grumbles.

"He's not a tool," I defend. "He's...I don't know what he is. Getting over someone maybe? Gah. He only wants casual, and he doesn't think I can be a casual girl."

"Can you?" Lynsey asks, her brown eyes curious.

"Fuck yeah!" I exclaim with a little dance I think a casual, cool girl would do. "I write casual sex like it's my job because it literally is." I smile lamely at my dumb joke, and my friends are super impressed.

"Screw it, you guys are good down here, right? I'm going to go upstairs and get ready because I am officially going to be late for my own party. Lynsey, start the music and hold down the fort while I go beautify!"

"On it, boss!"

"Dean...guard that shitty beer."

Forty-five minutes later, I stride down the steps to find my The End party in full swing. I'm dressed in a pair of lacy white shorts and a flowy nude tank with camel wedges. I've trussed my red hair up into a side braid down my shoulder, and I'm feeling footloose and fancy-free. I am ready to party.

Several of our old friends have made it out, as well as some new faces who Lynsey knows from grad school. I instantly get sucked into a conversation with a couple of girlfriends from college who all congratulate me on finishing. One calls me Kate, and I drag her into the kitchen to take a shot. Mostly because I think Dean might start crying if someone put their lips on his precious keg tapper.

Dean introduces me to his co-working space friends who won't shut up about this new bakery down the street from their building. Before I know it, I realize it's a couple of hours into the party and Miles still isn't here.

I excuse myself from some friends to go see who's out back. Maybe Miles has been here this whole time, and I didn't know it. I do a cursory sweep of the outside in hopes of seeing a tall, dark, and handsome fella but am disappointed just to find Lynsey and all her grad school friends.

She smiles brightly and comes striding out of her tiki bar to pass me a fruity beverage in a tall glass. "Drink it slowly, *Mercedes*. This shit is strong. I've had two, and I think I'm black-out drunk right now."

"Jesus," I exclaim, taking a sip and feeling an instant burning in my mouth. "No wonder. I think this might be worse than Dean's shitty IPA."

Dean's growl scares me from behind. "It's not shitty." Without warning, he dives straight for my legs, and I just barely hand my drink off to Lynsey before he tosses me over his shoulder. "*Mercedes* is doing a keg stand, everyone!"

Our friends all whoop with cheers, and I bellow over their voices. "Mercedes is *not* doing a keg stand because Mercedes likes Coors Light and complimentary coffee… and writing sex books!"

I hear cheers from both inside and outside, and because I'm feeling no pain, I decide to keep going. "And hard and fast wall sex!"

They all laugh and cheer out some more. This is fun! I have my own personal cheering track, so I continue, "And Mercedes likes a formal scene where the guy takes off a girl's panties and fingers them in his tuxedo pocket all night long!"

I'm met with crickets…until finally, Lynsey chirps, "That was really specific but, yay!"

Everyone joins in, but it feels obligatory and far less enthusiastic than before, so I give it one last go to save face. "And I *really* love to write about anal play!"

The crowd cracks up laughing even more, but more wonderful cheering follows. I can even feel Dean's shoulders shaking as he laughs and smacks my ass before dropping me back down to my feet.

When I turn around and right myself, I feel a head rush and try to focus my eyes on what's in front of me. I'm staring into the very broad chest of a very large man in a super-hot black leather jacket. I lift my chin and practically swoon when I see it's Miles. And he has a button-down on under his coat.

"Miles!" I exclaim and wrap my arms around his rock-hard body, still feeling euphoric from my version of a crowd surf I did a moment ago.

Dean clears his throat beside me and murmurs, "I'm going to head inside for a drink."

I pull back to wave hello to Sam, who looks a bit

uncomfortable next to Miles until he finally says, "I'm going to follow that guy."

Lynsey sidles up next to me in the same breath, not the least bit intimidated by Miles's statuesque posture. She thrusts her hand out and says, "Hi, I'm Lynsey, the best friend and neighbor. That's my tiki bar over there."

Miles slides his gaze to her and offers a small smile while shaking her hand. "I'm Miles."

"Nice to meet you. Can I get you a drink? My tiki bar is open!" She waves her hands out proudly.

"I'm good for now, thanks," Miles replies and looks back down at me. "Can we go somewhere and talk?"

I nod and grab his hand to lead him back inside. A group of Dean's friends is standing right in front of my bedroom door, so I decide to take him upstairs to where I was getting ready earlier. When we pass by Dean at the keg, I see him cut narrow eyes at Miles. I flash my own daggers at Dean, silently telling him to back the fuck off as we veer left.

I can't drag Miles up the stairs fast enough.

The light from the Edison bulbs is pouring through the back window into the dark bedroom, so I don't even bother with the light switch. Miles walks into the room behind me like a dark, thunderous cloud. When I turn around to look at him, I realize this room has never felt so small.

He looks around, noticing men's shoes on the floor in the open closet. "Do you have a roommate?"

My face heats instantly because this is nowhere near the conversation I want to have right now. Especially after Dean just flounced me around like a bimbo in front of everyone two seconds ago.

"Kind of?" I reply hesitantly.

"So it's a guy," Miles states, staring into the closet, then sliding his eyes to me.

There's no hiding that fact now. "Yes." I shrug.

He laughs and shakes his head. "It figures." He presses a hand to his forehead as he paces the room. "It's not that Dean guy, right? You said he was a neighbor."

"He is a neighbor. It's not Dean."

"Then who is it?"

"No one," I rush out, noticing that Miles is getting tenser and tenser by the second. The last thing he needs to hear is that I still kind of live with my dumbass ex-boyfriend. "He's away for the summer, so it doesn't matter."

"But it's a dude," he snaps, his hands balling into frustrated fists at his sides. "Damnit, Mercedes, I can't do this!"

"Do what?" I ask, my chest lifting with hope.

"I'm a jealous guy! You know that," he exclaims, throwing his hands out wide in surrender as he points downstairs. "This is not the kind of shit I handle well." He forks his hands through his hair, looking like he's about to bolt.

But I don't want him to bolt.

I want him to stay.

"I'm sorry, I should just go."

He moves toward the door, and I dash in front of him, blocking his exit.

"My roommate is…gay," I blurt, and my eyes fly wide at the lie that tumbled so easily from my lips. "And he's out of town for the summer."

Miles stares down at me, blinking. "Seriously?"

I shrug, completely unable to confirm it again because I still can't believe I lied in the first place. "Tell me why are you turning into such a maniac right now? I thought you only wanted to be friends."

He exhales heavily. "It's a lot harder than I thought it would be."

"Well, what can I do to help?" I ask, even though I don't want to help. *I want to bone.*

Miles groans and pins me with a serious glower. "Babe, jealousy is an issue I have to keep in check constantly. I try not to be like this, but it's virtually fucking impossible. I had almost ten years with a girl who took pleasure in fucking torturing me every chance she got."

"Well, I'm not that girl," I retort and step in closer to him, reaching my hands out to touch his forearms.

"I know you're not," he nearly cries. "But before we do anything, you need to know this about me. I'm overprotective. Overbearing. Over arrogant. Pretty much everything I do is to the extreme."

"Okay," I reply slowly and swallow a knot in my throat as he cups my face in his rough hands, looming over me like some sort of caveman staking his claim.

His voice is deep and melty as he adds, "And I fucking lose it if I think a guy is moving in on my property."

Okay, I *shouldn't* be turned on by that. I'm a modern woman. I'm independent. I think I could be a feminist if I ever knew exactly what the fuck that all entailed. But personally, I don't think feminism belongs in the bedroom. I think feminism is having license over your own desires, and Jesus, Mary, and Joseph, I think I just felt a gush of liquid between my legs, and I am so not mad at that!

I shake my head, trying to refocus my brain on the main point here. "But I'm not your property, Miles!"

"In my mind, you are," he replies, his jaw tight, his lips pinched. "And I really need you not to do things to make me jealous."

"Why?" I nearly sob.

"Because if you make me jealous, then I won't be able to stay friends with you."

"Why?" *Good God, man, just fucking take me!*

"Because it'll make me want to fuck you, so you don't ever want to look at another guy again."

Heavy breaths.

Thunderous heartbeats.

Noisy party downstairs...the real downstairs. That wasn't a euphemism for my pants, though, now that I mention it, I think I heard his dick grow. Like literally, I think I hear his jeans stretching between us.

I reach out and touch him with my hands and oh my God, yes. He's hard, and I'm hard, and I want him to just… "Prove it."

He shakes his head, severity to his brow that has a knot forming in my throat. "I hope you know what you're asking for."

With a feral sort of growl, he slams his lips to mine and plunges his tongue straight into my mouth. Deep. So deep. As if he's looking for tonsils deep. It isn't exactly sexy—it's uncontrollable. Heady. Toxic. I can't get away from him, and I don't want to. My arms wind tightly around his neck, holding him as if it's possible to merge our bodies together.

No more dead fish kiss. God, this is living!

Miles bends over, running his hands down my ass to the back of my thighs. He grabs me tightly and hoists me up, and my legs instantly wrap around his waist. I can't quite hook my ankles around his massive frame, so I just squeeze. Squeeze him into me as hard as I can because good Lord, this is what I've been missing. Strong, masculine, territorial *heat!*

I want his heat all over me. If he could unzip his skin and tuck me inside him, I'd want that. I want to be consumed by him in every possible way.

He combs his hands through my hair and yanks my head back so he can drag his tongue along my throat. I swallow against it, panting and writhing just from his wet tongue. He's ravishing, punishing, and claiming me with his mouth, and fucking hell, it's bliss.

He turns us toward the bed, and his hands drift down to my ass, his fingers greedily digging into the crease of my butt. "You said you liked anal play?"

I cry out loudly when his fingers slide along the lace of my shorts, and he presses hard through the fabric right on my puckered hole. "Jesus, I don't know. I just like writing it!"

He laughs, and it vibrates his whole body. I squeeze my legs tighter around him, trying to get that sensation inside me because fucking hell, I need to be fucked right now.

"Plenty of time for that later," he says, dropping me on the perfectly made bed and falling down on top of me, covering me with his warm, delicious weight.

"God, Miles," I moan, as he peppers my collarbone with kisses and bites. I kick my wedges off as my body rolls under his, my pelvis pressing up into the big hard appendage stuck behind his annoying jeans. "Take your jeans off. I want to see you."

"You first, babe," he husks and stands up, pulling me with him so he can pull my tank top off over my head. My braid flops back down over my bare breasts, and he drags his fingers along the texture of it. "Would you undo this?"

I nod absently. I'm pretty sure he could get me to run through that party naked if it meant I'd be getting laid by him tonight. I yank out the twist and shakily comb my fingers through my hair.

"I fucking love your hair." He slices his fingers through the thick tendrils and gives them a big sniff. *God, he sniffed me!*

"Now lie back," he says, hooking his fingers in the waistband of my shorts and sliding them down my legs as I do. He chucks them to the floor and grabs my lacy white thong. I moan as he pulls it down tantalizingly slow, his rough fingers caressing my legs with their descent.

When he slips the thong off my feet, he holds it out for me to see, then presses it to his nose and inhales deeply.

"Jesus fuck," I cry at just the sight of him sniffing my goddamned panties. "How are you real?"

"I'm completely fucking real, babe. And you're not

getting these back." He tucks the slip of white fabric into his jeans and pulls his wallet out of his back pocket, retrieving a condom from the inside flap before dropping it down on the bed.

He reaches behind him and pulls his shirt off over his head, and my eyes glaze over at the sight of him. He has lines in places that men were meant to have lines. A perfect outline of a six-pack, broad ribs hinting under his huge, meaty pecs. And then there's that *V*. Jesus God, the *V* that arrows down to his dick is enough to make me forget every man who ever came before him.

Miles could be on the cover of every last one of my books. In fact, maybe I should re-cover my books. I'd probably sell more copies. I want this man's perfectly sculpted body plastered all over my fucking world.

And if I thought his top half looked good, it is nothing compared to the bottom. He slides his jeans and boxers down, and the giant cock that bobs out has me more than a little terrified. Extremely aroused, but terrified.

It's a beautiful dick. Strong and proud. Straight and thick. But about twice the size I'm used to.

I clear my throat and say, "The cliché line you should say right now is, 'Don't worry baby, it'll fit.'"

He laughs at my man voice imitation, and his thick abs contract in a really sexy way. After he rolls the condom on, he steps between my legs and drapes his warmth over me. Our nakedness slides against each other like the most deliciously heated silk sheets.

Miles teases his covered tip against my slit. "But what if

I like it to hurt a little?"

In one fast push, he slams into me so fast I can't catch my breath for a moment. My hands grapple around the bed for purchase, for something to squeeze and hold as I fight this sudden, welcomed invasion between my legs. He offers up his own hands, sliding his fingers between mine in a gentle way that is at complete odds with the merciless tightness between my legs.

He squeezes my fingers and presses our hands to the mattress beside my head. "You okay?" He drops a soft, tender kiss on my lips.

I groan loudly, the tight ache building and begging for more. "I will be once you start moving." I grind my hips up to meet his with frantic need. "I need you to fuck me, Miles. Please, just fuck me."

"With pleasure," he replies, releasing my hands and sitting back on his knees. Throwing my legs up on his shoulders, he skims his rough hands down them at the same time. "God, these fucking legs are sexy."

And with that belly-flipping compliment, he begins thrusting into me so hard and fast, I can't even utter a moan. It's just a lot of strangled sobs that seem to bypass my voice box and come out straight from my lungs. He grinds and digs and punishes my pussy, and the orgasm that rips through me is completely ignored—like it's one of many he plans to give me tonight, so he's not even going to give it any attention.

A second orgasm climbs on top of the first, and I swear I can't take another when he reaches down and rubs his rough fingers on my swollen clit. My voice box finds itself at last, and I scream out in pleasure.

"Shhh," he growls and moves his naughty hand to my mouth, sticking his fingers in it so I can taste my arousal all over them. "You need to be quiet, babe. There's a party going on downstairs, and if they hear you like this, I'll get all worked up again."

He pulls his fingers out, and I groan, "Jesus, you're nuts." But in my mind, I'm saying that I never want any of this to stop.

"You make me nuts," he replies and continues pounding into me until I orgasm a third time.

"Think you've had enough?" he asks, bringing a finger underneath my ass and teasing my anus. "Or do you want more?"

"Later," I beg, moan, and whine a little. "More later, I just want to see you come, Miles."

I look down at his dick sliding in and out of me. It's so angry looking. It needs a release.

"Talk dirty to me again then," he quips, nodding his head at me in encouragement. "Talk to me like you did that night at the bar. God, I've jacked off to that memory at least a dozen times since then."

"Umm," I mumble, my brain needing to access a different vortex than where it's currently residing. "Okay, fuck. I loved when you stuffed your fingers in my mouth a second ago."

"Yeah?" he asks, his eyes ablaze and fixed on me. "Are you a dirty girl, Mercedes?"

"God, yes!" I moan because honestly, maybe this is what I've been missing all along. I should have been fucking Dryston as my alter ego, not boring Kate! Mercedes is a freak in both the real world and the fictional one. "I loved tasting myself on you. The sourness of me and the saltiness of you. God, we taste good together."

"Fuck yeah, we do," he replies, looking up at the ceiling and riding whatever wave he's catching, the cords of his thick neck bulging at the angle.

"I like your rough hands on my body," I state, grabbing one of his hands and placing it on my breast. He looks back down and watches his hand when I add, "See how hot we look together. Rough and soft. Dark and light."

He squeezes my breast and tweaks my nipple so hard I have to bite back another cry. "God, Miles, fucking come for me. Let that big dick come inside me."

"Oh God," he exclaims, freezing mid-thrust and exploding inside me like a fucking cannon. The veins of his long shaft contract and thicken inside my channel with each needy burst of seed he shoots into the condom. "Jesus Christ, Mercedes."

I laugh because what else can I do? I just fucked a guy who doesn't know my real name in the bed that I shared with my ex for almost two whole years. How much more fucked up can this situation get?

I tap his abs in appreciation. "That, Miles, was book-worthy sex."

He laughs at that while we clean up in the attached bathroom and quickly dress to head back downstairs to the party. I don't particularly want to go back down, but since it's sort of in my honor and we're not even in my bedroom, I don't see how I can really get away with staying up here all night.

Lynsey points out my hair instantly, and I close my eyes, wincing at the fact that I forgot to braid it back to how I had it earlier. Thankfully, no one else seems to notice.

I sip a drink and talk to my friends for the rest of the night, being really chill when I introduce them to my new friend, Miles from Tire Depot. Everyone laughs at how we're basically coworkers since I wrote the entire book there. If this was a book, I'd definitely brand it as an interoffice romance, for sure. *It all started with a cup of complimentary coffee.*

Throughout the night, I feel judgmental looks coming from Dean. He's most likely doing that overprotective brother thing again, but I don't want Miles to get the wrong idea, so I decide to keep my distance. Dean is a flirt, and while harmless, it's a difficult thing for outsiders to understand. I've even been accused by my college friends of having a romance with Dean. The idea is laughable.

By the end of the night, I am exhausted, and when Sam goes to leave, I frown, worried that Miles is going with him.

"We drove separately," Miles offers, and I glance out to see his motorcycle parked right in front of my house. "But I can go if you'd like?"

"No!" I exclaim and reach out to grab his hand. "You should stay…if you want, I mean." I am so uncool it's not even funny.

He nods, and that troubled look returns to his face. The one he's gotten every time he's rejected me or tried to reject me. It troubles me, but he seems to be ignoring it for the night, so I will too.

After a while, everyone clears out, including Lynsey and Dean. I shut off the lights, kill the music, and lead Miles to my bedroom off the kitchen.

"I'm really glad you didn't drag me in here before," he states with a smile.

"And why is that?" I ask, yanking my tank top off over my head and standing in front of him sans bra.

"Because then everyone definitely would have heard your screams." He quickly reaches for me, and I yelp as he picks me up in his arms so that my tits are pressed into his face. "I didn't get enough time to fully meet these girls earlier. Hello, ladies."

He nuzzles his whiskered jaw between my breasts, and I laugh and shove at him until he puts me down. With a blissful, sexy, indescribable smile, he tucks my hair behind my ears and kisses me so sweetly, I think I just experienced a type of orgasm I didn't even know existed.

Can you orgasm from happiness? I kinda think so.

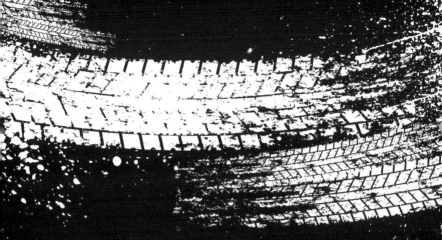

CHAPTER 15

Miles

I wake to the sound of bacon frying and sit up like a shot, completely forgetting where I am for a second. I blink rapidly, and Mercedes's bedroom comes into full view. I look over to see her side of the bed is empty, and I exhale as everything comes flooding back into my mind.

I had sex with Mercedes last night.

I had really fucking great sex with Mercedes last night... during the middle of a party.

I hunch over and rub at my eyes, trying to recall how bad I was last night. I came in hot, that's for sure. But seeing her draped over Dean's shoulder made it clear to me that he wants more from her—even if Mercedes doesn't see it yet.

I shouldn't have come. I knew I shouldn't have come. Sam was the one who forced me, making me feel guilty for not celebrating this achievement with her after all we'd been through together at Tire Depot. But somehow, I knew if I drove out here, I wouldn't be leaving. Now, here I am—butt-ass naked in her white, fluffy, really fucking comfortable bed.

This is going to be bad.

I stand and slide into my jeans, my mind clouding with my past and my present, creating this swirling fog of doubt. It's been a year since Jocelyn and I broke up, and I'm over her completely. Honestly, the bitch can live happily ever after with her old, rich geezer, but I'm still not over the stress of being in a relationship. Of caring for someone so much that you would literally do anything to protect them. That's why I'm only doing casual right now. I can't give myself to anyone again. Not yet.

And something about Mercedes screams way too good for casual.

I step into the kitchen, and Mercedes is at the stove in a pair of tight yoga shorts and my black T-shirt I had just been looking for. Just watching her with the morning sun slicing in through the window over the sink, I know damn well, this girl ain't casual.

I clear my throat. "Shirt thief," I tease and shuffle over to stand behind her. I put my hands on her cute little hips, and her entire body tenses. "What's wrong?"

She giggles nervously. "Are you in a pancakes mood? Or a chew your arm off mood? Because I haven't started the pancakes yet so now is the time to tell me if there's carnage in my bedroom."

I press a kiss to her temple with a laugh. "I could eat." *I could eat you* is what I'm really thinking. I move over to the barstool at the island to get a better view of her. How is it possible for her to look this cute in the morning? Her cheeks are flushed, and her red hair is tied up in a big ball on top of her head. And she doesn't look half bad in my giant shirt.

"How'd you sleep?" she asks as she begins whisking some pancake batter in a large glass bowl.

"Like a rock," I admit.

She bites her lip.

I smirk curiously. "Something I said?"

She nods. "You'd think I'd be more mature about it since I write about this stuff all the time, but I'm not. You had the biggest morning wood I had ever seen in my life when I got up earlier."

My brows lift. "Well, why didn't you wake me up so we could do something about it?"

Mercedes smiles a shy smile that is so cute, my dick jumps. My sex writer, fucking shy? Christ, she just keeps getting better.

"You were sleeping so hard," she explains. "And I figured three orgasms were enough for twelve hours."

I tip my head back and laugh. "I don't think you should ever put a cap on orgasms."

Her eyes find mine, and with one heated look, sexual tension begins to sizzle between us like bacon in a frying pan. She licks her lips. "Are you just going to sit there and make sex eyes at me, or are you going to help me make breakfast?"

I stand up and stretch. "I might need my shirt. It'd be a shame if I burned these with bacon grease."

I drag my fingers along the ridges of my abs, and Mercedes stares so hard, she starts spilling the pancake batter on the hot burner.

"Pancakes," I say, looking down at the mess.

"What?" she husks, still staring at my body.

"Mercedes, the pancakes!" I shout as smoke begins billowing up from the spot on the stove. I move quickly around the counter to grab the bowl out of her hand.

"Shit!" she exclaims, snapping out of her daze. She sets the bowl down, turns off the burner, and grabs a rag to clean up the mess. Her sheepish eyes peek up at me through her dark lashes. "Maybe giving you back your shirt isn't a bad idea."

Once Mercedes retrieves a shirt from her room, I slip mine on and finish helping her with the food. It's a very domestic, Saturday morning couple thing to do, and by the time we sit down to eat at her kitchen counter, my thoughts can no longer be ignored.

Drizzling syrup over my short stack, I decide to just come out with it. "I feel like I need to tell you that I did not come here last night to do…that." I point upstairs and into her room because those are the two places we've covered so far.

She frowns nervously. "Okaaay."

"I mean, it was good, don't get me wrong. Fucking great actually. But I want you to know that wasn't my plan."

She exhales heavily and focuses really hard on buttering

her pancakes. "Is this the part where you tell me you're not in a position to *like* someone again?"

I set my fork down and stare at her until she looks up at me. "Maybe?" I say, apology all over my face.

Her jaw goes tight, but she looks down, resuming her earlier food prep. "That's fine."

I huff, "Is it?"

"Yeah!" she exclaims and looks over at me with a smile. "This is no big deal, Miles. We had sex. You didn't ask me to go steady. I'm not getting this twisted up."

"Well...good," I reply, feeling a little confused as I eat a little more food and let the silence overtake us. Finally, I look up and add, "I just...I get the impression that you aren't a casual kind of girl, and I wouldn't want to put you in an awkward situation."

"Zero awkwardness!" she replies with a laugh, over an enormous bite of pancakes. She puts her fingers over her full mouth and mumbles, "I'm good...great even. I just had really good sex last night!"

My eyes narrow skeptically. She's acting weird. Weirder than usual. "So what does this mean then?"

She shrugs and takes a sip of her orange juice. "It can mean whatever we want it to mean. We can just stay friends, or not. We can keep having sex, or not."

I nearly choke on a bite of bacon. "Keep having sex?"

Her cheeks flush. "Yeah! *You* said I'm not casual, not me. I'm as casual as they come. Casual with a capital C. I write at Tire Depot, for God's sake."

My brows lift. "Good point."

She stands up and takes her half-eaten plate to the kitchen sink. "I'd be up for some casual…honestly. I'm a workaholic as it is, so it's not like I have time to devote to a boyfriend."

"Oh?" I ask curiously, annoyed that her comment also makes me feel slightly rejected. *I'm such a dick.* "But you finished your book. How much work can there be?"

She laughs at that. "Oh Miles, how little you know about my book world. The part at Tire Depot is the easy stuff. Now the hard work begins. Editing. Marketing. On top of that, I'm already starting the next book."

This has me sitting back on my stool. "Okay then, so what did you have in mind?"

She loads her plate into the dishwasher, her back to me for a good while before she suddenly turns on her heel with wide eyes and exclaims, "Book research!"

"Book research?" I repeat.

She nods. "I, umm…might need some help from you again for book research. Bedroom stuff, not motorcycle ride stuff."

My brows lift curiously. "What crazy shit are you writing now that you haven't already covered in your erotic novels?"

She rolls her eyes and moves to prop her elbows on the counter straight across from me giving me the perfect angle of her cleavage in that tight tank top. "It's not like that. I need help getting into the mind of a man. My *Bed 'n Breakfast* series was all told from a female point of view. But for my new book, I want to write in dual point of view. So one chapter will be in the female's voice, and then one will be in the male's voice. I'll alternate between the two."

My tone is flat when I reply, "I know what dual point of view is, Mercedes."

"Okay, sorry," she replies with an embarrassed smile, fingering the towel on the counter in front of her. "Do you think you might be able to help me?" She looks up at me with wide, nervous eyes, clearly anxious for putting herself out there like this.

I stare back and wonder if I can rise to the challenge. More sex with a girl I actually like, but no relationship ties? No strings. No commitment. Can it really be that easy?

I pick up my empty plate and stride around the counter to the sink. I can feel her eyes on me when I reply, "To be crystal clear, you're proposing friends with benefits, right?" I set the dish in the sink and turn to face her, leaning back against the counter and crossing my arms.

Her eyes stare at my biceps for a moment before she replies with a sweet smile. "It's a concept as old as time."

I chuckle and feel a sense of euphoria move through me. This morning is turning out a hell of a lot better than I anticipated when I got out of her bed earlier. In fact, it's pretty fucking fantastic.

I eliminate the space between us and cage her in, pressing my front against her front. "Should we start now? I mean, I'd hate to see your education suffer a minute longer."

She laughs and splays her hands flat on my chest to push me back. "Actually, since we're sticking with the whole friends thing, I was wondering if you could help me with a little project first."

I waggle my brows at her. "Like a naked kind of project?"

She frowns and bites her lip sheepishly. "You could be naked if you want, but I'm not sure how safe it would be."

My smile falls.

"Do you think you could help me move my roommate's shit downstairs? I'm going to get one of those pods delivered this week for his stuff. I want to make that upstairs room into a writing den."

My brows knit together. "You aren't going to keep writing at Tire Depot?" The disappointment I feel over that thought isn't lost on me.

"I don't know yet." She shrugs. "I might. But I want to try this out first."

"Okay," I reply with a frown. "But you know you could still write there. No one knows about you."

She laughs and frowns at me curiously. "We'll see." She shrugs noncommittally again, and it's annoying. Why doesn't she want to write there anymore?

Shaking off my agitation, I step back and spread my arms out wide to stretch. "So what did your roommate do to piss you off that you're moving his shit out?"

She rolls her eyes. "What didn't he do?"

I laugh at her cute little flash of attitude and reply, "Well, I'll definitely help you. This is the stuff guys like me were born to do." I give her a wink and flex my arms cockily. "Should we shower before or after hard labor?"

She smiles. "Why not both?"

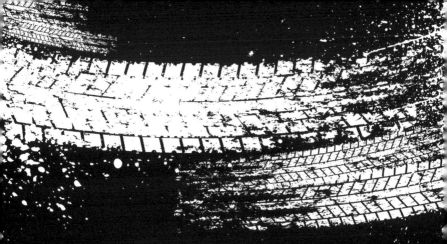

CHAPTER 16

Kate

"I've entered into a casual, friends-with-benefits situation with a mechanic from Tire Depot who thinks my name is Mercedes," I groan to my author friend, Hannah, on the phone while sprawled out dramatically on the now empty floor of the upstairs bedroom. "Tell me what to do."

"Okay, what book is this for?"

"It's not for a book."

"Wait, what?" she asks.

"It's not for a book. It's for me."

"This is actually happening to you?"

"Yes."

"Like in real life?"

"Yes, Hannah! And I like him way more than just a

friend so can you keep up, please? I'm in crisis mode, and I'm not sure what to do!"

"Besides bone him every chance you get?"

"Yeah. I mean…I'm kind of avoiding him this week to sort of play it cool, so he doesn't catch on that I like him."

"Which you do."

"Yeah, but I don't want him to know that!"

"Listen to me," she states, and I swear I hear her laptop close. "Here's what you're going to do. You're going to go camping."

"Camping?" I repeat.

"Camping."

"Why?"

"Cuz blue collar guys love that shit. Tell him it's for book research, and you need his help."

"Oh! That's good because I already used that excuse!"

"Perfect. I can see this playing out like a damn movie, and you know when I plot, and they play out like movies, it's a best seller."

"Yes!" I squeal excitedly, sitting up because now I'm too anxious to lie down.

Her voice gets mock high, like a Marilyn Monroe impression. "You're going to be adorable and fumbling and not know how to cast a fishing pole, and he's going to realize how much fun it is to go camping and get to fuck in a tent." She shifts her tone to hard butch at the end, and I'm literally clutching my belly from laughing so hard.

"Oh my God, this sounds good."

"But make him sweat it out for a while before you call

him. When was the last time you slept with him?"

"Two days ago."

"Perfect. Wait a few more days. Make him wonder for a whole week what you're doing. It'll drive him mad. Then when you do see him, play it super cool. Like you're just one of the guys."

"That sounds really good."

"See? Book ideas can apply in the real world."

"You're a genius, Hannah," I state, sitting up and looking around the empty room. Now's as good a time as any to redecorate. "I'm going camping!"

"Let me know where to have the pizza delivered to."

"Ha-ha. Bitch."

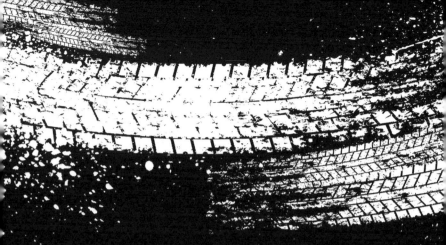

CHAPTER 17

Miles

"**D**ude, you are so screwed," Sam says, catching me totally off guard as I stare out the shop window into the alley.

"Jesus, fucker, warn a guy!" I exclaim, pressing my hand to my chest as I feel my heart rate pounding. "Why are you walking so softly?"

"I wasn't walking softly." He frowns down at his feet.

"Yeah, you were," I growl, tossing my impact wrench into my toolbox. "I didn't hear you because you tiptoed over to my station like a creep."

"I wasn't tiptoeing, moron. I was walking like a human. You've just been in your own little world all week, peeping out the window like a lovestruck teenager. If anyone's the creep, it's you."

I roll my eyes and have to fight the urge not to look out the window again, hoping to catch a glimpse of Mercedes. It's become a habit I don't even realize I'm doing anymore. Possibly even worse than licorice smoking.

It's been a week since her party, and I'm growing more and more frustrated by the fact she hasn't returned to Tire Depot to write. Or called me.

"I thought you said it was casual," Sam states, propping down on a metal shop stool and cranking the empty vise grip.

"It is. I'm not obsessing. I'm just…wondering why she hasn't come back. I probably fucked this up."

"Fucked what up exactly? You said you don't want anything more than casual with her."

"I want friendship," I reply through clenched teeth as I unzip my coveralls and step out of them. "I like her as a friend. She's not like anyone I've ever met. She's always saying something that surprises me, and she's really fucking cool in an unfiltered, real sort of way. She's cooler than you, that's for damn sure."

Sam clutches his chest at my burn. "So why don't you want more than friendship with someone that cool?"

"You know why," I nearly growl and then hear my phone chirp from the workshop bench. My nerves spike as I swipe my screen to unlock it, replying to Sam quickly, "I can't get wrapped up in drama again."

"Not all drama is bad," Sam mumbles as I stare down at my screen.

Mercedes: Want to help me with some book research? ;)

Me: Yes.

Mercedes: Jeez. What if I said it involves sex with an animal or inanimate object or something?

Me: Does it?

Mercedes: No

Me: Then yes.

Mercedes: Okay, can you come over tonight?

Me: Yep.

Mercedes: Cool, bring beer and pizza.

Me: Done.

Mercedes: And bring those book boyfriend arms. ;)

I'm smiling like a fucking goofball when I remember Sam's still sitting right in front of me. I look up and roll my eyes at his grim expression. "Let me hear it."

He cups his hands to his mouth and booms. "You are screwed!"

Pulling up to Mercedes's house, I feel nerves like I've never felt before. When I came to her place for her party last week, I had no expectations of the night. What happened between us wasn't planned. I had a feeling something might happen, but that's a hell of a lot different than sitting outside a girl's house and knowing when you walk inside, you're going to get laid. This feeling is equal parts thrilling and nerve-wracking.

Stop being a pansy, Miles.

I grab the pizza and beer off the seat of my truck and make my way to her front door. When she opens it, I remember exactly why I was so nervous tonight.

This girl is way too fucking hot for me.

She's dressed in a flirty little dark blue sundress with big pink flowers all over it. Her red hair is straight again, like that night at the bar when we first kissed. She's kept her makeup light, but her lashes are long and framing her blue eyes beautifully. Her lips are shiny with a pink gloss that makes me want to lean in and—

"Hey, bro!" she barks, punching me in the shoulder.

I frown and pull back. "Hey?" I say it in question because I'm not sure why she addressed me like that.

She reaches out and grabs the beer. "Thanks for bringing the brewskies." She turns on her heel and gestures for me to come in as she sets the beer down on her coffee table. She strides over and grabs the pizza box from me next. "I'm so hungry I could eat the ass end out of a dead rhino."

"Are you having a stroke?" I deadpan because seriously, what the fuck is going on here?

"What do you mean?" she chirps, her eyes wide as she clutches the pizza box.

"Why are you talking like this?"

"This is my casual voice."

My face screws up in disbelief. "I've heard your casual voice, and it usually consists of waxing poetic about complimentary coffee and cookies. Tell me what you're doing."

"I have no idea!" she exclaims and turns to set the pizza down by the beer. Looking back at me, she adds, "I was trying to be a friend. A bro. One of the guys. *Au casuale*."

I have to bite back a laugh. "Well, stop it. I'm not going to fuck one of the guys, and with how hot you look in that dress, I'd very much like to fuck you tonight."

"Hannah is an idiot," she growls under her breath.

"Who?"

"No one," she beams and slides her hands down her hips. "So you like my dress?"

I nod, my brows raised at the rosy hue creeping around her cheeks. "I'd like it better on the floor."

I move in and pull her body against mine, but she pulls back. "Well, it will have to wait because I really am famished."

I exhale through my nose, a low rumble vibrating in my chest. "Very well."

We get comfortable on the couch, and Mercedes places a couple of slices on a plate for me. I crack open both of our beers, and we proceed to wine and dine ourselves, Boulder style.

"So how have you been?" I ask as she takes a bite.

"Good! You?"

"Good," I reply, glancing down at her smooth, bare legs. "What did you do all week?"

Her brows lift curiously. "What do you mean?"

"I mean, I didn't see you come into Tire Depot, so I was wondering…where did you write at?" *Jesus, Miles, get a grip! Are you seriously jealous of where she's writing now?*

She licks some sauce off her finger before replying. "Well, I've been redecorating that upstairs bedroom."

Suddenly, I notice everything from that bedroom that we had stacked in a pile downstairs is gone. "When did the pod show up? I told you to call me, and I'd help you load it."

She bites her lip. "It came Wednesday, but it's fine. I managed."

"You managed?" I argue, my brows furrowing in disbelief. "Some of that shit was really heavy. How did you manage?"

She looks nervous for a second and straightens her posture to reply, "Lynsey helped. And Dean."

I sit back a bit, annoyance prickling my scalp. "I told you I'd help you."

She shrugs. "I didn't want to bother you."

"It wouldn't have been a bother," I snap back, my jaw tight with frustration.

"What's the big deal?" she retorts, her voice rising defensively.

I take a deep breath in and exhale slowly. This is not how I envisioned tonight going. I need to calm the fuck down, or I'm going to ruin both the friends and the benefits part of this arrangement. "Nothing, sorry." I clear my throat and take another bite of pizza. "So, you redecorated?"

This shift in subject brings a smile to her face. "Yes! It's looking pretty nice. I even got this new desk that rises and

151

lowers so I can write standing up if I want."

"Why would you want to write standing up?" I ask, dead serious.

She shrugs. "I don't know. Apparently, it's healthier. I'll probably never use it anyway since I can't seem to get into the writing groove again."

I shake my head. "Then why didn't you come back to Tire Depot this week? The coffee still tastes the same. I've checked."

She sets her plate down and reaches for her beer. "I don't know. It seems…unnecessary now. Overindulgent. I'm frustrated that I can't write in my own damn house. I redecorated that whole room, and that desk was frickin' expensive."

I nod and set my plate down to grab my beer as well. "So is that why you decided tonight was a good night for research?"

She nods and waggles her brows at me. "I thought maybe it'd get my juices flowing, literally." Her snicker afterward is so adorable, and I feel my own mood lightening with her.

But all humor is lost when I notice a naughty glint in her eyes as she wraps her pink lips around the amber glass and takes a long, cool drink. My body roars to life as memories of last weekend roll in and remind me just how great she feels naked against me.

"Let's get to work then," I nearly growl, staring at a liquid droplet of beer on her lower lip.

She swallows and licks it away while looking down at my plate. "You haven't even finished your pizza."

"I'm hungry for something else," I murmur, leaning

over and taking her beer from her hand and setting it down on the table next to mine with an audible thud.

When I sit back, I slide myself in closer so our legs are touching. Resting my hand right above her knee, I let my fingers press into her inner thigh and inch up ever so slowly. Her legs squeeze together as my eyes lift to hers. She trembles with an obvious shiver of anticipation.

"Okay, fine, I'm hungry for sex, too," she mumbles and sucks in a deep breath of air. "But I need to hear what you're thinking the whole time we do this...you know...for research and stuff."

"For research and stuff," I repeat, licking my lips and trying not to smirk.

"This is serious, Miles."

"Okay," I acquiesce. "But I have to warn you. I'm probably not going to be the most articulate when I'm buried inside you."

She swallows slowly and squirms in her seat as my hand inches up a little farther. Her voice is husky when she replies, "You had no problem articulating yourself the night of my party."

I chuckle at that memory. "Well, those were extenuating circumstances."

"Were they?" She bites her lip and stares down at my hand that's now disappeared under her skirt.

"Yes," I reply with a brazen squeeze of her thigh. "I was sexually frustrated beyond belief. I'd spent weeks watching you flounce into the comfort center looking so fucking sexy and unsuccessfully sneaky."

"Unsuccessful?" she exclaims defensively.

"Yeah, you weren't what I'd call stealthy."

"Shut up." She giggles, and her lower lip sticks out as she mock sulks.

"Then you kissed me at that bar and rode on the back of my motorcycle. By the night of your party, I was a sexually deprived madman. Then I catch you flirting with that guy—"

"I wasn't flirting!" she exclaims, shoving me hard in the shoulder.

I pull my hand from under her skirt and use her momentum to pull her onto my lap. She happily obliges, straddling me and resting her hands on my shoulders, mindlessly toying with the neckline of my T-shirt.

I slowly slide my hands up her bare thighs, and the movement has her legs spreading even farther. "I know you weren't flirting, but I wanted to fuck you so bad I couldn't think straight."

She pulls her lips in and rubs them together, seemingly appeased by that response. "Well then, what are we waiting for?" she asks, making fierce eye contact with me as she shamelessly grinds her hips down onto my groin.

My dick develops its own heartbeat as the heat of her center touches my erection. I reach up and cup her face, connecting our lips at last. Her gloss tastes like strawberries, and I swirl my tongue into her parted lips to taste more of her. She combs her fingers into my hair and gives as good as she gets.

Then…

She braces her hands on the back of the couch and begins full-on humping me.

I break our kiss, breathless and a little lightheaded. Tucking her red tendrils behind her ears so I can see her face more clearly, I ask, "Are you dry humping me?"

She smiles, her lips a little raw from my whiskers as she greedily thrusts her hips into me again. "Maybe."

My dick jolts, and my hands fall from her face to rest on her hips as I ride the motion like she's some sort of wave pool at a theme park. The texture of my jeans becomes painful as my cock pushes to full length.

"Tell me what you're thinking," she pants, dropping her forehead to mine as she continues working herself on top of me.

I press my head to her chest, the painful tightness in my pants unbearable, yet something I don't want to stop either. It's like an itch that feels so fucking good to scratch, but you know if you do it for too long, it will be raw and fucked by the end.

"Research mode already?" I ask, sliding my hands up the side of her ribs and cupping her breasts through the silky fabric.

"Oh," she moans loudly, her eyes closing as my fingers brush over her clearly unrestrained nipples. "And yes, tell me what's going on in your mind."

I nip at her breast through her dress as she grinds down on me again. "I'm thinking about how thinly veiled your little pussy is as it rocks on my thick, hard denim."

"So hard," she repeats, eyes still closed as she gyrates on

my lap.

"And it feels so good having you ride my cock, but I bet your little clit is just burning for release. All that friction and rubbing. I bet you've soaked through your panties."

"Yes," she husks and runs her hand through her hair as she grinds on me faster. "What else?"

My dick is getting angrier by the second, so I decide right then and there we're through with the dry humping session for this evening. "I want you naked and in a bed, *now*."

Her blue eyes pop open, pupils dilated and hair a wild mess as she drops her hands to my chest. "Very articulate," she says with a smirk and looks over her shoulder for a second. "But we're going upstairs. I want to christen that new bedding, and I can't think of a better time to do it."

With a half-smile, I help her off my lap and stare at her ass the entire walk upstairs. My dick is a fucking smashed-up mess in my jeans, and I cannot wait to let it free inside her.

When we step into the upstairs bedroom, I'm surprised at the transformation. On the right is a white desk with a gray tufted chair that looks really fucking comfortable. Her laptop rests closed on top of the desk. There's no clutter on it. No life. It was clearly set up and left completely unused thus far.

In the middle of the room is a giant king-size bed. Bigger than the one she has downstairs. Since I'm a big dude, this pleases me greatly. It's covered in a gray linen duvet with some colorful accent pillows strewn all over it. Overhead is a modern chandelier that Mercedes has dimmed, setting the mood for further "research."

Craving more, I reach out and grab her hand, pulling her to me for a kiss. She presses against my chest, pushing me backward until the back of my legs hit the bed, and I'm forced to sit. "Research first," she chastises like I'm some naughty schoolboy.

"You really are a workaholic," I tease.

"You really are a sex fiend," she teases back and moves away from me so she's standing all alone on the hardwood floor, fully out of my reach. "So let's start with something easy. What runs through your mind when I do this?"

She twirls in her bare feet, her dress fanning out all around her so high, I get a glimpse of her white thong and bare ass cheeks.

She stops, and I lift my brows. "You want the honest truth?"

"Of course," she replies, her brows furrowing like she's preparing to take mental notes.

"Honestly, because I am the way I am, all I thought about was the fact that I hope you never wear that dress in public again."

"What? Why?" She looks down at it accusingly

"Because when you did that, I saw everything. So either you can't wear that dress, or you need to wear big ole granny panties underneath. Or better yet, a pair of my basketball shorts."

She laughs at that idea. "Good God, you are too much. Good thing you're not my boyfriend."

Her response has my face tightening slightly, but I hide my reaction and repeat, "Good thing."

"Okay, let's try something a little harder. What are you thinking when I do this?" She bends over and peels her little white thong off, the one that I saw so perfectly only seconds ago. She stands back up and flings it over her shoulder.

"I'm thinking lots of things," I reply, running my hands down my denim-clad thighs. It's painful to be this far away from her right now, and I don't think I'm going to last much longer.

"Okay, like what exactly?" She gestures for me to elaborate.

I clear my throat, my eyes raking over her like a prize meant to be claimed. "I'm thinking about the fact that I can tell by the dampness on the front of my jeans that you are wet already. In fact, you've probably been wet all night. Same way that I was half hard just driving out here. So because you were so wet all evening, that means there's nothing to stop that moisture from running down your thighs."

She sucks in a big gulp of air, as if she forgot to breathe for a second. "And what would happen if you saw some of that wetness run down my thighs?"

I pin her with a wicked glare. "I'd have to lick it off you with my tongue, of course."

"Oh Jesus, Mary, and Joseph," she sings, her voice a mix of crying, moaning, and begging.

Unable to stay away a moment longer, I stand and take three long strides to tower over her. She's barefoot and completely naked under this dress—it's a fucking miracle I lasted this long.

I run my fingers down the sides of her arms and feel goose bumps erupt all along her skin. Lowering one of my hands past her fingertips, I touch the skirt of her dress, steal underneath the fabric, and find her smooth center with my fingers.

"Just as I suspected," I husk as my digits swipe along her folds. "Fucking soaking wet."

"Yes," she moans, one hand reaching out and clutching my bicep for support. When I sink one long finger into her heat, her other hand flies out to catch herself on my chest. "Oh my God."

"Let me take care of this," I husk against her ear as I remove my hand from between her legs.

I turn her in my arms and walk her back to the bed. She lies back, her head hitting the pillow, her red hair fanning out wildly. The bed dips as I press a knee between her legs and slowly push her dress up and spread her thighs apart.

I glance down at her needy center, practically quivering for more. I hit her with one last, smoldering glance before lowering myself and dipping my nose between her folds.

I inhale deeply. "Christ, you smell like sin."

"Oh God," she moans, and I really surprise her when my tongue darts out to tease that tight bundle of nerves. "And you taste like heaven," I add before flattening my tongue and licking the entire length of her.

"Holy shit," she cries loudly as I proceed to fuck her with my tongue.

God, she's responsive. It's been ages since I've done this

with a woman because I refuse to do it with random girls. But Mercedes is definitely not random. She's fucking perfect as she writhes against my assault on her pussy. Her back arching and flattening over and over as she squeezes the bedspread and struggles to handle everything I give her.

When I suck her clit into my mouth, her hands fork into my hair, nails scoring my scalp so harshly, I growl into her sweet cunt. "Jesus, Miles! Yes!"

The vibrations of my voice only drive her more wild because suddenly, her thighs squeeze so tightly around my head, I go deaf for a second—lost only to the sensations of my heartbeat racing and the interior, erotic noises of my mouth as I swirl my tongue all over her sweet center.

I can tell she's close to coming, but not because her cries grow louder. It's because they grow softer. In the short time I've spent with her, I know that she loses her voice when she reaches that point of no return. It's when she can see the finish line, and it looms over her like a ticking time bomb.

It's fucking glorious to witness.

I pull back to look up at her as I plunge two fingers into her wet heat. When she comes, I want to feel it. I want to feel everything from this woman. I seal my mouth back on her clit and suck, hard. And like a damn easy button, her spasming response is instantaneous.

She goes stock-still, tensing everywhere except her center as her muscles contract, pulling me into her. I have to bite back a proud laugh as I feel every single tremble of her pussy detonate against my fingers.

It's magnificent.

After a few moments, her voice returns with long, breathy moans of delirium. She's not saying anything. She's recovering. She's making up for the moans her orgasm stole from her and goddamnit, it's perfect.

"Want to know what I'm thinking now, babe?" I ask, staring up at her from between her thighs.

She looks down at me, her hair wild, eyes wide, lips parted. "Yes," she croaks, voice raw and overworked.

"I'm thinking your pussy is the best I've ever had, and I don't know if I'll ever get enough of it." My honest words take me by surprise, but I quickly cover them up by rising to my knees and pulling off my shirt.

When I undo my jeans, and my dick pours out long and hard and ready for its own release, we both forget my admission and get back to work. This is just for research after all.

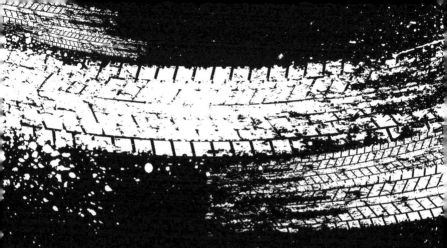

CHAPTER 18

Miles

The sound of soft tapping wakes me in the middle of the night. I assume it must be raining outside and maybe Mercedes left her window open, so I roll over to have a look. My eyes have to blink a few times to take in the sight of my redhead, sitting cross-legged in the chair at her desk. But she's not facing out toward the window, she's facing the bed. Her face is illuminated in the soft white light from her laptop screen, and she's so laser-focused on what she's doing, she doesn't notice me watching her.

She's wearing my black T-shirt, and I'm betting nothing else as the laptop rests squarely in the middle opening of her legs. Her tongue slips out of her mouth, running along her upper and lower lip, and I think I hear a little moan escape her lips, but that fact doesn't stop her fingers from flying across the keyboard.

It's an adorable sight, and one I'd be very inclined to sit back and enjoy if I didn't have a raging erection already. I prop myself up on the headboard and have to clear my throat before she even notices me in her eye line.

"Jesus Christ!" she exclaims with a jolt, her hand pressing against her chest. "How long have you been awake?"

"Only a couple of minutes." I frown at her wide-eyed, guilty expression. "What are you doing on your computer that's so important in the middle of the night?"

My hand instinctively fists around the blanket in preparation, because if this was Jocelyn, whatever she was doing wouldn't be good.

Mercedes eyes alight with excitement. "I'm writing!"

"At this hour?" I ask, dubiously, glancing over at the digital clock on the end table that displays 3:18 a.m.

"I couldn't get to sleep!" She shrugs. "The ideas have been flowing since the minute we shut the lights off."

"You've been writing since we went to bed?"

"Well, no, I was plotting in my mind for a good hour first. I was trying to whisper scenes into the audio recorder on my phone so I wouldn't wake you, but then I just couldn't take it anymore. I had to get up and frickin' write!"

She turns her laptop to face me, showing me a word document full of her efforts. "Five thousand words in three hours. That's Tire Depot magic right there!"

I half-smile, my entire body relaxing with a strange relief. "Maybe it's Miles Hudson magic."

Her eyes drift down to take me in more fully this time.

My bare chest is on full display, and the blanket is draped so low, she gets an eyeful of the deep *V* muscle of my obliques. The heated look in her eyes is not lost on me.

"Do you want to come back to bed so I can show you some more magic?" I waggle my brows at her suggestively.

She bites her lip and looks down at her computer, clearly warring with herself over what's more important. Apparently, it's a quick inner conversation because, in a flash, she sets down her laptop and jumps on top of me.

I laugh and roll us so that I'm on top, between her legs, nibbling at her neck and pushing her shirt up so I can feel her naked thighs all around me. "I think waking up hard is going to be a constant with you," I murmur, biting her nipple through my shirt.

She squeals and wriggles against my groin. "I'm super okay with that."

With all the wiggling she's doing, the tip of my dick connects with her center. She's wet and warm, and fucking hell, the direct skin-on-skin contact has me groaning. I press my face into her neck and groan, "Fuck, you feel so damn good."

"You too," she states, her hips pulsing up toward me, trying to take me inside her more.

"Babe, stop," I moan, sliding my forehead to her shoulder, my breath trembling with need. "I have to get a condom."

She whines out a little-frustrated noise as I move off her and grab my wallet off the end table. I lay on my back and roll the rubber on, feeling her eyes on me the whole time.

"This is my last one, so no morning sex for you."

"This is morning," she retorts, propping herself on her elbows so she can get a better view.

"No breakfast sex for you, then," I correct.

She laughs. "That's okay. You'll be too busy chewing your arm off anyway."

I growl at her smart mouth and roll back on top of her, tossing one of her legs up on my shoulder as I do. I press my now wrapped tip inside her and husk, "I think we're well past the arm chewing stage, don't you?"

When I thrust into her, this angle allowing me so far in, she cries out as my cock nearly kisses her cervix. Her fingers bite into my arms. "Jesus, Miles!"

"That's right, babe, let me hear you this time." I drop my head to her chest and nibble at her T-shirt covered breasts. I should have taken the time to rip that off, but desperate times call for desperate measures.

Her voice is hoarse when she replies, "You are so deep. This is so intense. I'm not sure I can—"

"You can," I encourage, driving into her slow and hard. Deep and long. My ass popping back and forth with every thrust. "You can take me."

"Oh God," she mewls, her other leg tightening around my hip, her heel digging into my lower back. "This is incredible."

"You're damn fucking right it is," I reply and realize with a sudden jolt that it's not like this with everyone. I've slept with at least a dozen women since my split with Joce, and no one has come even close to feeling this good wrapped around my dick. Not even Joce.

I increase the speed of my movements, trying to chase my wayward thoughts away and relish this sweet, sweet fucking I'm in the middle of. Between the wet, erotic noises of our breaths and the plethora of moans and grunts and pants filling the room, we're creating the best goddamn soundtrack to fucking I've ever heard.

Mercedes bucks beneath me, meeting me thrust for thrust. Growing quieter and quieter as she climbs along with me. We're in sync. Perfect, liberating sync.

She wraps her hands around my neck and presses her face against mine, crying out her orgasm right into my ear. It's a mixture of gasps and strangled breaths. It's otherworldly sounding. It makes no fucking sense, but my dick likes it, and with one final burst of energy, I'm following her, blowing inside the condom and knowing there's no way in fucking hell I'm not sticking around for pancakes with this girl.

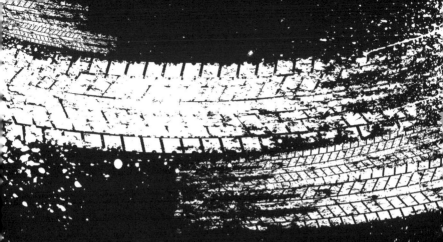

CHAPTER 19

Kate

I stride into the Rise and Shine Bakery, the cute spot on Broadway down the street from Dean's downtown co-working space. The smell of fresh donuts and coffee make my tummy growl excitedly as I head to the counter to order two croinuts. Croinuts are a croissant and a donut combination that this Boulder bakery is nationally famous for. A buttery and savory yet sweet and flaky combination that is basically like an orgasm in a carb.

The adorable little blonde behind the register smiles brightly and replies, "You'll have to take a number, I'm afraid. Our next batch isn't due out for another hour and a half. Are you planning to be here a while?"

"Yes, I have no problem waiting," I reply, clutching my satchel to my shoulder in confirmation.

She points at the little number machine that literally spits out a paper sheet with a number, so I give it a tug. I pay for two coffees and a brownie appetizer and move to find a table to wait for Dean.

Dean and I usually try to meet here once a week to catch up and check in on each other. This was the place where he asked me for advice on how to tell Lynsey he only wanted to be friends. They'd only been dating for a month or two, but he said that the more he got to know her, the more he looked at her like a sister instead of a woman he wanted to sleep with.

On the other end, I was getting panic-stricken texts from Lynsey saying Dean still wasn't coming on to her and what should she do so he would just man up and fuck her already?

The two of them parting ways, at least romantically, was definitely for the best. They were way too similar. I was just grateful they were able to actually continue their friendship. It took a little time, more so on Lynsey's part than on Dean's, but now it's almost like it never happened.

Ever since then, this bakery has become my sacred place with Dean. And it's the only spot in town I don't balk at spending $5.79 for a cup of coffee. Because…croinuts.

I make my way over to a dark red booth by the picture window that overlooks Broadway Street. I slide open my phone and see I missed a text from Miles.

Miles: My dick misses you.

Me: Your dick is insatiable. It's been two days.

Miles: Whatever. How are the words flowing?

Me: Good. Not as good as the other night though. ;)

Miles: Maybe that means you need to do more research.

Me: LOL, maybe. Actually, I thought I'd come back to Tire Depot tomorrow maybe.

Miles: Am I getting replaced by the Customer Comfort Center?

Me: Why can't I have my cake and eat it too?

Miles: I could think of something else I'd rather be eating.

Me: OMG, you are filthy.

Miles: Says the smut writer.

Me: If I say it, it must be true.

I throw my head back to laugh and nearly jump out of my seat when I see Dean standing next to me, looking over my shoulder. "Jesus, Dean, say hello or something!"

"I was literally standing here for almost five minutes," he retorts, an unamused look on his face.

"And reading my texts? God, you nosy jerk. Sit down."

"I need to go take a number," he says, gesturing over his shoulder.

"No, you don't. I ordered for you."

I push the second coffee over to his side of the table, and he looks relieved as he shrugs out of his sports coat. He's dressed in a matching navy linen suit today with a white button-down underneath. No tie. A bright pair of blue and white striped socks peek out above his expensive brown shoes. Even his dark hair looks expensive gelled neatly off to one side, a clean look that is in direct contrast to his masculine beard. I shake my head at how much money Dean must spend on his appearance alone.

Don't get me wrong. I make a really good living. But I spend it differently than he does. And I genuinely like Target's clothes.

He slides into the booth, draping his jacket over the far end of the table before pinning me with a look. "I saw his truck outside your place a couple of nights ago."

"Whose truck?" I ask, feigning indifference.

"Miles, who else?"

I narrow my eyes. "How do you know it was his truck?"

He scoffs. "Because I don't know any other guy in Boulder who would drive a beastly vehicle like that."

"Oh my God, you're such a snob."

"So he spent the night?" he snaps quickly, his hands reaching out to mindlessly move his coffee over to the side so he can fold his hands on the table in front of him.

My face contorts in disbelief. "What, did you come by to check back the morning after?"

He looks completely shameless when he replies, "Maybe."

This has me rolling my eyes. "Stop worrying. It's not serious. We're just…fooling around."

He shakes his head and laughs. "That's exactly what I'm worried about, Kate."

"Why?" I ask, dumping extra sugar into my coffee because with the way Dean is acting, I have a feeling I'm going to need my energy.

"Because for one, this guy rejected you once already."

"Thanks for the reminder!" I exclaim, stirring in the sugar with the spoon on the table.

"I'm sorry, but he did. And you were fucking pissy about it for days. A pain in the ass to be around."

"Well, please let me apologize for having feelings in front of my friends."

"It wasn't your feelings I was mad at. It was that idiot, Miles."

"You don't know he's an idiot."

"Oh, please." He sneers and drapes his arms over the back of the booth. Everything about him looks so pompous and arrogant that I want to punch him. "He's a mechanic at a Tire Depot. How bright can he be?"

I slam my spoon down on the table. "Are you frickin' kidding me with this shit?"

"No," he snaps, his jaw rigid beneath his beard.

"This coming from a high school dropout?"

"I earned my GED, and I'm self-educated."

"In what? Being a fucking asshat?" I snap and move to stand.

"Sit down, Kate." He reaches out to grab me.

"I will not!" I rear back and yank my wrist out of his hand. "This is total bullshit, Dean." I fume, feeling so hurt and upset by his snap judgment of Miles. A man he doesn't even know. It reminds me of the look I get from people who don't support what I do for a living or who think I'm only one thing. Miles is so much more than what Dean is giving him credit for, and if he can't see that, I don't want to be around him.

I pin Dean with a serious glower and say, "I surround myself with people who are inclusive and nonjudgmental because I have a weird job. I write frickin' erotic novels for a living, and I don't want judgy friends in my corner because that makes me a hypocrite to the characters I write about. And Miles is so encouraging about what I do. More encouraging than you've ever been, and that counts for a lot in my book! And he's not dumb at all. He's actually really fucking insightful, and you might know that if you'd quit looking down your nose at people."

Dean's face turns beet red, panic setting in over his features as I move to walk away. "Don't leave, Kate." He stands up and pulls me back to him.

"No," I exclaim, pulling out of his arms. "I'm sorry, but if you're going to start acting like this, then I don't see how we can continue our friendship."

"Kate!" he repeats my name so urgently I pause to look at him. His eyes are wide and more terrified than I've ever seen them, a sort of panic taking over his entire body when he finally stutters out, "I like you."

I shrug. "Well, I thought I liked you too until you turned into a douche-nozzle."

"No, I mean, I really like you." He closes his eyes and slides his hands into the pockets of his trousers, resignation all over his posture.

But for some reason, his words still don't fully sink in. My angry expression morphs into disbelief. "Like you really like me like a best friend or you…?"

He pins me with a severe look and replies, "I like you as more than a best friend, and it's not something I can ignore anymore."

"Dean," I say with a sigh, my stomach dropping like I'm on a damn roller coaster. "How long?"

"A couple of years?" he grinds through clenched teeth, drops back down into the booth, and runs a hand through his beard nervously. "But I was with Lynsey, and you were with that douchebag, Dryston."

I slide back into the booth, and my jaw dropped when I reply, "You never said a word."

"I was waiting for the right time." He shrugs.

"But Dryston and I have been broken up for months now."

"But he still lives with you!" he replies, leaning across the table with wide, urgent eyes. "And you were together for two years, Kate. You needed time to get over that shit. I wasn't going to be the rebound guy. I wanted more than that. Then this fucking mechanic comes out of nowhere, and suddenly, you're casual Kate. Wait, no…casual *Mercedes*."

I lean back, my teeth grinding at him throwing that in my face. "You know why I told him my name was Mercedes."

"I know it's ridiculous to be spending time with a guy who doesn't know the real you."

"He does know the real me!" I argue. "He knows more

about me than Dryston ever learned in our two years together."

"But you're hooking up with a guy who still doesn't know your real name. How do you think that's going to end, Kate?"

"I don't know. We're casual now, but maybe we could be more."

"See! That's what kills me. I thought Miles was just a rebound guy, but you're trying to force him to be more, and I'm right fucking here trying to offer you more! This guy doesn't even know your real name, and you're shocked by my hope? Come off your high horse, Kate."

"What high horse?"

"You're so blind and self-involved. You should have seen this coming."

My jaw drops. "Excuse me?"

"It's true. When you're in the book world, you ignore everything and everyone around you."

"It's my job, Dean!" I exclaim. "I can't help it. It's not a freaking switch I can click off."

He exhales heavily through his nose. "You honestly didn't see the signs?"

I close my eyes tight and cycle back through our friendship. Dean is a flirt. He's always been a flirt. He gets handsy, and he tosses my flip-flop out doors, and he gives me a lot of crap…*a lot more than he gives Lynsey.* He's like a kid on the playground who pulls a girl's pigtails because he likes her.

That realization hits me like a ton of bricks.

I look up at Dean who looks so defeated, it breaks my

heart. But I have to be honest with him. "I like Miles," I state with a simple shrug.

"But he only wants casual," Dean retorts, leaning toward me and grabbing my hand. "I want so much more with you, Kate. I'd want it all. The good and the bad. You said Miles doesn't want drama. I'll take all your drama because I care about you."

His words are killing me. Slowly slicing through me like tiny little pinpricks of anxiety because regardless of Dean's willingness to commit, I don't see him that way. I pull my hand out of his and reply, "I'm sorry, Dean."

He pulls back and exhales heavily with a tight nod.

"I still want to be friends," I add, but he cuts me off with a scathing look.

"I need you to go," he states, his jaw tight with anger.

"Dean—"

"I'm not kidding, Kate. This went worse than I could have ever imagined, and I need you to go before you ruin this bakery for me. We all have our own little places we vibe at, and this is my Tire Depot. So please, can you just leave?"

Seeing the resigned look on his face that I cannot ignore, I grab my satchel off the bench before sliding out of the booth. "I'm sorry, Dean."

He nods woodenly, and without another word, I turn and walk out, leaving Dean behind to wait with our numbers.

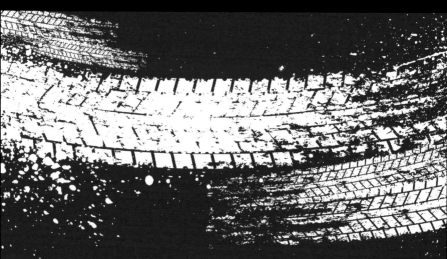

CHAPTER 20

Kate

"**H**ey!" Miles exclaims, his eyes wide and surprised as I stride around the hood of some sort of vintage blue truck he's elbows deep in.

He hits me with a megawatt smile, and I have to pause to stabilize myself on the toolbox beside me. Miles isn't dressed in his standard Tire Depot coveralls. He's dressed in a pair of worn jeans and a white tank top that looks about one size too small for his enormous pecs.

"I was just heading toward the comfort center, and I figured I'd stop and say hello since the garage door was wide open."

He sets down some sort of complicated-looking car thing and pulls the bottom of his tank top up to wipe the sweat from his brow. Jesus, Mary, and Joseph, even his abs have dirt and oil on them.

His entire body is glistening with sweat and oil, and his bright blue eyes are electric as ever. It's all doing serious things to my body.

I clear my throat and blink rapidly a few times to get control of myself. "What's that?" I ask, pointing at the contraption he set down. I need to distract my thoughts from how badly I want to bone him right here in this dirty garage.

"A carburetor," he answers, his mouth tipping into a half-smile.

"What does it do?" I ask like the good little student I never was.

"Uhh, kind of a lot." He scratches the back of his head and lifts it up to show me. "Do you really want to know?"

I nod because I do. I really, really do. I want to hear him drop some mechanical poetry on me right frickin' now.

He clears his throat. "Well, it mixes a proper ratio of gasoline and air inside an engine for combustion to occur. The correct proportion is needed on the basis of a car's speed, distance traveled, and other factors for better performance of the engine. Nowadays, most cars have fuel injectors, but the classics here still run with these."

"Interesting," I husk, moving in closer to him and pressing my back against the grille of the truck.

He moves in closer to me, his shoulder and leg brushing up against mine as he adds, "It's kind of like how a candle needs oxygen to burn. Combustion of an engine can't take place without the air the carburetor brings in."

I pull my lips into my mouth and rub them together

slowly, my gloss sticky in the summer heat. "Kind of like how an orgasm can't be achieved without friction."

His body shakes with silent laughter. "Sure, we could draw that parallel."

"I'd like to draw that parallel soon," I reply huskily.

His eyes heat at my very clear request. "Did you have something in mind?"

I wonder if a Tire Depot garage quickie is an option, but then shake that horrible idea out of my head as another thought bursts into light. "Yes, actually. I've been meaning to ask you if you ever go camping?"

His brow furrows at this request from left field. Clearly Miles was contemplating a garage quickie too. He clears his throat and replies, "I've been known to camp on occasion. Sam and I usually go to Rainbow Lakes a few times a summer. The fishing is really good there."

"Fishing!" I squeal excitedly. Goddamn, it's like this was meant to be. "I'd love to learn how to fish. Would you ever consider, I don't know, taking me camping, Miles? In the interest of book research, of course."

"Well, if it's for book research," he teases with a wink as he sets the carburetor down on a rolling cart. "Did you have a day in mind?"

"As soon as possible," I bellow and purse my lips closed, rolling my eyes to the heavens. This is not playing it cool. I'm so not being casual Mercedes right now. "My schedule is really flexible, so whenever it suits you."

He nods slowly and pulls a rag out of his back pocket to wipe his hands off. "Well, there are not a ton of tent camping spots at Rainbow Lake, and they don't take reservations. So we'd have to go out early on Friday if we want a chance of snagging a spot."

"Don't you have to work?" I ask, glancing around the enormous shop full of guys and cars.

Miles shrugs with a sheepish look on his face. "I have some vacation I could use."

I can't hide the pleased smile on my face. And honestly, I don't want to. "You'd use your vacation for me?"

He chuckles and shakes his head, shyness creeping over his features like a goddamn dreamboat. "Well, I'm very committed to your education, Mercedes."

I giggle at that reply and touch his arm in appreciation. "I'll make it worth your while."

I waggle my eyebrows suggestively, and he volleys back, "Oh, believe me, I know you will." He pulls back and shakes his head, clearly needing some space to get his mind out of the gutter. "Okay then, I'll pick you up Friday morning at eight."

"Eight sounds great!" I squeal and turn on my heel to leave. I head down the alley toward the employee entrance and can't help but notice the way his eyes drink in my bare legs. "I'd better get going...I'm suddenly feeling very inspired."

I turn to run and nearly smack into Miles's friend Sam, who's just come around the corner at the same moment.

"Sorry," I mumble with a shy, embarrassed smile and hustle my ass down my usual path toward the place that started me on this crazy fucking ride.

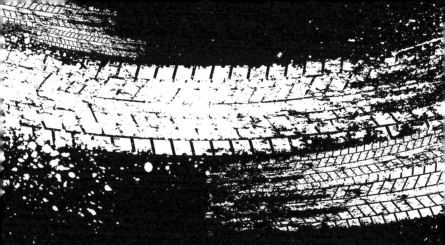

CHAPTER 21

Miles

D riving down the highway with Mercedes in my truck
and her smiling bigger than I've ever seen isn't a bad
way to spend a day of my hard-earned vacation. I didn't
know girls could be this excited about camping. Although,
in all fairness, my experience with women is pretty limited.
Jocelyn wasn't into the great outdoors at all, and my sister,
Megan, absolutely dreaded our family camping trips growing up. So I guess this will be a new experience for both of
us.

After a little over an hour's drive, we pull into Rainbow
Lakes, and I'm excited to see we're the first ones to arrive.
There are about twenty "first come, first serve" campsites
for tents and campers. Sam and I try to grab one particular
site every time we come because it has the best view of the

small lake with huge mountains in the distance. Plus, the spot offers a bit of seclusion from the other campers, and that's always a good thing.

It's not that I hate people, but I just like my space. It's why I ended up buying a house outside of Boulder. Everything in town seemed too crowded. I didn't choose Colorado for a city life.

We drive down a worn dirt path through some big trees and up onto the small hilltop of our site. Mercedes gasps when the view comes into her sight line. "Oh, Miles, this is perfect!" she exclaims, clamoring out of the car as soon as I put it in park.

She heads to the front of the truck to take in the view, and I have to fight the urge to yank her back inside and fuck the shit out of her right here and now. She looks so fucking cute in her short khaki shorts, white Chucks, and red and white flannel shirt. Her red hair is tied into two braids down over her breasts, and she's wearing a Yankees baseball cap pulled down low. I gave her some serious shit about that as soon as I saw her this morning. Seriously, how do you grow up in Colorado and not be a Rockies fan?

I get out to go stand beside her, sliding my hands in my pockets and take in a deep, cleansing breath. The air is fresh, the morning sun is warm, and I honestly can't think of a place I'd rather be right now. "This place is pretty perfect," I reply, seeing everything with new eyes. I point to an area off to the right. "There's a path here that leads right down to the water."

AMY DAWS

"Oh, that's convenient," she says, eyes bright, smile permanent.

"Yeah, you can swim in this lake too. The water is crystal clear."

She looks at me with accusing eyes. "You didn't tell me to bring my suit!"

My brows waggle. "I know."

She rolls her eyes and hits me in the arm. With a laugh, I grab her hand and pull her back toward the truck. "Come on, we have work to do."

We go about setting up our campsite. First, I lay out the tarp on the ground where we'll be staking down the tent. Then I have her help me push the tent poles through the slots and stake it down with a hammer. My tent is a nice-sized, two-room tent, which works well for Sam and me. But for Mercedes and me, one side will be for our bags, and the other side will be for us.

"This is brand new," Mercedes says from outside the tent.

Hunched over inside, I pop my head out through the door and see her holding the mattress pad I bought yesterday. I take it from her hands. "Yeah, I've never used it before."

"Why not?" she asks, bending over and coming in behind me.

I squat down to open the box. "I just do a sleeping bag usually."

"So you bought this for me?" she asks, brows furrowed.

I shrug. "It's not only for you. If I'm fucking your brains

182

out tonight like I plan to be, this will save my knees big time."

She laughs and shoves me on the shoulders, nearly knocking me backward onto my ass. "You are such a horny bastard sometimes, you know that?"

"Says the smut writer," I repeat my burn from our earlier texts. Her jaw drops as I add, "Seriously, how do you have any street cred in the romance community if you're this much of a prude?"

"You fucker!" she squeals and jumps on top of me, easily knocking me backward this time as she falls down on top of me.

I laugh and groan as my back hits a lump on the ground. "Ow!" I cry, my hand flying out to shove myself away from the apparent boulder below us. "See? This wouldn't have hurt if you could have kept your hands off me long enough to get the new mattress pad laid out."

"You are such a dick!" She giggles and digs her fingers into my sides to try to tickle me.

It's completely ineffectual.

I laugh at her tongue darting out as she focuses so damn hard to get me to squirm. But honestly, all it's doing is causing her to squirm. And with all this squirming, and her draped over the top of me, it's no wonder my body finally reacts.

Her hip catches on my erection, and she inhales sharply. She releases her lower lip from her mouth. "Seriously?" she asks, pinning me with curious eyes.

I reach up and pull her hat off, flinging it off to the side and cupping her stunning face in my hands. "Seriously." I pull her face to mine, connecting our lips and rolling us over, so I'm on top. I break our kiss and husk, "I'm only doing this without the mattress pad once, so I hope you can control yourself a little better once I give you an orgasm."

She giggles and gasps when my hand steals down the front of her shorts and swipes over her pussy lips. I push two fingers inside her, and she moans out my name right in my ear, the moisture of her hot breath sending a riot of need straight to my cock.

"Always so fucking wet," I growl and suck hard on her neck, knowing I'll be leaving a hickey.

I pull back and watch the angry red patch deepen in color. The image of my mark on her has my fingers working even faster inside her. She's rocking her sweet little hips up into my hands so shamelessly, I know she's dying for more. And fucking hell, so am I.

"Take your shorts off," I husk, pulling my hand out of her panties and grabbing my wallet out of my pocket.

She sits up and takes the foil packet from my hand. "I want to put this on."

My brows lift. "All right."

She bites her lip and unzips my jeans, her brows knitting together as she focuses. When my dick bobs out in front of her at eye level, I hear her inhale slowly. She's so fucking hot, staring at my cock like it's some sort of painting in a museum she wants to ponder for a while.

It's so sexy I have to look away.

When she takes me in her hand, I assume it's to finally

roll the condom on, but when my tip is hit with wet, hot heat, I look down to see her perfect pink lips wrapped all the way around my head.

"Fuck, babe," I groan loudly, my voice strangled in my throat as she sucks me into the back of her throat. She drags her tongue along the underside, stroking a vein that's sensitive to basically fucking everything. "Oh fuck, babe," I state again slowly, grateful I'm capable of forming coherent words right now.

She's got her tiny hand fisted around my base and is pumping me in perfect rhythm with the bobbing of her head. God, she's sexy. I reach down and grab her two braids, fisting them in my grip and guiding her motions on my cock. When I thrust gently into her throat one time, she moans loudly around my dick.

I think I might cry.

I do it again, and she moans some more, almost like me fucking her mouth like this is just as pleasurable for her as when I fuck her sweet cunt.

"Mercedes," I warn, but she ignores me.

"Mercedes," I say again, and she ignores me further, instead of moving her hands down to play with my balls.

"Babe!" I roar and yank my dick out of her mouth and away from her grip.

She's panting for air, taking in big gulps of oxygen, her mouth still hanging open. Lips still wet and raw from all the sucking and licking. "What?" she croaks, seemingly annoyed.

"You give a great fucking blowjob, but unless you want

me to blow it in your mouth, you have to stop, or I won't be able to fuck you."

"Blow it in my mouth," she states, reaching for me again.

I bend over and press my forehead to her shoulder. "Are you fucking kidding me?"

I feel her head shaking. "No, I'm serious."

Jesus fucking Christ, what am I going to do with this girl? I look up at her seriously. "Later," I snap, hunching over to grab the condom she abandoned on the ground and ripping open the foil packet.

I hold out the slick rubber to her. "Put this on me so I can fuck you from behind on your knees."

Her eyes fly wide with excitement. She's clearly okay with this change in direction now, and she focuses all her attention on my throbbing, wet dick as she rolls the Magnum over me.

I help her yank her shorts and panties down, and she quickly shucks off her button-down and turns on her knees in only a bra, her ass up in the air, poised and ready.

God, yes, she's so fucking beautiful. Perfect round ass. Small, bowed waist. I spread her knees farther apart and hike her hips up a little. Pressing my palm on her lower back, I glide my hand slowly up her spine so her chest drops to the ground. I position my fingers along her slit and find her pussy ready and waiting. Pressing my dick into her heat, I find where I need to be and thrust in, deep and fucking hard.

We both moan loudly in response to how deep I can get at this angle. When it's obvious she's not going to be quiet,

I quickly high-five myself for scoring the secluded campsite far away from nosy fucking neighbors.

"This isn't going to be soft, babe. Are you good with that?"

"Yes, Miles, fuck me!" she cries, her voice strangled, her need evident.

And that's exactly what I do. I grab her sexy little braids, and I drill into her sweet pussy until we both fall over the mountain…together.

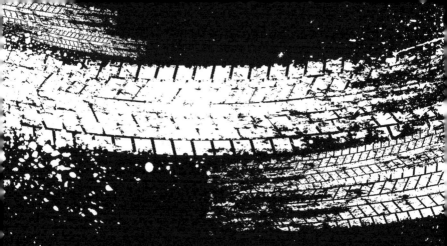

CHAPTER 22

Kate

M iles Hudson was meant for the wilderness. He doesn't have that mountain man look that so many Colorado guys have, but he has the look of a man who likes fresh air and wide open spaces. Probably because he's so big. But seeing him out here in his jeans, work boots, and a long sleeve, white Henley pushed up on his forearms in the setting of big pine trees, mountains, and lakes in the backdrop, it's like he's found his place in heaven.

And maybe the orgasms we both had earlier didn't hurt.

We finished setting up camp and made our way down to the lakeside with some fishing tackle. I'm actually excited that I don't have to fake the part of not knowing how to fish. My dad is a CPA and was more of a "resort vacationer" than a "let's go to a place that doesn't have electricity, running water, or showers."

So this really is a new experience for me.

We find a place on top of some big boulders along the shore to cast our poles out. Miles puts the worm on my hook, his manly hands grimy with worm guts and mud that he just rubs on his jeans like it's nothing. Then he wraps those same worm gut fingers around me as he shows me how to cast.

It's not gross at all.

It's manly.

It's sexy.

It's Miles.

After a while of watching my bobber float, Miles grabs the small cooler from behind his spot and opens it up to grab a beer. He twists the bottle top off and hands it to me.

"Thanks," I say, taking it from him and putting it to my lips for a drink.

"I figured you were thirsty." Miles winks and smiles. "All that deep throating."

I laugh loudly at that. "God! Get over yourself."

"Never," he retorts and looks over at me with a wink.

"Am I a better camping buddy than Sam?" I ask with a coy smile.

"Uh, yes. That fucker snores," he replies seriously. "And uses teeth."

I laugh again, so hard that tears spring to my eyes. Miles sits back with a smile and watches me regain control of myself.

"Mountain air makes you funny," I reply.

"I'm just in a good mood," he replies and reels his pole in to cast it out again a little farther this time. "It's amazing how much nicer life is with no drama."

I nod and ponder that thought for a moment. "Do you ever talk to your ex anymore?"

He shakes his head. "Not a word. And that's good."

"So you never told me what exactly broke you two up."

He shrugs like what he's about to say is no big deal. "She got pregnant with another dude's kid." My stunned eyes shoot to Miles, his profile strong and solemn as he looks out at the water showing no signs of emotion.

"That's awful," I reply and chew my lip for a minute before asking, "So you two were still together at the time?" *Translation: How did you know the baby wasn't yours?*

He shakes his head. "We were on one of our breaks. And the irony of the whole thing is that in the ten years we were together, we never went without condoms. Not once. Then she starts fucking some rich old guy, and suddenly, they have a whoops. You do the math there."

My brow furrows. "You think she got pregnant on purpose?"

"No," he replies glumly, picking at a rock. "Yes. I don't know. Probably. I hate to think of her like that because then I have to wonder what kind of fuckwit I was for staying with someone who turned out to be such a blatant gold digger."

He sighs heavily and continues, "But it makes sense because Jocelyn always had issues with what I did for a living. She thought being a mechanic was too blue collar of a profession. She wanted me to do something where I made more money."

"You look like you do just fine to me," I state firmly, annoyed at this bitch for projecting such superficial bullshit on the man she was supposed to be in love with.

"See? Thank you," Miles states, tossing a rock into the water. "That's how I've always felt. I want simple things. Family, friends, a home with a view. A place to go to let off steam every once in a while. Everything I really want, I have. Even my house in Jamestown…it needs work, and I knew when I bought it that it was a TLC project. But that works for me. I like making things my own, and the bones of the place are fucking awesome. It's a great house, and it's going to be a really great flip if I ever decide to sell. But it still would have never been enough for her."

"I think people like that will never be satisfied with anything in their life, regardless of the money," I state, pulling my baseball cap down so it blocks the sun enough for me to see Miles. "Motherhood, friendships, relationships, jobs. If she's always green-eyed and gawking at what other people have, she's missing what's right in front of her."

"Exactly!" Miles states, looking over at me with a sideways glance. "Now I'm just pissed off that I never saw that and wasted the best years of my life with her."

"Who says they were the best?" I state, feeling a little smarted over that comment. "Look around, Miles. This is a pretty fucking beautiful day." I pin him with a serious look, and I hope this gets through to him because I mean it one hundred percent. "You want for nothing, and that is an incredible quality in a person."

His frown turns into a smile. "Thanks."

"Anytime," I beam with a wink. "And look at you... you're smoking hot, you have a great job, a house, friends, and a really sexy fuck buddy."

He laughs loudly at that. "Is that what you're calling yourself now?"

I shrug and give him a squinty smile. "I guess. It just kind of rolled off the tongue there."

"I like it," he replies.

"Me too," I state, carrying my pole to sit next to him on the rock. I nudge him with my shoulder. "So don't sweat the past. Focus on the now. Because seriously, right now, I need help. My bobber disappeared several minutes ago, and I don't know what the fuck that means."

"Shit! You got a bite!" he exclaims and stands up, dropping his pole and wrapping his arms around me. "You gotta set the hook." His hands squeeze around mine on the pole, and he pauses to wait for the bobber to disappear again. After a few seconds, it drops under the water, and he yells right in my ear, "Now jerk it back!"

His arms tense around me as I yank the pole back, and the line goes taut. "You got it! Now reel it in," he says excitedly and pulls away to watch me with a giant smile.

But honest to God, I'm fucking terrified.

What is going to be on the other end of this hook? It feels massive and heavy, and it's bending my pole way too much. That can't be good. How strong are these poles? What kinds of fish live in this lake? Not sharks, of course, I'm not that stupid. But what if I'm going to reel in some disgusting swamp creature that's like a beaver and a bass that fucked during a full moon and created some kind of terrifying swamp thing that eats people like piranha. Oh my God, are there piranha in Colorado? I should have googled!

"I don't know about this, Miles," I whine, cranking the handle and reeling the line in inch by nerve-wracking inch.

He grabs the fishing net behind us and shuffles down the boulder to get closer to the water. He looks up and gives me a thumbs up. "You're doing great! You look so fucking hot!"

"Really?" I smile a little, then frown at how shallow that is to make me happy at this moment. *I need to read more literature.*

My face contorts when the end of my line pops out of the water at last. "Are you kidding me?"

Miles's raucous laughter echoes off the fucking mountains as he leans out to scoop my catch into the net. "Babe, you did it! You caught something!"

He pulls my catch up onto the rock, and he's laughing so hard, he can't speak. He keeps starting a sentence and then stopping, his body buckling over with hysterics.

I'm not laughing.

My tone is flat when I say exactly what he's trying to say. "I caught a fucking bicycle tire."

He's roaring now, dropping down on his haunches and covering his eyes with his hands.

I'm glad he's having such a great time because I am pissed. Really frickin' pissed. "A tire? What the hell, Colorado? Way to keep it classy!" I shout to no one in particular. "God, I thought this was some great outdoors experience, and I seriously just reeled in a lousy old tire. My hands hurt!"

My last comment sets Miles off again, and I start to worry about him getting enough oxygen during his fit down there. Finally, he swipes tears away from his eyes. "Babe, how can you not see the irony of this moment? It's a tire! You're a smut writer who writes in a Tire Depot. This is fucking kismet."

Well, when he puts it like that, I can't help but see a little silver lining. I set my pole on the ground and move down the boulder to inspect my catch. I look up at Miles and ask, "Think I can mount this in my new office?"

He nods and smiles. "Fucking right, you can. I'll help."

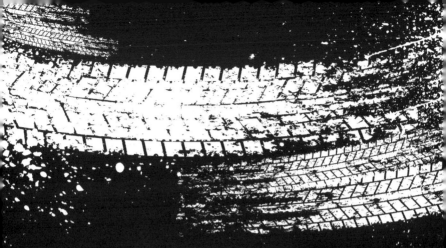

CHAPTER 23

Miles

"**A**re you ever going to tell me about this new book you're writing that requires all this painstaking research?" I ask Mercedes as I scrape away the remnants of our burgers on the grate over the fire.

It's dark out now, the night air full of the sounds of nature. Crickets chirping, owls hooting. The wind rustling the trees in the distance. Occasionally, you can hear the gentle waves lapping on the shore of the lake. And with the way the wind is blowing, I can't even hear the other campers at their sites, so I get the illusion of complete and total privacy. All-in-all, a perfect day off work.

Mercedes and I went camping.

And fuck me, it was fun. She's got a great attitude about pretty much everything. She even tried to bait her own hook at one point. She failed, but at least, she tried. We had some lunch, then went for a hike and worked up a sweat. Then we worked up another sweat back in the tent. We napped after that, and honestly, it was just one of those perfect summer days that you never want to end.

But looking at her in the lawn chair next to me, her red hair out of her braids, face glowing in the campfire light, cold beer in her hand, full moon above—I think the nighttime is shaping up pretty perfectly as well.

"It's about a mechanic," she answers finally.

"Your book is about a mechanic?" I ask, my eyes wide with total disbelief. "You're fucking with me."

She shakes her head. "Nope. The idea just sort of hit me."

"When did it hit you exactly?" I ask, taking a sip of my beer while blatantly baiting her. She blushes, full-on blushes, and I feel a strong desire to pull her onto my lap just to feel the weight of her on top of me. "Tell me," I urge.

She rolls her eyes. "I, um, was maybe ogling at you in the shop one day." She covers her face with her hands and pulls her plaid shirt up over her cheeks to hide her mortification.

"Which day?"

She shrugs. "It was before you and I started…friends with benefitting. You looked so hot and sweaty, and suddenly, this character exploded in my head, and before I knew it, I had outlined a new story." She pins me with nervous eyes.

"So it's about me?" I ask, brows furrowed cautiously.

"No." She scoffs. "It's just about a mechanic. Get over yourself. Not everything in my life is about you, Miles."

I chuckle at her eye roll but feel a sense of relief at her reply. "It's going to be about a kinky mechanic. I like it."

"Actually, it's not going to be heavy erotica like my *Bed 'n Breakfast* series."

My brows lift. "No?"

She shrugs. "No. I mean, there's still going to be sex, lots of sex, but it will be sweeter sex. Like, maybe I won't write anal in this book."

I mock gasp. "How will you handle that?"

She rolls her eyes. "I'll probably still write it, but I'll give it to my readers as bonus content or something."

I chuckle at that idea. "You wouldn't be you if you didn't do something a little bit different."

"Okay, enough about me," she states, shaking her hair out. "Let's play a game."

"Like what?" I ask, looking around. "I didn't bring any cards."

She rolls her eyes and props her head on her hands. "Miles, we don't need cards to play Truth or Dare."

I sit back in my chair and take a drink of my beer. "Who goes first?"

"Me, of course. I'm the guest, and this is all still in the interest of research, so…Truth or Dare?"

I exhale heavily. "Truth."

She jerks back, seemingly surprised by my selection. She taps her finger to her lips and says, "Okay, do you ever get horny in the garage at Tire Depot?"

Her question has me barking out a laugh. "What?"

She smiles a sly smile. "You know, are you ever working

on a customer's car and your hands get really dirty and you're really digging into a repair, and you pop a boner?"

I laugh and shake my head. "I'm afraid not."

She looks dejected.

"But classic car work, on the other hand…" My voice trails off as her eyes light up. With a chuckle, I add, "If it's a classic car and I'm elbows deep in it, and I connect two pieces, and someone is behind the wheel, and I tell them to try to start it…and an old car that hasn't run in fucking decades suddenly roars to life? Then hell yes, my dick totally gets hard."

"Ha-ha! I knew it! Perverts attract perverts. My writing makes me horny way too much."

I laugh at her and say, "Truth or Dare?"

"Dare," she replies instantly.

I quirk a brow. "Oh, someone has secrets they want to keep in the dark. Interesting."

Her face seems to flush, even in the firelight.

But I decide we've talked enough for one night. "Okay, I dare you to go skinny dipping in the lake."

Her brows shoot up into her hairline. "The lake that birthed my blessed tire? No way! Who knows what the hell else is in that thing?"

I shake my head. "I knew you wouldn't do it."

"Oh, and you would," she grumbles back.

"I've swum in that lake before. It's not disgusting. One little bicycle tire doesn't change my opinion on its cleanliness."

She pouts. "But it's probably going to be cold."

I shrug. "It's fine. I knew you wouldn't do it. You're all talk, no action."

"Are you serious?"

"Yep," I reply, pinning my eyes to her.

"Need I remind you who's been sneaking into Tire Depot for weeks on end now?"

I scoff. "You call that dangerous?"

"I'm consuming those complimentary beverages without a service, Miles." She waggles her head back and forth with some serious sass. "That's basically just as bad as thieving."

I laugh at her choice of words, then narrow my eyes and reply through clenched teeth, "Such a cold, hard criminal."

She narrows her eyes back at me, clearly not enjoying my sarcasm. "Fine, I'll do it, but you have to do it with me."

"And why would I do that?"

"Because I'll be naked," she replies, taking her shirt off and flinging it at me. When the fabric falls down from my face, I see the complete outline of her nipple through the sheer pink bra she has on.

When I see my hickey, my dick jumps to life. "Fair point."

I stand, and we both make our way down the path toward the water to our earlier fishing spot on the boulder. It's a perfect jumping-off point.

Mercedes takes a deep breath in and ditches her shorts and flip-flops, kicking them off behind her, her arms crossed in front of herself for warmth as she stands before me, slightly hunched in a matching pink panty set.

I reach back and yank my shirt off over my head and toss it over by her shorts. She eyes me brazenly and waggles her brows at my package. "Jeans too, buster."

"Buster," I mimic her word with a shake of my head and push the denim down off my legs and kick it off along with my shoes.

She reaches back and unclasps her bra, flinging it over with the rest of our stuff. She's no longer hunched and hiding now, though. She's standing proud and poised, perfectly at ease with herself as she bends over and slides her panties off.

When she rights herself, my jaw is slack. The moonlight, the sound of the water, and the view of her completely naked, red hair blowing in the night breeze…it's too much. It's too sexy. It's fucking dream-worthy.

"Come on now. We've come this far," she says, pointing down at my boxers.

Mindlessly, I push them down, my eyes still completely locked on her.

She glances down. "Is that going to hurt when you jump in the water?"

I shake my head. "Not if you hold it."

She laughs, and Jesus Christ, she actually gets more beautiful at this moment. And without a look back, she runs and jumps off the boulder and into the water.

No graceful dive.

No demure leap.

She fucking cannonballs like the original, magnetic, real girl she is.

I dive in after her and take three hard strokes to get to her. I pull her into my arms, her hard nipples brushing against my chest as she wraps her legs tightly around my hips.

She folds her hands behind my neck and kisses me sweetly, giving me just a tiny sample of her tongue as I tread water and turn us in circles. She pulls back with a smile and lets go of my shoulders as she stretches her upper body backward to float. Her arms are fanned out wide. Her bare, beautiful breasts shiny in the moonlight. She's stunning.

My bare dick is hard and pushed up between us, but I'm not thinking about fucking her right now. All I'm thinking about is how quickly I'm liking this girl. About how confusing these feelings are for me because even though she's so cool and awesome and sexy and fun, I still don't know if I'm ready for more. My heart and my head are at complete odds with each other, and I don't know which one knows best.

My heart says, *yes, take more, take a lot more. She's perfect!*

But my head says, *as soon as you do, everything will change, and you'll be inviting drama right back into your life. Just like before.*

"Mercedes," I husk her name, and her head lifts up from the water, all her strands slicked back perfectly, her blue eyes wide and curious. "Do you feel like—"

"Did you feel that?" she asks, her face bending in a weird, pained way.

"Feel what?" I ask, hopeful that maybe she's having the same confusing thoughts as I am, and we can talk them out together.

And then the floodgates open.

Literally, it starts pouring rain on us.

"Oh my God, that rain is freezing!" she squeals, unwrapping her legs from me and sinking down into the water as deep as she can so only her face is out.

"No shit." I squint, looking up at the sky. "I never saw rain in the forecast."

"Should we just stay in the water until it passes?" she shouts, because the downpour on the lake water is deafening now.

A flash of lightning illuminates us both in the darkness, and I shake my head. "Bad idea. We gotta get out."

She nods, and we both swim to the shore and pad carefully up the rocks to our soaking wet clothes.

She struggles with her soaked clothes, then shouts, "Fuck it, let's make a run for it. No one will be walking out in this."

I nod and place my hand on the small of her back to guide her through the trees and back to the trail we walked down on. It's a muddy, slippery mess, but we manage to make it back to our tent without taking a tumble, thank fuck. That would have hurt, being butt-ass naked.

We rush inside the tent, and the rain is still deafening as it pounds against the thin nylon. But we're kneeling in front of each other so close, we can hear our ragged breaths, heavy and labored from our climb. Adrenaline coursing through our bodies from the storm outside.

It's overwhelming in the smallness of the tent. It takes up all the air and space and funnels in tightly around us like a spring-loaded coil, ready to explode.

Our eyes meet, and just as there's a crack of thunder and a flash of lightning, we slam into each other, like two storm clouds colliding in the starless sky.

My arms wind around her waist, and I kiss her with my tongue as deep as she can take. Her hands are all over me—on my face, my arms, my head, my back. She can't get enough. It's like she's trying to feel every square inch of my body, and I want to give it all to her.

We're a mess of rain, mud, and lake water, but it doesn't stop me from falling back onto the mattress pad and taking her with me. Her thighs are shaking under my hands as they spread over the top of me. My red, throbbing cock bulges up between us as I put my hands on her ass and squeeze her to me.

"Take me inside you, babe," I state, voice ragged, nearly lost in the rain. "Take me as deep as you can."

She nods and looks over in the dark at the tipped over box of condoms we left out this afternoon. She shakily grabs one and opens it up to roll it down my length.

Rising up on her knees, she positions me perfectly before dropping down and impaling herself in one, glorious motion. My fingers bite into her hips, and she uses my wrists for balance as she grinds into me, waiting for her body to adjust to the fullness.

She rears back and slams down again, crying my name

as she throws her head up to the sky.

It's the most beautiful sight I've ever seen.

Her wet hair and naked body, her arched back and flushed skin. It's all more beautiful than the lake and the mountains. The trees and the moon. Mercedes riding me is more beautiful than pretty much anything I've ever laid eyes on.

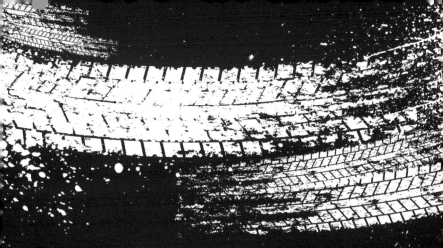

CHAPTER 24

Kate

Y ou know that saying, rode hard and put away wet? Well, that's me when I wake up the next morning to birds chirping and the sun shining. The tent is about half as warm as usual because I don't have a huge hulk of a man sleeping next to me. But I can hear Miles outside, making the noises of breakfast, so obviously he's not hemorrhaging blood from chewing his arm off or something.

That thought makes me giggle, so I quickly tuck my head under the blanket and bite back a squeal of excitement.

Yesterday was amazing. Last night was even more so. The way Miles looked at me when we closed ourselves inside this tent and away from the storm outside.

We were the motherfucking storm.

We were thunder and lightning, and we created the

most beautiful swirl of passion I've ever experienced with a man.

Like I'm talking three orgasms.

To top off an already perfect day, we cuddled. We cuddled good. We stayed completely naked and let the delicious skin-on-skin comfort lull us into the best sleep of my life. It felt like I was meant to fit on his chest and his big arm was meant to wrap around me and keep me warm. It was magic.

This camping trip is shaping up even better than I could have hoped for. In fact, I think I might actually like camping!

I mean, sure, Miles still doesn't know my real name yet. And yes, technically, my ex-boyfriend still lives with me and is coming back eventually, and Miles has made it crystal clear that he has issues with jealousy.

But beyond all of that, he knows what's important. He knows what I'm passionate about. He knows how I take my coffee and how to tease me. He knows where my G-spot is, that's for damn sure! Dryston never found that even with explicit directions.

Surely, the whole different first name thing is a minor detail that won't have much relevance when I do, in fact, tell him. I mean, we're genuinely connecting, so surely, that's what's most important. Not what first name he calls me.

I quickly dress in a pair of jeans and a T-shirt, opting to let my air-dried hair run wild. I slip out of the tent and note that Miles has packed up a lot of our stuff already and loaded it into the back end of his pickup.

"Good morning," I say brightly as he flips a couple of

eggs on a portable skillet.

"Morning," he replies with a shy kind of smile, almost as if he can't make eye contact with me.

Is he feeling weird about last night? God, if he is, that could be so bad. I need to defuse the situation. I need to be casual Mercedes again, so he doesn't think I'm like falling in love with him or something.

I walk over to where he's working on the picnic table and grab his arm tightly. "Whew! It's not a prosthetic. He didn't have to chew it off, folks!" I shout to no one in particular.

He shakes his head, and his shyness falls away instantly. "Still very much intact. But I didn't bring any pancake mix, so don't read into that, all right?"

I smile and nod, then look around with a big stretch. "You've been busy this morning."

He looks back over his shoulder at his truck. "Yeah, it's going to be a muddy mess all over today. I figured we may as well leave early."

I nod and pull my lip into my mouth, feeling a bit of disappointment over that. But since I need to play it cool, I reply, "Well, I'm starving. How can I help?"

A short while later, we're back in Miles's truck and on the way back to reality. As silence envelops us inside the cab, I can't help but wonder where we go from here. Did last night change what we are? He's sure acting the same. Are we still

AMY DAWS

just friends with benefits? Do I go back to Boulder and start writing at Tire Depot again?

After a painfully quiet car ride, Miles finally pulls up in front of my house. We both jump out and move to the back of his truck where he reaches in and grabs my bag.

I take it from him, and our hands brush together as I say, "Well, thanks for helping me with the research." I half-smile up at him, his steely blue eyes intense on me.

"Anytime," he replies, his voice deep and melty.

"You okay?" I ask curiously, shielding the sun from my eyes so I can get a better look at him. "You seem quiet."

He shakes his head and offers me a lopsided smile. "Just tired."

"Shouldn't have gotten the mattress pad." I give him a playful shove that doesn't move him an inch.

A shuffling noise from behind has both our eyes swerving toward my front door. My anxiety sparks to life when I see Dean standing on my front step. He adjusts his glasses while watching us carefully. His arms are crossed over his chest. His body is propped up against a support beam.

Miles clears his throat from behind me, and I look back at him as he mumbles, "Looks like you've got company. I'll see you later, Mercedes."

"Bye," I reply, wistfully watching his back as he moves to get back into his truck. For a jealous guy, he sure has no problem walking away from me. Though he has no idea that Dean told me he wanted more than friendship only a few days ago.

My life is getting seriously complicated.

208

With a rumble of his truck, Miles pulls away, and I exhale heavily. Turning on my heel, I walk up to my front door. "Hey, Dean," I murmur, fishing out my keys and unlocking the deadbolt.

"Hey, Kate." Dean looks awkward as he scratches his fingers through his beard.

I take pity on him and ask, "Want to come inside for a coffee?"

He smiles. "Is it complimentary?"

I pin him with a look. "For people who aren't assholes, yes."

His eyes cast downward. "I won't be an asshole, I swear."

"You sure?" I ask, gesturing down the road. "Nothing to say about Miles's truck? Did you hear how loud that muffler was?"

His brows lift. "I'm surprised you even know what a muffler is."

I frown at that comment. "Me too, actually. I guess some of my research has been sticking."

The corner of his mouth tips up into a smile. "I'll be good, I swear."

Dean follows me inside, and I drop my bag on the floor and set about making us a couple of coffees. Exhaustion begins to overtake me as well, but I know I need to talk to Dean. I've been avoiding his calls and text for the past several days, and I don't want this to completely ruin our friendship.

He props himself on a barstool and takes the coffee from my hands. "Did you spend the night at Miles's house last night?" he asks, his eyes staring down at my neck.

I look at him and blink a few times. "Are you really asking that?"

He rolls his eyes and points at a spot on his neck. "You may have a little something…"

My eyes fly wide at the memory of Miles sucking hard on my neck. I move to cover the mark, and Dean quickly says, "I'm not judging, Kate, I'm just making small talk. Work with me here, okay?"

I take a deep breath in and pull my shirt up to try to cover it. "We were camping."

"Camping?" The disbelief in his voice isn't lost on me.

"Yes, camping," I reply, dropping my hand. "It was for book research, and it was really fun."

Dean shakes his head. "So I take it you're writing something quite a bit different from your other series?"

I shrug. "I'm trying to."

He stares down at his drink. "Inspiration must be flowing."

"It has its moments." Even if they do involve sneaky little hickeys.

"And Miles is the guy who brings that out in you?" Dean asks, looking up at me. I look closely for a sign of judgment in his expression, but I don't see anything. It's a genuine question.

"He's certainly not hurting things." I shrug and prop my elbows on the counter, hunching over with my coffee mug between my palms. "He's not like anyone I've ever hung out with before. He's a salt of the earth kind of guy. So different from Dryston."

"So different from me," he adds, a pained look behind his dark-framed glasses.

I pin him with a look. "Dean, look…I never had a clue you had feelings for me. If I had, I would have done so many things differently."

"Like what?" he asks, his brows pinching together in confusion.

"I don't know. Maybe come over less often. Acted differently." I run a hand through my hair and sigh. "I love you as a friend, but I just don't see us that way, and I'm sorry if I led you to believe otherwise."

"You weren't leading me on, Kate. You were being yourself. And that draws people in." He stares at me through wide, understanding eyes, then adds, "It's the same reason Miles can't stay away from you even though he's told you he doesn't want a relationship. You're so…magnetic."

It's really weird getting a compliment from a guy you've just rejected, but I can tell Dean is trying really hard here to make amends, and I'm so relieved. "Well, Miles is still keeping me firmly in the casual corner, so apparently, I'm not a strong enough magnet."

Dean thinks on that for a second while taking a sip of his coffee. "I think if you really like Miles, you need to come clean with him. If you guys develop into more and he finds out you're keeping stuff from him, it's not going to end well, Kate."

"I know," I groan and run my hands through my hair. "I just like who I am with him. I like having no baggage."

"You still technically live with your ex, Kate. That's about the worst kind of baggage you can carry. No guy is going to take that information well, and the longer you wait, the harder it will be."

"Are you sure I can't keep pretending to be Mercedes? She never would have gone out with dippy Dryston."

"You're not pretending to be anyone," Dean corrects, adjusting his glasses to pin me with a serious look. "You are Mercedes. You are Kate. You need to quit looking at them like they're two different people because they are both you. You're the porn writer and the friend. You're the bestselling author and the neighbor. You don't have to keep the two sides of yourself separate. Let them merge. Maybe the Kate part of yourself that you're holding back will be exactly what brings you and Miles together."

I look over the counter at Dean. My friend. My true friend who I've become so comfortable with the past couple of years. He's sitting here, giving me advice on how to win over a dude that I'm rejecting him for. Whatever asshole tendencies he may have on occasion, he's still a really frickin' good person as a whole.

"Thanks, Dean." I smile softly.

He exhales heavily. "Does this mean we can we go back to being friends again? You're like one of four people I actually like in Boulder. Losing you would be a huge deficit in my social life."

"Of course, we're friends." I smile and shake my head. "Because there's no way in hell I'm going to start cleaning my own gutters."

He laughs and rakes his hands through his hair in frustration. "I'm hoping you can work out this thing with Miles. I'm tired of being Lynsey's and your damn handyman. Especially because I'm not fucking handy. I've told you both this. If you need help with investments, I got you. But pretty soon, I'm going to start drawing the line at favors that make me sweat."

"Yeah, yeah…whatever, Dean."

With double smiles, we clink our coffee mugs and get back to being exactly what we were always meant to be. Just friends. Great friends.

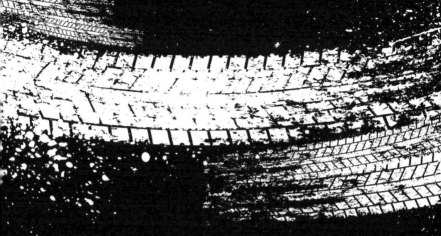

CHAPTER 25

Miles

I'm stir-crazy this week at the shop. Something is off between Mercedes and me, and I can't quite put my finger on it. She's been in and out of the comfort center. We do our regular flirting thing where I come in and eat cookies, and she asks me about my day. It's nice. It's friendly. But it's limited. She hasn't asked me to help her with any more book research, and I guess I'm just wondering what she's waiting for.

Our camping trip was amazing. More than amazing. Spending a full twenty-four hours with a person and not wanting to kill them means you've really found a true friend. And that's how I see her still. A friend. So why does it feel like she's still holding a part of her back from me?

I head up to the counter to find Sam and see if he wants

to go get a drink this weekend. I need to talk this shit out, so I'm not fucking up vehicles or losing any fingers this week with my wandering thoughts.

Sam's standing at the end of the long, high top counter where the customer service agents all check people in. I sidle up next to him, my coveralls still on, but not so dirty that I felt like I had to take them off first.

"Hey," I say, and he looks up from his computer.

"Hey, man," he says with a smile that's practically hidden under his red beard.

"What are you doing this weekend?" I ask as he pulls the Bluetooth device out of his ear.

"Nothing," he replies with a shrug. "Beers?"

I nod and slow blink.

"That bad?" he guesses.

I inhale deeply and finger the piece of red licorice behind my ear. "I'm just…in a rut, and I don't know. I need something."

"I've been seeing Mercedes in the comfort center," he says, clearly already picking up where my mind is at. "Is she here today?"

I shake my head. "I haven't seen her yet."

He furrows his brow. "You guys good?"

I shrug. "I think so? I don't know. That's partially why I need a drink."

"Say no more," he replies with a congenial smile.

A light reflects off the front door as two blond guys walk into the reception area. They look about the same age as Sam and me. Maybe a little younger. They also look like they do nothing but lay out because their tans are way too perfect.

But above all that, there's something about the way they hold themselves as they walk that has my alerts pinging. I decide to stick around and hold my spot at the counter.

Sam is busy typing something into his computer when the guy in a pink polo flicks his keys up on the counter. "I have a flat. I need it fixed."

I cringe at his rudeness and slide my gaze to the other guy who's decked out in a bright, neon green golf shirt. It's fucking blinding.

Sam smiles politely at Pink Polo. "Okay, what's your name and what kind of car are we talking about?"

"Why does that matter?" the guy snaps. "It's a tire. Just need it repaired quickly because I have a tee time to make."

The guy's condescending tone has me shifting out of my leaned position to stand at full height. Green Shirt eyeballs me.

Sam is not the least bit put off as he smiles around his beard and replies, "We just need to know if you're in the system. Because if for some reason your tire can't be repaired, we can prorate it with your warranty to get you a new one at a discount."

"Why could my tire not be repaired?" Pink Polo snaps.

"If there's a puncture in the sidewall of the tire, those are unfixable, unfortunately." Sam offers an apologetic look.

"What a rip-off," the guy snaps. "What kind of business are you running?"

I glance down at this asshole's shoes and know instantly

money isn't the problem here. Privilege is.

"Hey brah, who's that chick?" Green Shirt asks, leaning over the counter closer to me as if we're a couple of bros or something.

I look over at where he's gesturing to Alexa who works two computers down.

I shrug noncommittally. "She's a customer service rep."

Green Shirt smiles. "Perfect, we'll take her."

Sam clears his throat. "I'm afraid you don't get to pick. And you've got me already."

Pink Polo apparently wants to pick up where Green Shirt left off. "I think we could pick if we really wanted to."

"And believe me, we want to pick at every part of that." Green Shirt leers at Alexa so hard, my teeth grind.

I slam a fist on the counter in front of me and say, "Hey! This isn't ordering a girl off the internet, moron. Do you want your fucking tire fixed or not?"

Pink Polo's eyes fly wide. "Who's your goddamn manager? I want to speak to him."

Sam's voice cuts in, telling us to calm down as Green Shirt and I stare at each other over the counter. He's a good five inches shorter than me, but his privilege makes him think he's untouchable, and I can't stand douchebags like that. It's exactly the kind of dude Jocelyn was looking for and found apparently.

"Manager. Now," Pink Polo states again, and Sam presses a hand to my chest.

"Just go back to the shop," he says, turning his back on the two douchebags and shoving me backward a few steps.

Through clenched teeth, he adds, "I'll let my uncle deal with these fuckers."

I narrow my eyes one more time at the pair and exhale heavily, turn on my heel, and make my way out of the reception area and back into the alley for some air.

I take a deep breath of the balmy summer air and bite off the ends of my licorice. "I really wish this was a cigarette," I mumble to myself as I suck air through the hole.

Frustrated that it has zero effect, I chuck the piece of stupid candy on the opposite wall. I'm so in my own head I didn't even hear Mercedes approach when her voice says, "Whoa, whoa, whoa, what'd that licorice ever do to you?"

I swerve my eyes to her and eye her outfit. It's that blue summer dress with the pink flowers. The one that shows her whole ass if she turns in it.

"Nothing," I reply through clenched teeth.

"What's going on with you?" she asks, her blue eyes looking me up and down. "You look like you're ready to rip someone's head off."

I shake my head and drop my eyes to her dress. "Nice dress."

She half-smiles. "I thought you might like it."

"So long as you don't twirl in it," I state firmly.

Her brows pull together. "What's going on with you?"

"What's going on with *you*?" I volley back.

She frowns in confusion. "Excuse me?"

"What's your deal lately? You're not into me anymore? Someone better come along to help you with your research?" *Dean maybe?*

"Miles, you're acting crazy. I was actually going to ask you if you'd show me your place tonight."

"Tonight?" I ask, pressing a hand against the brick and trying to calm myself down in some small way.

"Yeah, after work, maybe. I want to see your house, specifically your garage. You know…research. Get our hands dirty." She waggles her brows suggestively.

I nod, my jaw tight. "Fine."

"Well, don't look so thrilled," she balks.

I blink slowly, knowing she doesn't deserve this. Those two douchebags set me off, and her timing was just too close on the heels of that bullshit. "Sorry…I'm good with this."

"Good!" she states and gives my arm a shake. With that simple touch of her hand on me, my mood lightens as she adds, "But I have to say there's something seriously hot about seeing you in a mood…I hope that works to our advantage later."

She winks, and already, I can think of about five different places I want to lose myself inside her at my house. I feel this strange desire to claim her further. I pin her with a serious look and reply, "Babe…having you in my house gives us all sorts of advantages."

Her eyes alight with anticipation as she replies. "I can't wait. Now, go take your anger out on some poor car and pick me up back here after you're done."

I nod and watch her skirt sway in the wind as she strides back toward the employee entrance of the comfort center.

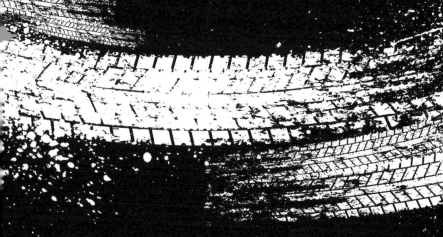

CHAPTER 26

Kate

I could have picked his house out by a mile. Pun intended. With my arms wrapped tightly around his waist, Miles pulls down a short gravel lane that's tucked away from the main highway that runs through Jamestown. When a rusty, shabby chic ranch nestled right in some beautiful foothills comes into view, I know it's his place. It just screams, Miles: masculine, rustic, and a little overgrown.

The outside is stained cedar plank siding, and it has two tuck-under garages beneath a huge wraparound porch. He has a couple of Adirondack chairs positioned by his front door, and I can so easily picture him sipping a cup of coffee and gazing at the creek that runs through his property.

He stops his motorcycle in front of the garage and kicks out the kickstand before cutting the motor.

"Oh my God, Miles!" I exclaim, shaking his shoulders a little to show him my enthusiasm.

"What?" he asks, pulling down his aviators and looking over his shoulder at me. His mood seems slightly better than earlier, but I have a feeling I know what will turn him around completely.

"Your place is stunning!" I exclaim, gazing at his face in the setting sun. The golden colors really making his blue eyes pop.

"Eh." He shrugs and climbs off the bike, turning around to take the helmet from me.

I comb my hair out with my fingers, my eyes wide in disbelief. "Are you kidding? It's gorgeous!"

He props the helmet under his arm and looks out toward the creek. "I couldn't find anything in Boulder, at least nothing I could afford that gave me a little land and some privacy. I really hate neighbors."

I laugh and look around to see he's completely secluded here. His own private little sanctuary plunked onto a stretch of the wilderness a mere twenty minutes from Boulder. "Well, this is perfect. Something like this would easily cost two million in Boulder."

"No shit," he replies instantly and rubs the back of his neck. "As I said, it's a work in progress, but it's mine."

I smile brightly and throw my leg off the bike. "Show me the inside!" I have to stop myself from jumping up and down like a doofus.

He chuckles softly. "Okay, but then we're getting dirty in the garage."

"Okay," I chide and let him drag me upstairs and through his front door.

He's in a hurry to get back down to the garage, but as I take in the space through his rushed tour, I can see that Miles has vision. Most people probably wouldn't have looked twice at this property, but he's already turned it into something really unique and special.

He first points at where a big wall was knocked out last summer that originally separated the dining room from the living room. Since it was a load-bearing wall, he put in knotty wood support beams stained a deep espresso color that contrasts nicely with the white shiplap on two of the living room walls. The desired effect is a rustic, shabby chic farmhouse feel that oozes charm and natural light.

His furniture is minimal. Masculine. A leather couch and loveseat face a giant big screen TV. His kitchen is his current work in progress, but the new slate countertops were just installed last week, and now, he's refinishing the cabinetry. The cupboard doors are all removed and apparently down in his garage awaiting their next coat of varnish.

He shows me to his bedroom, and it has a giant bed screaming practical comfort. But when he walks me around the corner to his master bath, it's clear where all his money has been going.

A huge two-headed waterfall shower occupies one whole wall of the bathroom with a perfectly clear glass door to showcase his incredible tilework. I may have sprouted a lady boner when he told me he did the work himself. He also removed the wall that separated the bathroom from the spare bedroom so he could turn that space into an attached walk-in closet.

Honestly, his ex is a fucking idiot. This man is husband material right here.

He quickly shows me a spare bedroom adorned with shag carpet and wood paneled walls. He says it's next on his list, but it's kind of fun to see because it shows how much work he's already put into this house. Miles is clearly not someone who sits idle.

As we walk down the interior steps and he opens the door to his garage, he smiles over his shoulder and tells me *this* is where the magic happens.

You know the kind of sex that's fumbling and messy and shit gets knocked over a lot, and you feel like you're apologizing for everything the entire time, but you still somehow manage to have an epic orgasm and break something?

No?

Yeah, me neither…until tonight.

Not only did Miles show me his filthy garage and list all of his tools that seriously sound like they were meant for a sex toy room. He also gave me a hard and rough quickie by bending me over his toolbox and getting my arms all grimy from some spilled brake fluid. I had to wash up in his paint-splattered work sink afterward just to get the smell off me.

Whatever was bothering Miles earlier, the tour of his

house and the quickie he gave me seemed to have helped calm him down immensely. And considering I had a glass-shattering orgasm, I'm not complaining one bit.

Before heading upstairs to clean up in that stunning fucking shower, Miles walks me over to his second garage to show me a project he's been working on.

He pulls on a couple of metal chain switches on the ceiling, and the illuminated bulbs swing over our heads, showcasing a stunning classic truck.

"It was my grandpa's," he states, sliding his hands in his pockets, his muscles extra veiny from our efforts in the other garage. "It's a '65 Ford pickup. I just got the white paint completed a couple of months ago, and the interior done last week. All it needs now is this special carburetor that only works in this particular model. It's really hard to find and crazy expensive because of that. Most of my money has been going into house renovations, so I'm waiting until I have the funds to get it up and running again."

"So it looks pretty, but it's not functional," I state, sliding my hands over the glossy white paint. It's perfect. The chrome finishes shinier than a mirror. I smile and add, "It's like art."

"You could say that," he replies, watching me curiously from the doorway.

I continue my perusal. "It looks like it belongs in a Pixar film," I muse with a smile, checking out the front end and imagining the grille opening up to talk.

This makes Miles laugh, which is nice because I've missed the happy-go-lucky demeanor he had when we were camping. I should have guessed classic cars were boner-worthy for mechanics.

"You said this was your grandpa's?" I ask, walking around the hood toward the passenger side door to check out the interior a little closer. The white leather bench inside the cab is beautiful.

"Yes." Miles nods, his posture visibly tensing as he adds, "He passed away two years ago."

My eyes lift to his, and instant sympathy casts over me. "I'm so sorry to hear that."

He exhales heavily and offers a sad smile. "Yeah, it was a shock to all of us. I mean, he was seventy-seven, so it's not like he didn't live a good, long life. But he was one of those guys who seemed like he'd live forever."

"Never aging? Always just in that perfect grandpa look?"

"Yeah," Miles agrees. "Do you have a grandparent like that?"

I laugh softly. "My grandma who schedules meetings for me with her priest. She's going to live forever, I'm sure of it. And if she dies, she'll definitely haunt me from her grave." Miles shakes his head, but I stave off his sympathy. "In some ways, I like pushing the old bird. It's like our special connection, you know?"

He nods, moving to the front of the truck and staring down the hood. "I get that. For my grandpa and me, it was cars. I remember working on this with him as a kid. He taught me so much. I knew the names of tools before the names of my cousins. Drove my mom nuts."

I giggle. "God, I bet you were a cute kid. Dark hair, bright eyes. I bet you got whatever you wanted from your grandpa."

Miles lifts his brow. "Well, he always kept candies in the glove box for me." He walks over to where I stand and moves me out of the way so he can open the passenger side door. Leaning in, he presses the button to the compartment and grabs a bag of round, pink candies.

"Want one?" he asks with a tipped smile, the scent of wintergreen hitting me right in the nose.

I laugh and shake my head. "No. If those were your grandpa's, they should stay right where they are."

He nods and replies, "They're so old, but I can't bring myself to eat them or throw them away." He leans back into the truck and puts them back where he found them.

When he pulls back to close the door, I think I see a sheen to his eyes that wasn't there before. He props himself on the door and pinches the bridge of his nose. "I think that brake fluid is still stinging my eyes."

I reach out and rub my hand on his arm in a smooth, comforting motion, a knot forming in my throat at the pain he's trying so hard to hide.

"What is it?" I ask, my thumb rubbing the inside of his wrist in slow, gentle circles.

He shakes his head with a sad smile. "Nothing."

"Miles," I repeat, looking up at him encouragingly. "Just tell me."

He exhales and leans his back against the open door. "I wish I had it running already." He looks up at the ceiling as if he's trying to get the sprouting tears to go back into his body. "It was kind of a dying promise I made to him, and I feel bad I haven't finished it yet."

"Miles," I say with a sad laugh. "Look at this thing. It's gorgeous. It's art! You've already done so much to it."

He shakes his head and gives me a laugh. "He'd give me shit for not having it done, though. He liked to pretend to be this grumpy old man, but he had a soft side he only showed to a couple of us."

This image makes me smile. "Those are the best kinds. It means more when you're one of the lucky ones who get that side of them."

"Exactly," Miles replies, looking back down at me.

"Did he like your ex?" I ask, the question tumbling out of my lips unexpectedly.

Miles seems puzzled by this question but shakes it off. "Nah, he pretty much hated her. The first time I'd ever heard him use the word bitch was in reference to her."

This makes me giggle so hard I have to cover my mouth. "I think I would have liked your grandpa a lot."

Miles tilts his head thoughtfully at me, assessing me up and down for a moment. "For some reason, I think he would have liked you, too."

"Oh?" I reply, crossing my arms over my chest and leaning on the car. "Why would I get special treatment, you think?"

He shrugs. "I think because you're so real, Mercedes. You don't put on a show for people, and everything you say is exactly what you are. It's a rare quality—to be exactly what you show people."

Guilt crushes down on me at his words. Then the words from Dean the other day pile on top of that. I need to tell him my name. This was the point of tonight. It's gone on long enough. I'm playing games, and when you play games, someone always loses.

Miles's stunning blue eyes are full of pain and passion, and so open to me that I feel like I can see his entire soul. I know the time for the truth is now. I need him to know all of me. The boring and the brave. "Miles, I need to tell you—"

I can't finish my sentence because his mouth is on mine. His huge frame hunched over, and my face cradled in his hands as his tongue sweeps between my lips to caress my tongue.

My hands reach up and grab the back of his arms, holding on for dear life as his lips possess me in such a tender way that I feel butterflies erupt in my toes, in my legs, in my belly, my head. Even in my chest. Especially in my chest, right in the place that thumps harder as he presses my backside flush to the cool metal behind me.

He tilts his head and deepens the kiss, thoughtfully paying homage to both my upper and lower lip before his tongue dives into my mouth, massaging against my own, artfully giving and taking. Ebbing and flowing. A gentle claiming.

I feel his arm shift and flex under my hand before hearing the audible opening of the truck door. Without taking his lips from mine, he slides me over so my butt hits the soft bench of the truck. He kisses me all the way into the truck until I'm laid out flat on my back, my thighs squeezing tight around his sides as his weight presses down on me, hard and heavy.

Finally, I break away, our bodies rolling uncontrollably into each other. "Miles, are you sure?" I croak because I want him to be aware of where we are right now. "You want to, here?"

"Shhhh, Mercedes," he husks, dropping a soft kiss to my lips before opening his pleading eyes to mine. "Just give me this moment. Please. No research. No thinking. I…you feel so good, and I need to feel good right now." He exhales heavily and adds, "I need this."

I swallow down the agony of his voice, my own guilt consuming me entirely as he pulls back and undoes my jean shorts, slowly pulling them down and off my legs along with my underwear. He presses his palm to my mound and swipes between my folds. "You're always ready for me. Always." He says it with such reverence that I almost feel guilty.

He falls back down on me, taking my lips again and kissing me feverishly, unceremoniously shoving my shirt up and pulling my bra cups down to pull a nipple deep into his mouth. So hard.

My hands slice through his hair, raking through the thick, short tresses as I pump my hips up into him, riding the delicious punishment he's giving to my body.

We grind against each other so much my clit is almost raw from his jeans. "Miles, I need you," I husk softly, no longer able to withstand another moment of this painful torture.

He lets out a deep grumble. "I don't have a condom on me." He presses his forehead against my chest, clearly tortured by the idea of having to go upstairs.

I don't want him leaving me like this, so I reply quickly, "I'm on the pill." Miles's head pops up, his eyes so serious on mine. It makes me nervous, so I quickly add, "And I trust you."

He stares at me, blinking several times and taking me in for a long moment before asking slowly, "Are you sure?"

I nod because honestly, I'm the untrustworthy one here. Miles is perfect.

I reach down between us and begin shakily fumbling with his jeans, a frenzy overcoming me with every minute that ticks by that he's not filling this ache inside me. I need him just as badly as he needs me. Pleasure will take away the guilt and anguish consuming me. I need to lose myself with his weight and his body and not think about everything I'm hiding from him and how badly this could all come to an end.

I push his jeans down his butt cheeks and fist his girth tightly in my hand, positioning him between my slit and right where I need him.

"Miles," I cry out in a beg. "Do it."

"Mercedes," he growls and thrusts into me. Deep. So deep.

"Yes," I cry out because the flesh against flesh contact is wonderful. The fullness is miraculous. The pressure is life-affirming.

"Mercedes," he moans again and again, alternating

between my name and kisses to my neck and collarbone. And it isn't long before I feel tears prick the backs of my closed eyes. Tears of my impending doom.

He's never going to forgive me.

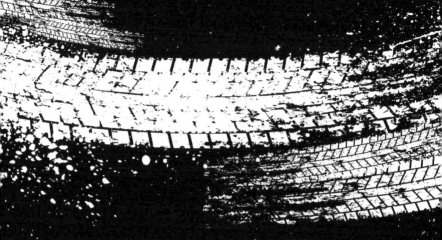

CHAPTER 27

Miles

I frown down at my phone clutched tightly in my hand, mindlessly willing it to ding. To ring. Something. Anything. It's been days since I took Mercedes out to my house, and I haven't heard a word from her.

I know going without a rubber is dangerous, but is she worried she caught something from me? I'm fucking clean. We even spoke more about it afterward. I never go without a condom. Even in all those years with Joce, we still always used condoms. She was so paranoid about getting pregnant, which is ironic, considering it was an accidental pregnancy she had with that rich fucker.

And I know I've slept around some since then, but I've always been careful. So fucking careful. I don't know what came over me that night in my grandpa's truck. I guess I just had two worlds collide. The old and the new and it felt so right, so natural, so…real. I had to have her. There. In that truck.

My gramps would have been fucking proud, too. He'd have patted me on the back and probably told me to put a ring on any girl's finger who'd spread her legs in a vintage truck.

I laugh at that thought and take a long pull of my beer, then gesture to the bartender for another.

"Dude, have you been listening to me at all this entire time?" Sam says, turning to face me, his ginger beard long and scraggly, his eyes narrow and angry.

"Yes, I listened to you. Your uncle wants you to buy him out at Tire Depot. That's fucking awesome, man."

"It's awesome for both of us, numbnuts."

"Huh?" I reply, mindlessly ripping apart a Pearl Street Pub coaster. "What do I have to do with anything?"

"If I'm running Tire Depot, I want you by my side. Maybe as a manager or a fucking parts director. I don't know, man. Shit, maybe you can open that vintage garage under the Tire Depot umbrella. You can finally work on classic cars more often. We can advertise it and shit. Could you imagine how cool your gramp's truck would look in our showroom? Fucking white wall tires. Goddamn, I get hard thinking about it."

I shake my head and hand the bartender my empty bottle when he hits me with a fresh one. "I guess that wouldn't suck."

"You're damn right, it wouldn't," Sam bellows and clinks

our bottles together. "Jesus Christ, we'd have everything in one shop. Tires, auto repair, and antique car restorations. We could advertise in Denver for that because you know people with classic cars will drive for good work. And you're a fucking king at the classics, bro. You know this."

I nod mindlessly, knowing what he's saying is something we've dreamed about together a lot, but for some reason, I can't get my mind off Mercedes.

"Dude!" Sam punches me hard in the shoulder.

In a flash, I'm on my feet, my rage billowing up faster than anticipated. My jaw is clenched so tight I think I hear my teeth crack.

Sam holds his hand back in surrender. "Chill the fuck out. I'm just trying to get you to snap out of this pissy mood. You need to get laid."

"Fuck off," I growl and drop back down on my barstool.

"It's true. You're pining over a fuck buddy, and it's stupid."

"She's not a fuck buddy," I growl and shove him in the arm. "Watch how you fucking speak about her. I'm not joking, man."

"Okay, okay. But you gotta get your priorities straight. Don't let that girl get in your head and force you to miss out on a great opportunity. I'm saying we can be business partners in the near future. I'm saying we're going to make Boulder our bitch, and it's going to be fucking fantastic."

I nod solemnly and let his words sink in. It's clear that Mercedes has been occupying all of my thoughts tonight, and that's exactly the kind of shit I don't need in my life. If she's not going to call me, I'm not going to fucking stress about it. We're casual. That's what I wanted.

I did *not* want drama.

With a renewed sense of purpose, I smack my hand on the bar. "You're fucking right, Sam. This is going to be awesome."

"You're goddamn right it is!" He clinks his beer with mine and watches me with confusion as I stand. "What are we doing?"

"We're leaving."

"Leaving? Leaving to where?"

"We're celebrating, bro. We have a new future to look forward to, and it's time we get out of the same old scene. Let's head down Pearl Street and see what kind of trouble we can get into."

Sam laughs hard and claps me on the back. "I'm in!"

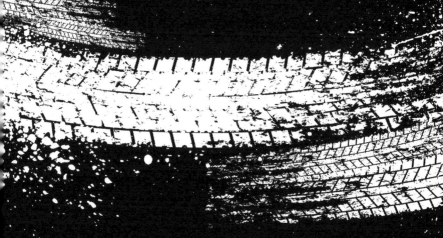

CHAPTER 28

Kate

"Oh, I see a table that just opened up!" Lynsey squeals, rushing off with her Long Island Iced Tea and practically falling over the top of a stainless steel table before the couple currently occupying it have even grabbed their jackets to leave.

I cringe at the scene and look around to see how many people are looking. Not too many. Could be worse. But I appreciate Lynsey's efforts because tables are tough to grab at West End Tavern. It's a bar in Boulder with three levels of outdoor seating, and their rooftop patio is always packed in the summertime. It has a stunning view of the mountains, and it's one of those places that's always noisy, so you feel like you're a part of something.

I head over with a sheepish look on my face and mouth,

"Sorry," to the couple who's backing away slowly. Lynsey finally slides down off the tabletop and into a chair.

"Okay, so finish where you left off," she says as I take a seat opposite her.

"Where did I leave off?" I ask, sipping on a glass of wine because beer won't cut it after the week I've had.

"Well, Dryston is back…" she begins, repeating my earlier story.

I bark out a laugh. "Yeah, well, that's pretty much all I know. I got a text from him a couple of days ago while I was at the supermarket that said in all caps, WHERE IS MY SHIT. And he put a period instead of a question mark… idiot."

"Clearly he's been back to the house then," Lynsey says, brown eyes wide and worried.

I shrug. "I guess so. He said he's been staying with his friend, Mitchell."

She shakes her head, little wisps of her brown hair falling out of the messy bun on top of her head. "That's eerie."

"Super eerie," I agree, grabbing my own hair and pulling it off to one side to cool my neck down. "Dryston wasn't supposed to come back for another month. I thought I had time to break it to him that I moved all his stuff into a storage unit." *Translation: I thought I had time to tell Miles the truth about my roommate.*

"So what did you say?" Lynsey asks, taking another drink of her Long Island.

"I told him where the pod was and that I could have it delivered wherever he intended on living because now that he was back in town, I was going to change the locks."

Her eyes alight with excitement. "Oh my God, you didn't!"

I nod. "I did. Fuck him. He comes sneaking back into town without even an announcement, thinking he can just stride into my house like he's been paying rent all summer? That's bullshit because he most certainly hasn't been sending me checks. I'll pay him the deposit we split on the townhouse if that's what it takes. I'm not moving!"

"Good for you!" Lynsey exclaims, slapping the table in excitement. "You're finally taking a stand."

"Damn right, I am," I reply with a smile and take a drink of my wine. "So talk to me about you. Where have you been the last few days? I've stopped by and you're never home."

Lynsey's face flushes a crimson color at my sudden change of subject. Her eyes are practically twinkling in the swooped Edison bulbs overhead. "You're going to be so proud."

"Tell me."

She sighs heavily. "Well, my thesis was going horribly, so I decided to go back to the hospital cafeteria to see if I could have a Tire Depot moment."

My smile is enormous. "And did you?" I nearly squeal.

"Yes," she squeals back and covers her face like the monkey emoji.

"Why are you acting embarrassed? That's awesome!"

She rolls her eyes. "Well, gosh, I eat there every day now, and I feel like the cafeteria people think I'm there for some really tragic reason. They normally scream 'next in line' when it's your turn to pay, but whenever they see me, they say 'Come on up, sweetheart.' It's so weirdly obvious. I think people are starting to notice."

I scoff, "Like who? Other patients' families that are all temporary? They'll be gone in a week."

"Well…not only patients' families. There's this older doctor who is kind of a dick. He keeps scowling at me every time he sees me. I can't tell if that's his face or if he thinks I'm a freak."

"Just ignore him. If he's a doctor, I'm sure he's way too busy to worry about you."

"Yeah, you're probably right. I'm only noticing him because he's fucking *stupid* hot. Like take McDreamy and McSteamy and rub their penises together. That's how hot he is."

I nearly spew wine out my nose. "Lynsey! That was scandalous!"

She shrugs. "I know this girl who writes the best kinky books. You should check her out sometimes, broaden your horizons." She shoots me a wink and adds, "So now that Dryston is finally officially gone, does that mean there's nothing to stop you from pursuing more with Miles?"

"Except for that whole pesky first name business," I reply, pursing my lips off to the side because I already miss him like crazy. I've been avoiding Miles for fear of Dryston stopping by unexpectedly. But I'm not going to be able to stay away much longer. I need to come clean about everything. Get it all out there and hope he understands.

She shakes that off like it's nothing and sucks down

the rest of her drink. It's nearing eleven, but I can already tell this is going to be one of those nights we have to cab it home.

Lynsey looks around with a pinched expression. "Do we not get a waitress over here?" She lets out a little growl and stands up. "I'm going to go pee and grab drinks at the bar. Another wine?"

"Please!" I bellow at her retreating back.

And no sooner do I sit back in my chair to ponder what I should text to Miles now that Dryston is somewhat squared away, than the man himself sits down right next to me.

"Honey, I'm home!" Dryston laughs obnoxiously and grabs my wine glass. He tips it to his lips, guzzling down the last remaining drops and hits me with a half-lidded stare. "How are you, Katie?"

I roll my eyes and shake my head. He's the only one in my life who's ever called me Katie, and I can't believe I ever thought it was cute. "I'm fine, Dryston. How are you?"

I eye him up and down for a minute, noting that he's clearly drunk. His body is swaying slightly as he props his arms on the metal table. It's been two months since he left for the summer, and I haven't missed him one bit.

And he's clearly still trying to come off like some Hamptons big shot, which means absolutely nothing in Boulder. I glance down and see he's got his typical boat shoes on with no socks and his standard khaki chinos. On top, he has a white button-down with at least five buttons popped open to reveal his ridiculously perfect summer tan.

His blond hair is styled into a mess of over-gelled spikes with his sunglasses propped on top of his head even though it's been dark out for hours.

He is the exact opposite of Miles in every possible way.

What the fuck was I ever thinking?

My only defense is that it was before I even knew that guys like Miles existed. And even though Dryston was a pompous ass a lot of the time, we still had some fun times together. I can't deny that fact. We traveled the world, went to crazy parties, and experienced a lot. I think he kept me around because my job was so flexible that if he wanted to fly to the beach for the weekend, we could. It was easy to get swept up in the excitement of travel and ignore everything else that was missing between us.

The connection. The emotion. The passion.

We never had any of that. I've known Miles a fraction of that time, and we have that in spades.

"Goddamn, Katie. Did you look this good when I left?" he asks, his brown eyes lowering and taking in my tight olive green tank dress. It's ruched on the sides, and the scoop neck goes low enough to show a little cleavage, but I mostly love it for its color. Green complements redheads, and I had some sick hope of ending up at Miles's place tonight.

"This is so typical."

"What?" he leers.

"You come crawling back into town and think you can get whatever you want." I shake my head in disgust.

He doesn't seem the least bit put off. "What? I don't remember your tits looking this good. I need a refresher."

"Don't be a pig, Dryston."

"Don't be a bitch, Katie."

I eye him with a cold glare, my posture stiffening at his combative tone. Through clenched teeth, I ask, "What do you want?"

He leans across the corner of the table and slides a finger along my upper arm. "I want to come home."

"No!" I exclaim, yanking myself back from his touch. "Dryston, we're broken up. Your shit is in storage. There's absolutely no reason for you to come back to the house."

"Well, it's fucking bullshit that you moved it without my permission. If anything is damaged, I'm making you pay for it."

"Fine! Send me the bill. I don't care."

He laughs haughtily. "So I suppose you're fucking someone new now, and that's why you're giving me the cold shoulder?"

"That's not why," I snap, my eyes fierce on his. "I want you gone because I can't stand you, and I don't feel like living with my ex who turned out to be a total douchebag."

"How was I a douchebag?" he asks, his jaw dropping with indignation.

"Many, many reasons!" I exclaim, feeling the veins in my neck bulge. "But the one that is my absolute favorite is you being ashamed of me to your family. We'd been together for almost two years, and you wanted me to lie to them about what I do for a living."

He shakes his head. "Well, my family is religious, and what you do isn't exactly wholesome, Katie."

I roll my eyes, murmuring under my breath, "Frickin' weak."

He growls back, "Well, you don't get to just kick me out of our house. Our lease doesn't end for another seven months."

"Let me buy you out then!" I exclaim, my eyes wide and accusing on him. "My best friend lives next door. The only reason I even found that place was because of her. Stop being so selfish and find somewhere else to live! Or move in with your buddy. Your stuff is all packed up and ready to go."

He sits back in his chair and snaps, "I don't even have a car that'll tow a storage pod."

My face crumples with disbelief at his idiotic comment. "They deliver it, Dryston. And don't worry, I'll pay for that too. Heaven forbid, you have to dip into your trust fund."

He cuts a mean look at me. "You can be a real cunt, you know that?"

"And dirty, so you better run away before you catch my erotica stank!" I wiggle my fingers toward him in dramatic fashion when a deep, familiar voice sounds off from beside me.

"What the fuck did you call her?"

I look up, and my heart falls through the floor when I see Miles Hudson standing right next to me.

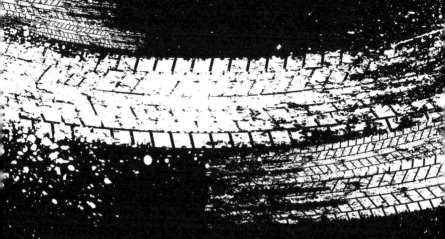

CHAPTER 29

Miles

Normally, I avoid places like West End Tavern. They're usually overflowing with people who are all trying too hard to have a good time. A good time shouldn't be something you have to go to great lengths to have. It should come naturally.

But tonight, I'm itching to get my mind off Mercedes and her lack of communication, so I follow Sam up the stairs to the West End Tavern's rooftop. The noise and music are lively, and it's busy, but not so busy that I regret my decision to venture out.

Sam sees a couple of guys we know from the shop, so we make our way over to the bar. After ordering a couple of beers, I look to my right and see a familiar brunette down at the end of the bar.

Mercedes's friend's eyes find mine at the exact same time and go wide with surprise. "Miles?" Lynsey says with a smile and waves her hand at me.

I give her a nod and hold my place at the bar as she makes her way over to me. The bartender is just handing me a bottle when she reaches me.

She presses in beside me and beams up excitedly. "What are you doing here?"

"Here with my buddy," I reply, gesturing behind me to Sam. "What about you?" I ask, fighting the urge I have not to do a sweep of the patio in search of a redhead I miss more than I'm even ready to admit.

Lynsey pokes me in the stomach and replies, "I'm here with Kate! What are the odds?"

I frown down at her. "Who's Kate?"

Her eyes go wide, and her smile falls as she looks down for a moment. Slowly, her eyes lift to an area over my shoulder, so I turn to see what's got her so freaked out.

At that moment, I see red.

Literally and figuratively.

My hand tightens around my beer bottle when I spot Mercedes sitting at a table with some guy. This would annoy me under normal circumstances. But that fact that I recognize this douchebag from the tire shop, Mr. Green Shirt Fucking Prick, means that I'm not just annoyed. I'm fucking pissed.

And they aren't merely sitting across from each other like a couple of old friends who ran into each other. He's sitting right next to her, his seat scooted over, so their legs are touching. And he's leaning in so goddamn close he can smell her lip gloss.

Sam must pick up on my mood shift because he catches my eyes with a confused frown. I head nod to what I'm looking at, and I know he instantly recognizes the prick too.

Sam looks back at me. "Is that…?"

I nod slowly.

"And is she talking to…?"

I nod slowly again.

"What the fuck, bro?"

My jaw is tight, and a muscle is reflexively ticking away on my cheek like a madman ready to hulk out on this entire bar.

When Green Shirt Douche-canoe's hand reaches up to touch Mercedes's face, I'm moving across the patio in huge, hacked-off strides.

"Miles, it's not what you think," Lynsey's voice chirps from behind me as I struggle to get through a pack of people. Lynsey's hands wrap around my bicep as she tries to hold me back.

I turn and loom over her to reply, "It looks pretty crystal-fucking-clear to me."

"He's no one," she states, chewing her lower lip nervously.

"Then why are you holding me back?" I snap, looking down at her hand on my arm. She smartly lets me go, and I murmur a thanks and resume my earlier pace.

I didn't really make the conscious decision to come over here and approach them. It was an instinctual, knee-jerk response that I really couldn't fight.

Green Shirt's voice catches my ear just as I'm close enough to hear, "You can be a real cunt, you know that."

Mercedes replies something snappy and wiggles her fingers in his face right before I add, "What the fuck did you call her?" I nearly growl, moving up close to stand on the other side of Mercedes.

Green Shirt looks up at me with an annoyed expression painted all over his face. "Excuse you?"

"Excuse you," I snap back and lean down, splaying my hands out wide on the table.

"Miles," Mercedes says, her voice strained. I can feel her eyes on me, but I can't move my laser focus off douchebag here.

"What the fuck did you call her?" I repeat my question earlier and add, "I won't ask again."

Green Shirt, who's actually in a white shirt tonight, just laughs. "This conversation has nothing to do with you, grease monkey. Why don't you take a walk? You've clearly been sniffing too much gasoline."

"Dryston!" Mercedes snaps at him and just the way she says his name seems familiar. Like this might be a person she knows more than I'd like to believe.

"You know this fuckwit, Mercedes?" I ask, sliding my eyes to her. She's twitchy and nervous, struggling to make eye contact with me. Her chest is flushed with hives like I've never seen.

The guy barks out an obnoxious, pompous laugh. "Mercedes?" He looks at me with raised eyebrows. "You think her name is Mercedes?"

My brows furrow and look at Mercedes for approval. She shakes her head quickly and rushes out, "I was going to tell you everything."

"Tell me what?" I snap, my hands turning into fists on the table. "Who the fuck is this guy?"

"He's no one!" she states adamantly through clenched teeth, her eyes flying all over my face as she reaches up to touch my arm.

Green Shirt hoots out another obnoxious laugh and says, "No, I just lived with you for two years."

"Lived with you?" I ask, completely confused because this fucker did not give me a gay vibe at Tire Depot. "Is this is your gay roommate that you kicked out?"

Green Shirt leans across the table and murmurs, "I didn't fuck her like I was gay, brah."

Rage. Undiluted rage rips through my body, and I straighten, chest heaving. Mercedes rises to grab my arm and stop me from walking around this table and ripping this dick's fucking throat out.

"Miles, please, if you'll just let me explain," she rushes out, her voice shaky and garbled.

"Yeah…*Katie*," Green Shirt adds, "explain to him how I was your boyfriend for two years and still basically live with you."

"You do not live with me, Dryston!" she shouts, her own hand fisting at her side as she stomps her foot.

My face twists up in confusion as I turn my shoulders to face her. "Why is he calling you Katie?" I grind through clenched teeth that feel like they could crack any moment. "Your name is Mercedes."

"Her name is Kate Smith, moron. Mercedes is basically the hooker name she made up to write those god-awful things she calls books."

Now I'm done. I'm done with this douche. He's said the last asshole thing I can handle.

I reach across the table and yank him up onto his feet by the collar of his shirt. Sidestepping, I wrench him right up to my face so hard, he has to stand on tippy toes to just reach my chin. "Call her a fucking name again, and you will regret it."

The dude is like a limp sack of noodles in my arms, his eyes half-lidded as his lip curls up and whispers, "You can have the trashy cunt. She's not suitable for mixed company anyway."

My eyes fly wide, and before I know it, I rear back my arm and send my fist flying into this fucker's pompous nose. A satisfying crack vibrates against my knuckles, and blood sprays out all over his face.

He howls in pain and crumples to the ground, his hand covering his nose. "You fucking ape!" he shouts, his voice cracking at the end. "I think you broke my nose!"

"Good," I grind through clenched teeth as Sam wraps his arms around me and hauls me backward. My shoulders rise and fall rapidly as I suck big gulps of air and stretch and flex my fingers on the hand that made contact.

"You won't be saying good when I fucking sue you!" Green Shirt bellows from the ground on his knees.

But his words don't even register in my mind as I slide my gaze to the left and see Mercedes standing there with her hands over her wide open mouth. Obvious tears have sprouted in her eyes.

Are those for this douchebag?

She looks up at me and drops her hands, her chin quivering uncontrollably, and she croaks my name. "Miles."

She moves out to touch me, and I yank back from her and shake off Sam's grip. I pin her with a serious stare. "Don't talk to me."

"Miles!" she exclaims with a shout. "I need to explain."

"Explain this?" I roar, pointing down at her idiot of an ex weeping into a cocktail napkin. "Explain why I punched a guy for a girl whose name I don't even know?"

A sob bubbles up her throat, and I can't even look at her anymore. I turn, powering my way through the crowd of people who have all pressed in around us. I pass Lynsey near the bar, and she looks at me like a whipped puppy, but thankfully says nothing.

As I make my way through the doorway toward the stairs, my mind begins racing. You think you fucking know someone. You think maybe you've been wrong all along, and there are good people out there who can be honest and up front with you. Real.

But then you find out you were wrong , so fucking wrong that you have the bloody knuckles to prove it.

I pause in the stairwell and send my bloodied fist flying into the concrete wall. It does zero damage to the wall, but it takes the sting off the pain in my chest, and that's better than nothing.

"Goddamnit," I growl, shaking my hand, my knuckles cracking painfully into each other as I stretch my fingers out.

"Miles, wait," Mercedes voice echoes in the dark stairwell, illuminated only by a sconce on the wall.

I'm tempted to ignore her and keep going, but I catch sight of her fumbling down the stairs in a pair of tall wedge sandals. She looks like she could fall at any second, so I stop just to get her to stop chasing me.

"What, Mercedes?" I growl, my hand clutching the metal railing so hard, it aches. "Or is it Katie?"

She stops two steps above me, her chest rising and falling rapidly. Her blue eyes are sad when she croaks, "It's Kate. I was going to tell you."

"When?" I ask, my voice ragged now that my adrenaline has slowed and I'm staring up at the woman I've bared my soul to these past several weeks. I look straight into her eyes and add, "After I fell in love with you?"

She sucks in a sharp, shaky breath and replies hurriedly, "I'm still the same person, Miles. I'm as much Mercedes as I am Kate. Mercedes is still my name, it's just used on my books."

"It's your pen name?" I ask, and she nods her confirmation. "Then why fucking lie about it?"

"I don't know!" she replies with a flick of her hands. "Because with my ex, I got used to hiding that part of me. But with you, I didn't have to do that, not ever. Kate Smith is who I am when I'm not telling people about what I do. One of our first nights together, you told your sister about me. That's something I've never experienced before, Miles."

I shake my head in disbelief. "If I'm so open and accepting, then why hide your real name? You had so many chances to tell me. Do you know what an idiot I feel like for calling you Mercedes all this time? Every time we slept together. I feel like a fucking joke to you!"

"You're not a joke, I am!" She steps down one step so she's eye level with me and reaches her hands out to grab my face. "I liked you so much. All this time I liked you as more than a friend with benefits. I'm the joke because I thought I could be cool and casual Mercedes with no strings attached, but that was the biggest lie of all. I'm plain old boring Kate Smith, and I'm totally fucking falling for you, Miles."

Her words have me yanking my face out of her embrace and dropping backward a few steps. I don't care if she's falling for me. I mean, look what happened tonight. She's worse than Jocelyn. She's going to rake me over the coals, and after going through all that shit for a second time, there will be nothing left of me.

I turn and look away from her emotional, tortured face. "I told you I don't want drama, Kate. My ex did that to me over and over, and I'm done with that shit." I look back and point up at the door at the top of the stairs. "I've never punched another guy in my life, and I just fucking broke that dick's nose."

"I'm sorry!" she exclaims, grabbing the railing and squeezing so hard her arm begins to tremble. "But I'm not perfect. I'm going to have drama in my life. And you can't give me a zero-tolerance policy for drama because of your freaking baggage!"

I shake my head, refusing to hear any more. My mind is full up of bullshit tonight, and I can't take another second. "I'm out, Kate, Mercedes, whoever you are. You can keep your drama and your lies. Keep living your life as your author name, your real name, with your boyfriend or ex-boyfriend. Gay, not gay. Whatever."

"Miles, please—"

"No, I'm done." I point at the area of space between us like it represents everything that's happened since the moment she ran into me in the alley of Tire Depot. My tone is deep and final when I add, "This…is officially the end of our story."

And then I turn my back and walk down the stairs away from the girl I thought I fucking knew but was, in fact, writing fiction the whole damn time.

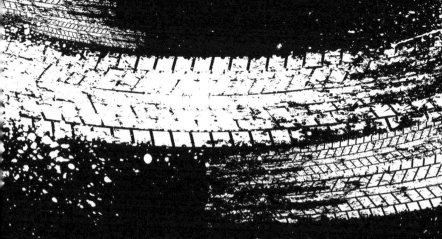

CHAPTER 30

Kate

You know that point in a romance novel where the girl bares her heart to the guy, and he tells her that he's loved her since the first moment he laid eyes on her?

That's not how my story with Miles went.

In fact, my story with Miles went from an epic love story to a tragic women's fiction. Because what do you call a love story with no happy ending?

Fucking pathetic, that's what.

There are two black moments to my story with Miles Hudson. And if I thought black moment number one—when he rejected me outside of Walrus Saloon—was bad, it's nothing compared to black moment number two.

Make a note to never write another fight scene outside a bar in any book ever again.

I stare at the blinking cursor in my manuscript and will my fingers to begin typing. I shift uncomfortably in the beach chair on the back patio of Lynsey's townhouse, just trying to find a sweet spot that'll help things start clicking into place.

It's useless.

I've tried every spot in Lynsey's home to find my writing mojo again, and nothing is flowing. Nothing. And the fact that I can see Dryston's stupid face upstairs in the window of the bedroom that I once had my mojo in makes me vibrate with rage.

I ended up giving Dryston the townhouse so he'd stop threatening legal action against Miles for punching him in the nose. It was a no-brainer because Miles would never have punched Dryston if it wasn't for me. But now I've spent the past two weeks struggling to find my vibe while living with Lynsey. As far as roommates go, she's great. But she doesn't inspire me the way Miles did. Not even close.

Hell, I even went with Lynsey to the hospital cafeteria one day to try to find a new vibe. When that didn't work, I tried hanging out at the bakery by Dean's office.

Nothing worked.

Because I already found the place that I vibed in.

Tire Depot.

But I burned that bridge. Miles hasn't returned any of my calls or texts, and that's all there is to it.

In my mind, I am having a Rita Hayworth moment. She was a stunning, old Hollywood actress who said men would go to bed with Gilda, the beautiful icon, and wake up to the reality, a lot less glamorous version of the dream.

Mercedes Lee Loveletter is Gilda. Kate Smith is reality.

I wasn't brave enough to find out if Miles would accept less than Gilda, and now I've ruined my chances of ever knowing for sure.

I slam my laptop closed and let out a mighty growl just as Lynsey and Dean come striding out onto the back patio with drinks in hand.

Dean smiles down at me as he hands me a margarita. "Drink up, it'll help."

I take the glass from his hand and watch Lynsey stride over to her tiki bar to set an enormous full pitcher of margaritas down. She looks at me excitedly and says, "We're brainstorming!"

"Plotting," Dean corrects with a wink and takes the beach chair beside me.

Lynsey flops down on the other one, so now I'm sandwiched between my friends with drinks in hand, a far improvement to my state only a few minutes ago.

"You guys are right," I reply and take a sip. "Maybe a new book idea is just what I need to get my mojo back. Something about a pilot or a series that features British soccer-playing brothers, perhaps! You guys know I love a British accent."

"Kate," Dean cuts me off.

"Sorry," I cringe. "It'd be football if they're British."

He rolls his eyes. "We're not plotting a new book series. We're plotting how you can get Miles back."

I deflate instantly and take a sip. "That ship has sailed,

my friends. Miles made that perfectly clear."

"Oh, stop," Lynsey chastises. "He was upset. Guys don't like to be made a fool of, and you made him feel like an idiot. He'll get over it."

"He's not returning any of my calls," I correct. "It's been two weeks."

"That's because you haven't made your grand gesture yet," she says, pulling her sunglasses down off her head and over her eyes as she sits back.

"I'm sorry, what?"

"Kate!" Lynsey exclaims, hitting the side of her chair in frustration. She flails her hands out to gesture while she continues, "You write this shit, now you need to live it. You need to make a grand gesture that shows your hero you care in a deeply personal way that makes it clear that while you know you fucked up royally, you still know him. You know him and care about him, and the grandness of this gesture will prove that."

"Wow, that was a mouthful," I quip and take another drink.

"She's right, Kate," Dean interjects, and I look over and see the seriousness in his eyes. "You know he cares about you, so just talking to him isn't going to be enough. You have to make it big."

I bite down on a chunk of ice for a moment while pondering this. "In erotica, the grand gestures are usually like a power flip. Like, oh, okay, I'll let you put a horsetail butt plug in me just this once."

Lynsey and Dean erupt into laughter, and I frown back

at them, stating, "I'm serious."

They roll their eyes, and Dean says, "Think more romantic, less farm animal."

I remain silent for a few minutes as I scroll through everything about Miles that I love. Then I think about everything he loves, and my eyes alight when I recall the night we shared in his grandpa's truck.

"His grandpa has this old truck that he's dying to fix up. But he's dumping all his money into house renovations, so he's holding off on it for now. He said the carburetor needed replacing."

Dean's eyes brighten at this revelation. "You just had seven months' worth of rent open up."

"You think this is a good idea?" I ask, chewing on my thumbnail nervously. "Can you just buy a carburetor for a car? Wouldn't he have to like…I don't know…repair it or something?"

"That's what Google is for!" Lynsey squeals and reaches out to grab my computer.

"Wait, will this be emasculating?" I say, stopping her mid-Google. "If I buy some expensive part for his grandpa's truck, is he going to be like, 'Fuck you bitch, I pay my own way?'" Lynsey and I both look at Dean for an answer.

"Not if you give it to him naked." He simply shrugs.

My first reaction is to laugh, but when Dean doesn't join in, my face drops. "Wait, seriously?"

He lifts his brows and pins me with a look. "I'm not even into cars, but if you came at me naked with a carburetor in your hand, I'd probably be all over that."

I look over at Lynsey, who gives me a shrug as well.

"We'll figure that part out later," I state with a laugh. "Let's find this orgasm-maker!"

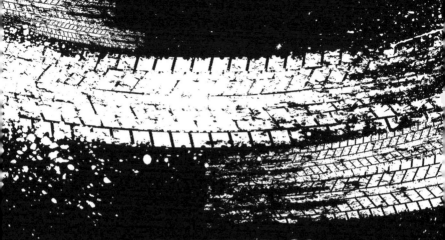

CHAPTER 31

Miles

"**B**ro, what the hell is your deal?" my sister, Megan's voice cuts through the phone line, waking me out of a deep slumber.

I scrub my hands over my face and check the time on my phone. "Jeez, why are you awake? It's 6:30 in the morning. My alarm hasn't even gone off yet."

"I thought you worked for a living," she retorts.

"I don't leave my house until 7:15. I had a good thirty minutes before I had to get up, you brat."

She sighs heavily. "Mom's worried about you."

I stretch my arms wide and throw my feet off the side of the bed to make my way to the bathroom. "Why?" I ask, pulling myself out of my boxers.

"Because you haven't sent her an email in two weeks.

Are you peeing?"

"No," I lie.

"Liar."

"I'm not peeing. It's just the creek by my house. It runs really fast and hard in the morning."

"You're disgusting. Have the decency to mute the phone line next time."

"But then you wouldn't be able to hear me pee." A lazy grin spreads across my face as I tuck the phone against my shoulder to wash my hands. "What's Mom's deal?"

"You go from emailing her on Sunday nights like clock-work to radio silence on all of us for two weeks. We talked about this, Miles. One email a week means you get to avoid the two-hour phone calls with her where she threatens to come stay with you for a week. Why are you slacking?"

I exhale heavily and make my way down the hall out into my kitchen. My timed coffee pot has finished brewing, and I pour myself a cup. "I've been busy."

"Bullshit," she snaps as I open my front door and step outside onto the porch. The sky is a mixture of blue and golden sunrise, illuminating the treetops in front of my house.

"I haven't felt like talking, Meg."

She groans loudly. "Don't tell me you got back together with Jocelyn. I'm telling you, Miles, our family will not be able to stand this again. I thought she was married and had a kid anyway."

"It's not Joce," I snap, rolling my eyes and taking a sip. "It's that…author girl," I admit because I know my sister, and she won't quit until I fess up.

"The one you called me from the bar about?"

I clear my throat and reply through clenched teeth. "Yes."

"Oh man! I didn't know you were seeing her!"

"I'm not…I mean, I was. But it's over now."

"Why?"

"Because she lied to me about some shit, and I'm not bringing noise like that back into my life again. Been there, done that."

Megan's little growl on the other line surprises me. "Don't think every girl who isn't perfect is like Jocelyn, all right? I don't know this author chick, but I do know you, and you sounded so crazy happy that night you called me to talk about her, Miles. Happier than I'd heard you in like…forever. I'd say since Joce, but honestly, you were never happy with that girl. Not a day in your life. I know I haven't met this author, but I called Mom the very next day to tell her about how you sounded because it was so night and day different. We were excited."

"Seriously?" I state, my jaw dropping. I knew my family had issues with Jocelyn, but they rarely ever voiced them to me. They were always blindly supportive of my decisions. "You guys never said anything."

"Miles, Joce was the worst, and she made you miserable. You were moody for years because of that girl. God, every time you guys broke up, we all prayed it'd be the last time."

"Why wouldn't you say something to me about that?" I

exclaim, wrapping my hand around the railing of my porch and squeezing it in frustration.

"Because we never knew when you might get back together with her! And if we admitted how we really felt, and you stuck with her, it could ruin our relationship with you. We actually used Grandpa to tell you she was a massive bitch because we knew you couldn't hate him."

"Oh my God," I exclaim with a shake of my head. "Grandpa was in on it?"

"Oh yeah," she replies with a giggle. "I remember him saying to Mom one time…'If you guys are too weak to tell Miles to drop that girl, then I'll do it.' Mom was super insulted, but it was Gramps…ya know."

I laugh loudly at that. "God, I can picture him saying that."

"Needless to say, I'm glad your silence isn't because of her. So what's going on with the author girl then? What's her name again?"

I shake my head and reply, "Kate." It feels weird to say out loud when she's been Mercedes in my mind for so long, but honestly, it suits her a hell of a lot better than Mercedes Lee Loveletter.

"What did she lie to you about?"

"A couple of different things," I reply, really not wanting to get into the details because it makes me feel pathetic.

"So what happened when you found out?"

My brows lift. "I punched a guy."

I'm met with silence on the other end.

"Megan?" I ask. "Megan!" I say a little louder.

"Sorry, I was processing. So you actually punched a guy?"

I nod. "Yeah. I'm not proud."

"Jesus, I am…impressed. Dad always said the only woman who would ever make you violent to another person was me. You're sort of one of those 'all bark, no bite' guys. Your bark is usually scary enough because you're basically a giant. So the fact that you punched a guy over this girl makes me think you must really care about her."

This is a concept I have been pondering for the past couple of weeks. "I think I was really starting to," I admit. "But it's over now. She lied, and I'm not doing the Joce bullshit again."

"There's one big difference here that I think you're not considering, Miles."

"What's that?"

"Joce made you miserable, and this girl makes you happy, true or false?"

I swallow around a knot in my throat. "True."

"So you're going to let one bad night discredit several moments of happiness?"

"I don't know if it's that simple, Meg."

"It's only as complicated as you make it, bro. I think you're overreacting because you've been burned. And that's understandable. But don't throw away a good thing because of your past. It's already taken enough from you."

I run a hand over my head and sigh heavily. "How did you get so fucking insightful?"

"I'm wise beyond my years." She giggles, and I hear a

rustling in the background. "I'm just getting to my kickbox-ing class. I gotta go. Call me after you quit being an idiot and make up with that girl!"

She hangs up without another word, and I can't help but smile. And part of my smile is because for the first time in two weeks, I think maybe I was wrong. Not about being up-set with Kate for lying to me about some pretty major shit, but about the fact that I never really let her explain her side of things. I never fought with her. I shut her down like I chose to shut down drama in my life after being burned so badly with Joce.

But the fact that I'd never punched another man until that night with Kate says something.

It says that Kate Smith is a woman worth fighting for.

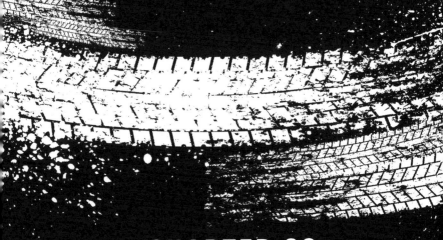

CHAPTER 32

Kate

"I'm sweaty. I'm tired. And I stink in places I really shouldn't be stinking." I whine and shoot a glare to Dean, who's sitting in the passenger seat looking sheepish.

"What?" he exclaims with his hands raised. "I didn't know we'd have fucking car trouble. Your car isn't even a year old."

"I know!" I snap, hitting my hand on the wheel and growling in frustration. "Stupid old lady car!" I exclaim and push my head closer to the window for a breeze. "The frickin' air conditioning isn't even working anymore. Me and this car are officially in a fight."

"I think we all just need to remain calm," Lynsey chirps from the back seat, leaning forward so her head comes between Dean's and mine. "Because, as horrible as this trip was, after everything that's happened between the three of us the past couple of years, I think this was really healing."

I close my eyes and shake my head, ruing the moment I agreed that a road trip to the Rocky Mountains to pick up this four-thousand-dollar carburetor from some hick who apparently didn't know how to *'mail things so they don't get lost.'*

Honestly! How are people who don't use the mail a thing? Though, admittedly, when we got to the man's mountain home, I realized that he was probably more familiar with the Pony Express. And I couldn't be sure his wife wasn't his cousin. But that's me being judgmental. Still, though, it's no wonder he wouldn't let me PayPal him the money. I had to get an actual cashier's check from a real bank.

Then on our way back down the mountain, I got a flat tire. Dean, Lynsey, and I set about changing it together, thinking three heads could figure out how to put a spare tire on better than one.

One minute, I'm snapping at Dean to hand me the tire iron, and the next minute, he's asking me if I'm being a bitch because he told me he had feelings for me. Then Lynsey chimes in, hurt and dismayed that neither of us told her about our conversation at the bakery, and it was a mess. On top of all of that, my car wouldn't start back up! It was a disaster.

The three of us fighting with each other on the side of the road looked like a bad episode of Sister Wives: Colorado Edition.

I should probably make more friends.

"God, I hope this thing is legit," Dean states, turning the carburetor over in his hands.

"Put it down. You're making me nervous," I snap, eyeing him cautiously.

We're only five miles from Tire Depot, and they close in ten, so my nerves are freaking fried. "I just want to drop this thing off and forget this whole trip ever happened."

"No!" Lynsey exclaims. "Stick to the plan. This is your grand gesture! Your get out of jail free card."

"I don't want a get out of jail free card," I cry back. "The longer we spent on that hot highway trying to figure out what was wrong with my car, the more ridiculous this plan became in my head. I don't want to buy Miles's affection back. I want him to want me for me. Flaws and all."

"So what are you going to do?" Dean asks, and I feel his concerned eyes on mine.

"I'm going to drop this expensive hunk of metal at the counter and leave. I'm not giving it to him naked or holding the thing above my head like John Cusack in *Say Anything*. I'll drop it off at the front counter, and then we'll go. End of story."

Lynsey's voice pipes up from behind. "That sounds like the worst ending to a book I've ever heard."

"This isn't a book!" I shriek. "This is my life, and it's no wonder this plan has turned into such a mess. It has desperation stamped all over it. I just want to go home, eat some pizza, and cry a little, okay?"

The car is dead silent as we enter Boulder until Dean's

voice pipes up. "Hey Kate, I know you're a little emongry right now, but I really don't think you should drive on this spare tire anymore. They're only manufactured to drive for so many miles, you know."

I turn and glower over at him. He shrinks down into his seat a little bit. "Fine, I'll leave it at Tire Depot overnight. One of you needs to call a cab because we're almost there."

"They have a courtesy vehicle that will take us home!" Lynsey chirps up helpfully from the back seat.

"Fine," I mumble as we pull into the Tire Depot parking lot. I glance through the glass front side of the building and see Sam alone at the front counter. "You guys, go flag down the courtesy driver. I'll be out in a minute, okay?"

They both nod and fold their sweaty bodies out of my vehicle, tails tucked between their legs. I owe them copious amounts of alcohol after this shitstorm of a trip.

When I walk inside, Sam's eyes fly wide at my appearance. I haven't looked in a mirror lately, but I'm betting I look a bit like Ronald McDonald after a bender.

I hold my hands up and say, "Don't ask," as I place the carburetor on the desk in front of him and my key fob.

"This can't be from your Caddy," Sam exclaims, a puzzled look at his brows as he turns the hunk of metal over in his hands.

"It's not," I reply flatly. "It's the carburetor Miles needs to get his grandpa's truck running. Can you give it to him, but not tell him it's from me please?"

"Are you kidding me?" Sam asks, his face incredulous.

"Mer—Kate, this thing costs a shitload of money. Where did you find it?"

"It's a long story. Just take good care of it and make sure it gets to Miles, okay? Oh, and my Cadillac needs a new tire and a service. It's started stalling on me. I'll call you tomorrow with the details."

Ignoring his perplexed expression, I turn to leave, but before I get more than a couple of steps away, he calls out, "Hey, Kate?"

I turn on my heel and prop my sweaty hands on my hips. "Yeah?"

"Why don't you want to give him the carburetor yourself?" He scratches his beard nervously.

I shrug. "Because I don't want him back like that." I turn to leave again, but he stops me one more time.

"Hey, Kate."

"Yes?" I ask, turning back to him again.

"You know Miles paid my uncle for every week you were here using the comfort center, right?" Sam's sheepish expression is saying even more than his words could right now.

"He what?" I ask, confusion all over my face.

"My uncle is the owner of Tire Depot, and Miles worked out a sweat equity deal with him in exchange for him looking the other way while you worked in the comfort center."

My eyes go wide. "I thought I was flying under the radar."

Sam laughs. "Everybody saw you walking in and out of

the employee entrance, Kate. You know you're not invisible, right?"

I inwardly deflate.

Sam shrugs. "At first, my uncle was just giving Miles shit. He had him stacking tires upstairs in the storage room after a big shipment came in. He said he wanted to see how far he'd go for a pretty girl."

My jaw drops.

Sam rubs the back of his neck sheepishly. "But now I think my uncle's taking advantage of him because he's still got Miles doing shit, even tonight."

"Miles is still here?" I ask, my voice rising in pitch, my belly doing that fireworks thing again that sounds like diarrhea but feels like delicious anticipation.

Sam nods. "He's upstairs."

"Upstairs," I ask, my brows furrowing.

Sam walks toward me and hangs a left to the door that enters the garage. He points to a set of industrial stairs. "He's up there stacking tires. You should give this to him yourself." He hands the carburetor over to me, the corners of his mouth tipping up into a smile. "He knows you're not like Jocelyn, Kate. Go put the boy out of his misery."

I take the carburetor from Sam, my tummy literally up in my throat as I do. My nerves are intense at what I'm about to do, but Miles wouldn't have done that if he didn't care for me. This must mean more than casual to him.

I make my way into the quiet garage, but before I head toward the stairs, I call back to Sam, "There's a couple of sweaty friends of mine waiting in the courtesy van. Will you tell them to go on ahead without me?"

Sam frowns at the parking lot but gives me a thumbs up. I turn back to the stairs and take a deep breath.

I'm a mess, I'm disgusting, and I've had a horrible day. There's only one person who can make it better. Time for my book-worthy moment.

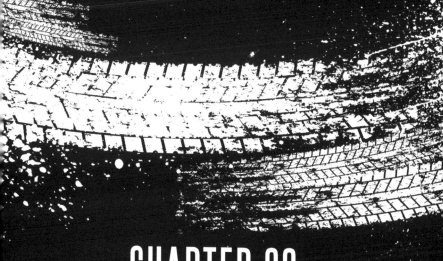

CHAPTER 33

Miles

I was laser focused through my work day at Tire Depot because all I could think about was finishing here and going straight to Mercedes's house when I was done. Or Kate, I should say. I need to talk to her. I need to make sure that what we had was real. I also need to tell her that I don't want casual anymore either. I want her. Only her.

I'm done with this half-ass attempt at making up for my twenties that I missed. I just want her. She's right, I can't compare her drama to Jocelyn's drama. I've been fighting my feelings for Kate for all the wrong reasons, and I'm done with that shit now.

I sling a tire up onto a stack of eight that are set to go on a semi tomorrow morning when I hear a voice behind me. "I'm wondering if you can help me with some more book research. It has to do with a happy ending."

I turn and see Kate standing by the stairs about twenty feet away from me. Red hair stacked up in a ball on top of her head. Curly tendrils slipping out all around her face. She's wearing a T-shirt that's tied in a knot off to the side, revealing a strip of flesh right above her Daisy Dukes. She looks dirty and sweaty and exhausted.

She looks perfect.

With a soft smile, I grab the bottom of my white tank top that's covered in black from tire rubber and swipe at the sweat running down my forehead. "What are you doing here?" I ask, licking my lips and trying to stop my blood pressure from spiraling out of control.

She moves something metal back and forth in her hand that I can't see from this far away as she says, "Did you pay off Sam's uncle for me to write inside the comfort center?"

My face falls, my brows furrowing when I realize she must have spoken to Sam. "Not in money but in labor, so yeah, I guess so." I look around at the sea of tires surrounding me in answer.

She nods and chews on her lower lip as she walks closer to me. "Do you know what this is?"

I frown down at the hunk of metal in her hands. "That looks like a carburetor."

"Do you know for what kind of vehicle?" she asks, her blue eyes pinning mine in place.

I shake my head and shrug. "I can't tell from here."

She pauses and sets it down on a cart next to the clipboard of tire orders that I check off as I stack. "It's for a

1965 Ford F100."

My jaw falls open.

"That's the one you have at home, right?" she asks, blinking her wide eyes at me.

I nod.

She smiles.

"Where did you get it?" I husk, my voice raw with shock and disbelief.

"It's kind of a long, crazy story." I see her throat swallow slowly. "But I'm hoping it has a great ending."

My stunned expression morphs into wonder. "What kind of ending?" I ask, wiping my hands off on my jeans as she stops ten feet in front of me now. I can see the brilliant blue of her eyes and the light sheen of sweat all over her body.

She's stunning.

She exhales heavily through her nose, a flush crawling up her cheeks as she replies, "The kind where you let me apologize for lying to you." She hits me with a serious look and says, "I'm Kate Smith from Longmont, Colorado, whose ex technically still lived with her until two weeks ago when she moved in with her best friend, Lynsey. I'm not some brave erotic romance author who's into kink and cool with casual and uses a mechanic for 'book research.' I'm a girl who's been falling for a guy who works at Tire Depot and would really like to go home with him and just take a frickin' shower."

She exhales heavily, clearly out of breath from her long-winded confession.

I'm out of breath too.

Because suddenly, with one intense look, I'm transported back to that night when there was a storm overhead and I crashed into her like I was the thunder to her lightning. Everything around us disappeared.

Now in a sea of tires, all I see is her.

In a flash, I'm striding toward Kate, and she's striding toward me. We connect, and within a single breath, she's up in my arms, both of us covered in sweat and dirt, my left arm circling her waist, my right hand splayed wide on her back, holding her flush to me as her legs wrap and tighten around my hips.

She feels good and light in my arms. Warm and soft. The heat of a woman fucking made for me. At first, I press my forehead to hers and breathe in the smell of her. Amongst all the shop smells, nothing beats this girl's scent. I press my lips to her damp forehead, then her temple, then the curve of her earlobe. I trail my lips along her jaw and sample the corner of her mouth with mine.

She lets out a soft moan, which parts her lips to me, and I take that as an invitation to feast as I connect our lips straight on. My demanding tongue thrusts in to meet her eager one, our flesh dancing against each other with desire. With apology. With two weeks' worth of anxiety, stress, and confusion.

She sifts her fingers through my short hair, humming her appreciation into my mouth and squeezing me into her center so tight, I pulse inside my jeans with need.

I pull back to look at her. "Were you serious about

that shower?"

Her mouth tips up with a breathy laugh. "God, yes."

"Good, because I'm disgusting, and all I want to do is bury myself inside you right now."

She laughs and releases her legs around my hips, sliding down to the ground. I grab her hand with mine, hauling her behind me as I approach the carburetor she placed on the cart.

"I can't believe you did this," I state incredulously, picking up the rare part in my hand. "This had to cost a fortune."

She lifts her shoulders. "I needed you to know that everything we experienced together wasn't fiction. The important stuff mattered to me. A lot."

My eyes soften with emotion as I take in the sincerity on her face. I should have never doubted her. I should have never put her in the same category as anyone else. Kate Smith is in a league all her own.

I crook my finger under her chin and brush her lips with mine. It's not a sexy reclaiming like I want the minute we get to my place. It's a tender thank you.

"You're amazing," I murmur against her lips.

She smiles softly. "So are you."

I slide my hand into hers as we make our way down the stairs to my shop station where I grab my helmet and the keys to my bike.

"Where's your car?" I ask, as we step out into the back alley where my bike is parked.

"It's staying here overnight. It needs a service, and I got a flat."

My eyes pin her with a curious look.

She brushes me off. "I'll tell you about it later. Now, I really want to climb on the back of your bike."

With a smirk, I pass my helmet to her and help her aboard. With a thunderous start, my bike roars to life, and I pull out of the parking lot, out of Boulder, and head to the little place I call home.

Our lips are locked on each other's all the way up my garage steps, all the way through my living room, my kitchen, down the hall, and into my bedroom. We break our kiss briefly to ditch our shirts. We resume said kissing as my hands reach behind Kate's back and unclasp her bra. In one swift motion, her breasts are bare, and I'm crushing her to my chest. Lifting her feet off the ground so I can reconnect our lips and feel her bare skin against mine.

She fumbles with the button on my jeans, so I set her down to help rid her of her shorts and panties. Turning to get the showerheads started, I kiss her for a minute longer, then pull away to guide her into the shower with me. Placing her under her own spray and myself under mine, I stare down at her as the hot water pours over her face and down her body.

She tips her head back, her red hair slicking to her head. She drops her chin and her blue eyes are bright and rapidly blinking against the water as she looks at me looking at her.

I step into her spray and run my hands along her

collarbone and shoulders. "I fucking missed you, Kate." My hands slide lower to run over the swells of her bare breasts, cupping them to test the weight of them. "It's weird to call you Kate."

Her breath quickens as I pinch her pink nipples between my thumb and index finger. "You can call me Mercedes if you want," she says with a soft moan.

I shake my head slowly, gliding my hands down her ribs, over her lower belly and teasing the slit at her mound. "I like Kate. It suits you."

She bites her lip as I increase the pressure and then croaks out, "You don't think it's boring?"

I shake my head and wait for her to open her eyes to look at me before replying, "No, I think it's sexy. And shower sex with Kate is just what I want."

She squeals in surprise when I haul her up against me and press her back against the cool tile wall. Her legs wrap around me as I position myself between her thighs.

I find where I need to be, and with one strong thrust, I push into her, hard and bare, my head pressing down on her shoulder as I stretch her.

She cries out, her voice echoing off the walls. "Oh God, Miles!"

My fingers bite into her ass as I pull back and thrust in again. "Kate."

"Miles!" she screams again.

I grind up into her deeper and growl, "Kate," one more time. It's a claiming. An ownership of her name in my mouth. And it feels right. "Kate," I state again huskily,

AMY DAWS

licking a trail up her neck to her ear. "Kate, this isn't casual."

"No?" she cries out in question against another hard thrust.

"No," I confirm with a growl. "This isn't fiction, and I don't want to be casual anymore. I want you to be mine."

"Okay!" she cries, her hands tightening around my neck as she scrunches her eyes shut and tries to find release against the tightness between her legs.

I pull back to look at her. "Babe, open your eyes and look at me."

She rolls her head against the wall and finally flutters her lids up, but she doesn't look happy about it. "Yes, Miles," she says, stroking her hands down my cheeks like she's trying to appease me.

"I'm serious. I want to be your man. And I want you to be my woman."

The smile on her face is stunning, and the giggle that rolls through her body does seriously awesome things to my dick. "You want to be my boyfriend?"

"Yes," I reply with a frown at her choice of word. "But none of that book boyfriend bullshit. I'm as real as they come, and I'll put all your fictional studs to shame, you got that?"

She bites her lip and runs her fingertips down my face. "You already have."

"Good," I reply, grinding my hips up into her further. "So we're in agreement?"

"Totally," she moans out loudly, making weird, uncontrollable noises in her throat.

But she grows more and more silent as I slam into her again and again until we're both floating somewhere up in the hot shower steam clinging to the ceiling and at last falling down like rain.

Together, as one.

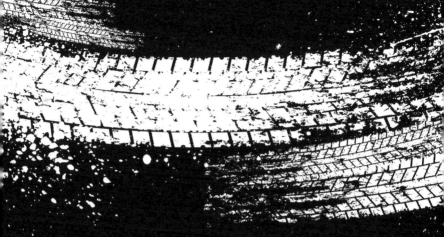

CHAPTER 34

Kate

Clean and with damp hair, Miles turns me on my side in his big, manly bed that smells delicious, like him, and pulls my naked back to his naked front. He kisses the top of my shoulder, his mouth warm and lingering as he presses up against me, leaving absolutely no space between us.

"Are we going to bed already?" I ask, my voice soft in his cozy room as the faint glow of the setting sun outside grows darker and darker.

"This is just intermission," he replies, his deep voice vibrating against my back. "We're not even close to being done making up yet."

I pull the blanket to my mouth to stifle my excited giggle. "Is that what happened in your shower? Makeup sex?"

He groans his confirmation and thrusts his hips into my rear end. "If you have to ask, then I didn't do a good enough job."

I turn so I'm lying on my back and can look up at him. "You did a superior job. But I guess I would have called that more of a welcome home session."

His eyes are closed, but his brow furrows cutely. "Are you moving in?"

My cheeks burst into flames. "No…God, that's not what I meant. I just…I meant that like, we'd been apart for a while and now we've been reunited and—"

"Babe," he says, cutting me off mid-rant. "Shush. You're getting tense, and after the best sex of my life, I really don't want you to harsh my vibe."

I giggle and pull the blanket over my mouth before mumbling. "Best sex of your life?"

He cracks one eye open and looks down at me, removing his hand from my belly and pulling the blanket down off my face. He tucks back a loose strand of hair and confirms his statement with a sexy, "Fuck, yes. Now talk to me about your townhouse. Why are you living with Lynsey?"

I groan loudly. "Now you're harshing my vibe."

He pins me with a look.

I exhale. "Dryston was threatening to sue you for breaking his nose. I offered him the house in exchange for him promising not to come after you."

Miles's entire body goes hard, his hand gripping my shoulder as he pins me with a serious look. "You gave up your house for me?"

I shrug. "It was my fault you were blindsided in the first place. I should have been honest with you from the start."

"Oh, you mean like not lie to me that your ex-boyfriend still lived with you and wasn't, in fact, gay but a super douche?"

My shoulders shake with a sad sort of laugh. I groan and try to hide my face, but Miles won't let me. "I'm so sorry. That was completely idiotic of me. I just really, really liked you and was so freaked you were going to bolt that night. You were going on and on about being jealous."

His lips form a thin line, a look of disappointment clouding his features. "I shouldn't have scared you with all that. I put way too much pressure on you with talk of my past. I'm a protective guy, Kate, but I hope you know I trust you."

I give him a small smile and take a deep breath in. "Good, because I have another confession."

"Christ, what?" Miles asks, running a hand through his hair.

"Dean told me he liked me as more than a friend."

"What?" Miles snaps, popping up on his elbow so he can see me more fully. "Are you fucking serious? Goddamn it, I knew it!"

I sit up, clutching the sheet to my breasts with one hand and reaching out to run my hand down his tricep. "We talked it out, and he knows I don't feel the same. We're just friends. He knows that now."

"God, any other guys lining up I need to be aware of? I might need to start wearing boxing gloves!" Miles deadpans.

"No, only Dean," I reply with an awkward shrug. "And you're not going to punch him because he's still my friend. And he only told me because he had no idea that I was completely in love with you."

Miles's bright blue eyes flash up to connect with mine. His body even more tense than it was before. "What did you just say?"

My heart is in my throat, but I know there's no going back now. "I'm in love with you, Miles. Like, completely."

His mouth falls open as he expends all the air in his lungs. "Now I need to fuck you again," he murmurs and moves over on top of me, between my legs, his hardened erection nudging my entrance as he rests his elbows on either side of me and looks straight into my eyes. "How do you keep getting better and better?"

I purse my lips together and touch his face with my hands. "I'm being myself, finally."

The edge of his mouth tips up in a small smile, then falls when he replies simply, "I love you too, Kate."

And without a moment's hesitation, I yank his face down to mine, and I kiss him. I kiss him as if my happiness depends on it. Because at this point, it completely does. Miles Hudson is the sun and the air and the moon and the stars. He's fucking wonderful, and he loves me.

How much more book worthy can it get than that?

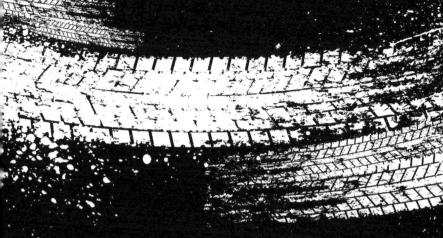

CHAPTER 35

Kate

3 Months Later

I hear the familiar purr of the '65 Ford driving into the garage under my feet just as I pull the homemade pizza that I spent forever making out of the oven. I know it's not necessarily a romantic meal, but it's sort of what started our relationship. I gave him leftover pizza in exchange for his silence about me sneaking into Tire Depot to write. He ended up being the man of my dreams, and the type of guy I have to celebrate three-month anniversaries with.

I can't help myself.

I even have licorice ropes for dessert because, like any good novel, full circle moments always make a scene extra special. And since I've just completed my mechanic romantic comedy, I'm ready to celebrate The End with the man I love.

But for fun, we're calling tonight "date research," and Miles obliged almost instantly.

The past few months have been a blur of a wonderfully uncomplicated relationship that consists of morning coffees on his porch, quiet dinners out, and sex pretty much anywhere we can get it. Oh, and words. So many words! I'm constantly taking notes with Miles wrapped around me at night. He's not even surprised anymore when he wakes up to his alarm clock to find me in nothing but his clothes, clacking away on my laptop and watching the sunrise on his front porch.

Miles Hudson's house makes Tire Depot look like a little bitch.

Just kidding! I take it back. I still come creeping in there for work at least three days a week. Those complimentary beverages and cookies won't consume themselves! And Sam's uncle finally introduced himself to me and told me I could come in as often as I like.

Life is good. And being committed to Miles is great. But tonight will be fun to think back and remember how oddly our relationship started out.

I'm shocked to hear the doorbell on Miles's front door chime. I guess he's taking this "research" seriously. With a smile, I hurry over in my platform sandal wedges to open the door and nearly fall over dead when I see my man standing in front of me wearing a frickin' button-down with a rose in his hand.

A single, red rose.

But I'm looking beyond that now because he clearly did a lot more than just wash up at the shop. His dark hair looks like it has some gel in it, and his dark jeans are worn in all the right place. The places that a man's jeans wear when he works hard in them. And good God, he even has dress shoes on.

He looks good enough to eat.

"Jesus fuck," Miles drawls, taking in my short red dress. It was an impulse purchase and way too slutty to wear out in public. But I'm committed to my research this evening.

Miles looks like he more than appreciates it as he steps inside and drops the rose on the side table. In one long stride, he kicks the door shut with his heel and cups my face in his hands.

Hunched over me, he husks against my lips, "First thing I have to say about what I'm thinking right now for your research is that when a girl who you've been fucking for months still makes your dick hard just by wearing a cute little dress, it makes it really damn hard for a decent guy to be a gentleman."

With a soft yank of my hair, he tips my head back and crushes his mouth to mine. My hands fist into his shirt by his sides as I open my lips to him and welcome his hot, wet tongue inside me. He caresses his tongue against mine, and I feel a pooling in my belly that is so intense, I moan into his mouth.

He growls in response, sounding feral and animalistic as he walks us backward toward the nearby wall. He plasters me up against it, one hand letting go of my cheek as he reaches down to pull my leg up onto his hip, my dress riding up all the way to my waist. Lowering his body, he presses his front to my center, and I cry out when he rubs himself against me, showing me how hard he is already.

Seriously! How did he get that hard this fast?

"Holy shit!" I exclaim when he breaks our lips to run his whiskered jaw down my neck, his tongue trailing a delightful path of goose bumps the entire way. He gets low to my breasts and plunges inside my cleavage to suck hard.

"Oh!" I yelp and shove him softly.

He pulls back with a proud smile. "That's going to leave a mark."

"You jerk," I husk, pushing him away. My man has an affection for leaving marks on me, and even though I pretend to hate it, I actually frickin' love it.

His chest vibrates with laughter as he holds me to him. "I can't help it. I like marking you."

I roll my eyes. "What was it you said when you came in? Decent guys are gentlemen or something."

He lifts his brows. "Who said I was decent?"

I glance down at my cleavage and pull my dress back to see the red mark already showing. "Clearly not you."

The hungry look in his eyes is not at all apologetic, and I can't help but love him a little more for it. On wobbly legs, I extract myself from his embrace and grab my flower from the table he unceremoniously tossed it to.

"You brought me a flower." I smile and press it to my nose while walking back toward the kitchen.

His grin is sheepish as he rubs the back of his neck. "I thought the flower was very date-like. Book boyfriend worthy, as you say." He shrugs his shoulders like it's no big deal.

I shake my head. "Quit acting like you're too cool for this stuff now. You love book research."

He chuckles softly and props himself on the counter by the stove while I search for a pizza cutter. "Actually, I just love watching you work."

"Yeah?" I reply, abandoning my task to grab a couple of beers out of the fridge. I hand one to him that he cracks open, handing it back to me so I give him the other.

He clinks bottles with me, takes a drink and points to his front door. "And the fact you can sit out on *my* porch and create your stories is enough to make my dick hard."

"Brake fluid makes your dick hard," I reply with a dramatic eye roll.

He pins me with a look of warning and sets his beer down, reaching out and yanking me into him. He twirls us so his arms cage me against the counter and he's pressed up against me in that really delicious, big way he has about him.

He looks into my eyes with such sincerity when he says, "I'm not joking. I like you writing here, Kate."

"Well, the vibe here is good. Even better than Tire Depot."

He gasps at that and smiles. "What if I want you to spend your days and nights here?"

"Well, you pretty much have all my nights on lockdown already," I state with a laugh. Lynsey's house is not conducive to noisy sex, so we inevitably end up at Miles's place more often than not.

"I mean permanently." His smile falls, his eyes grow serious.

I frown up at him. "Like move in with you?"

"Unless you prefer sleeping next door to your ex-boyfriend?"

"Wait, is that the only reason you're asking me to move in with you? Because you're trying to keep me far away from my ex?"

"Nah," he replies casually, splaying his hands over my hips and pulling me to him. "I'm asking you to move in because I want you in my bed every night, Kate. Not just when it works for you. I want to carpool together to Tire Depot where you can write all day, and I can come in and sneak a kiss whenever I want. And when I get off work, you'll climb on the back of my bike and squeeze yourself around me as we ride home together. Honestly, I can't think of a better way to spend *some* of my time with you."

"How would you spend your other time?"

"Buried inside your sweet little pussy."

My breath inhales sharply at his dirty promise. It sounds perfect. It sounds like he just described heaven, and I'm standing at the pearly gates waiting for entry.

But I try to play it cool when I reply, "I think I could like the idea of moving in with you." I bite my lower lip and run my hands up his chest, stroking his full pecs appreciatively. "You are certainly my best writing inspiration to date."

"You'd better not be using me for your fictional stories,

babe," he drawls, dropping a tender kiss on my lips. One that's full of warmth and respect and adoration. It's not a hickey, a claiming kiss. It's not a sex-crazed, lustful kiss. It's got nothing to do with book research.

It's one that I can see him giving me every day for the rest of our lives.

"Never, Miles," I murmur against his lips and run my hands through his hair. "Although living with you will definitely help me finish my book quicker than anticipated."

He pulls back with a smile and asks, "So are you ever going to tell me what this book is about?"

I shrug my shoulders. "It's our love story. No big deal."

He laughs against my body. "Interesting, how does it end?"

I smile brightly up at him. "Happily, of course."

THE END

MORE BOOKS BY
AMY DAWS

The London Lovers Series:
Becoming Us: Finley's Story Part 1
A Broken Us: Finley's Story Part 2
London Bound: Leslie's Story
Not the One: Reyna's Story

A London Lovers/Harris Brothers Crossover Novel:
Strength: Vi Harris & Hayden's Story

The Harris Brothers Series:
Challenge: Camden's Story
Endurance: Tanner's Story
Keeper: Booker's Story
Surrender & Dominate: Gareth's Duet

Payback: A Harris Brother Spin-off Standalone
Blindsided: A Harris Brother Spin-off Standalone
Replay: A Harris Brother Spin-off Standalone
Sweeper: A Secret Harris Brother Standalone

The Wait With Me Series:
Wait With Me: A Tire Shop Rom-Com
Next in Line: A Bait Shop Rom-Com
One Moment Please: A Hospital Cafeteria Rom-Com
Take A Number: A Bakery Rom-Com
Last on the List: A Boss/Nanny Rom-Com

Pointe of Breaking: A College Dance Standalone by Amy
Daws & Sarah J. Pepper

Chasing Hope: A Mother's *True* Story of Loss, Heartbreak,
and the Miracle of Hope

For all retailer purchase links, visit:www.amydawsauthor.com

ACKNOWLEDGEMENTS

I feel like the acknowledgements for this book are uniquely important because so many people know that this story was very loosely based on my real life experiences and I want to make some things clear while I have you here!

First of all, yes, I snuck into a tire shop waiting room. Yes, I took countless people's cars in, and yes, my author friend really did have a pizza delivered there, and I even got a fake invoice in the mail from my friends. It was all mortifying.

But basically, the love story that happened between Miles and Kate is one-hundred-percent fiction. I'm a happily married woman and my hubby and I have a child that is our whole world. There was never any flirting I did with a tire shop employee. Or any hot mechanic who noticed me sneaking in. Frankly, the guys at my local tire shop remind me of a bunch of really sweet uncles.

Also, my family is incredibly supportive of my writing. My mom reads and loves every one of my books and my dad gets copies for his female coworkers with every release. Even my grandma is awesome! She enjoys Amish romance and is the epitome of a wholesome farm wife, but that wonderful woman buys two copies of every single book I write: one for her bookshelf at home and one for her local library with a population of 800 people. My family is amazing and I've never once felt shamed the way Kate did in this story. In fact, the pride my family has for how hard I work is beyond measure. They are the best.

I had a blast writing about this unusual start to a love story. I'm so grateful to everyone I've met through this unorthodox process. The guys at the tire shop have been especially welcoming of me and I'm so excited they have given me the green light to write there whenever I like. The town I live in is bigger than Boulder and it's pretty cool to see adorable, small town charm in a bigger city.

But ultimately, I want to thank everyone who followed along with me on social media and had a laugh with me through my tire shop antics. This story never would have been imagined if you guys weren't all so fun and engaging with me on social media. And I had a blast writing this book.

I'm a firm believer in the fact that your best connections with people happen when you're being real. And the truth is, there's a lot to be sad about these days. There are horrible things happening in the world all the time.

But sometimes, all it takes is a fun book and a cup of really good complimentary coffee to make a dark day just a tiny bit brighter.

MORE ABOUT THE AUTHOR

 Number 1 Amazon Bestselling author Amy Daws writes spicy love stories that take place in America, as well as across the pond. She's most known for her footy-playing Harris Brothers and writing in a tire shop waiting room. When Amy is not writing, she's likely making charcuterie boards from her home in South Dakota where she lives with her daughter and husband.

Follow Amy on all social media channels, including Tik Tok under @amydawsauthor

For more of Amy's work, visit: www.amydawsauthor.com or check out the links below.

www.facebook.com/amydawsauthor
www.twitter.com/amydawsauthor
www.instagram.com/amydawsauthor
www.tiktok.com/@amydawsauthor

29051008R00178